BY JULIA SEALES

A Most Agreeable Murder
A Terribly Nasty Business

A TERRIBLY NASTY BUSINESS

A BEATRICE STEELE NOVEL
JULIA SEALES
A Terribly
NASTY
BUSINESS
RANDOM HOUSE NEW YORK

Published in the United States by Random House,
an imprint and division of Penguin Random House LLC,
1745 Broadway, New York, NY 10019.

Random House and the House colophon are registered trademarks of
Penguin Random House LLC.

Library of Congress Cataloging-in-Publication Data
Names: Seales, Julia, author.
Title: A terribly nasty business : a Beatrice Steele novel / Julia Seales.
Description: First edition. | New York, NY : Random House, 2025.
Identifiers: LCCN 2025006974 (print) | LCCN 2025006975 (ebook) |
ISBN 9780593450017 (hardcover; acid-free paper) | ISBN 9780593450024 (ebook)
Subjects: LCGFT: Detective and mystery fiction. | Novels.
Classification: LCC PS3619.E25514 T47 2025 (print) |
LCC PS3619.E25514 (ebook) | DDC 813/.6—dc23/eng/20250214
LC record available at https://lccn.loc.gov/2025006974
LC ebook record available at https://lccn.loc.gov/2025006975

Printed in the United States of America on acid-free paper

randomhousebooks.com
penguinrandomhouse.com

2 4 6 8 9 7 5 3 1

First Edition

Book design by Diane Hobbing

The authorized representative in the EU for product safety and compliance is
Penguin Random House Ireland, Morrison Chambers, 32 Nassau Street,
Dublin D02 YH68, Ireland. https://eu-contact.penguin.ie.

To the friends who made a small-town girl
feel at home in a big city
It's the joy of life to Sing with you all

A TERRIBLY NASTY BUSINESS

PROLOGUE

Walter Shrewsbury had never cared for music; he did not see the point in it. Women always ruined perfectly good dinner parties with the grating tones of the harp. Ladies were meant to create background noise, not claim center stage with experimental nonsense. One would be enjoying a dish, until a shrill glissando interrupted the precious moment between man and stewed cucumber.

Tonight, Mr. Shrewsbury simply could not bear it, so he retreated to the lounge and slammed the door to muffle the melody emanating from the dining room.

Lately, the ladies of London seemed emboldened by some unwelcome muse. They played songs of their own selection, instead of what their husbands requested. These were full of disgustingly dulcet tones that might be called heartfelt, if one were prone to movement by music. The women wore bizarre fashions, with more regard for comfort than a gentleman's preference. Worst of all, at tonight's dinner, he had heard a woman venture a joke—*at his expense*. Walter had excused himself the moment it was explained to him.

Now he sank into an armchair, pining for the vegetables he had left behind, lost in troubled thought. He was not naïve; he understood the danger of art, of this ridiculous concept of "expression." It was the root of all these terrible developments. It gave any random person a voice, making them believe they had the power to effect change. As a wealthy gentleman, Walter Shrewsbury had no need for change. It would benefit him as much as a well-composed symphony: which was to say, not at all.

He put his hand into his pocket and withdrew a letter. It had been delivered weeks ago, a nasty little note that had compounded his growing unease of late. He unfolded it and stared at the words on the page:

Confess, or die. You decide.

In case the meaning wasn't clear, the unknown sender had drawn a sketch below the words: a moth, with a pin stabbed through its thorax.

Walter crumpled up the paper and flung it across the room. He had made up his mind. He would not be threatened. He would not be laughed at. He would not be forced to listen to music that brought up emotions and memories and unrequited loves and made his upper lip tremble when he had specifically vowed to keep it stiff. Whatever change was happening, he would stop it the way he had once stopped a too-long orchestra performance: with threats, yelling, and smashing violins when necessary.

The study door creaked open, and Walter whirled around.

"Can't I have just *five minutes* to myself—" he began, and then broke off. "Oh. It's you. We should talk. Fetch the port. . . ."

He rose to his feet but fell back as the intruder delivered the first blow. Walter Shrewsbury put a hand to his nose, stemming a sudden flow of blood.

"What are you *doing*?" he sputtered. But before he could comprehend what was happening, the intruder hit him again, and again, finally producing a knife and plunging it into Walter Shrewsbury's chest.

The last sound Walter heard before taking his final breath was the distant, taunting trill of the harp as the door opened and the intruder slipped away.

He would never hear another sound, not even the scream some time later when a maid discovered his body splayed out on the armchair in a pool of blood.

"Murder!" she cried out. "Murder at the Rose!"

The Neighborhood Association of
Gentlemen Sweetbriarians (NAGS) Presents:

THE LONDON SEASON

Miss Beatrice Steele and her chaperone, Miss Helen Bolton,

are invited to attend the Season
at the local assembly rooms of Sweetbriar.

Enclosed in this invitation,
you will find a map of the neighborhood,

as well as a schedule of upcoming events.

We look forward to your introduction into London society!

Note: This invitation is for
the Tulip and Carnation Club Seasons only.

Invitations to the Rose are handled separately,
in the very unlikely chance you receive one.

We advise young ladies not to get their hopes up.

Cheers!

CHAPTER ONE

An Exit

In the northwest corner of London was a neighborhood called Sweetbriar, known for its theater, its pleasure garden, and an unfortunate infestation of flying squirrels. This is where Beatrice Steele had taken up residence with her chaperone, Miss Helen Bolton. Except for the squirrels, it was just the sort of neighborhood in which Beatrice had always dreamed of living—that is, when she wasn't dreaming about solving murders. But so far, her new life wasn't quite what she had imagined.

Beatrice had grown up in a small, manners-obsessed town called Swampshire, where she always feared that her reputation would be ruined if her secret true-crime obsession came to light. (Her horrifically bad skills at sketching, embroidery, non-macabre conversation, and most other hobbies suitable for an "accomplished woman" hardly helped the matter.) But when a gentleman dropped dead at a country ball, she finally got the chance to put her detecting skills to the test and caught the killer alongside the haughty but admittedly perceptive Inspector Vivek Drake.

Was it unfortunate that the dead body had been a wealthy man and presumed match for Beatrice's sister? Yes. Was it even worse that Beatrice had determined the killer to be her own childhood best friend and potential betrothed? Of course. Was it devastating that a lovely ball had been ruined by a corpse? Perhaps, though not for Miss Steele.

Drake showed up on her doorstep shortly after their investigation concluded, asking if she would partner with him to open a detective office in London. The venture was funded by Drake's newfound half sister (newly found by Beatrice, a fact she would not let Drake forget). Beatrice's future had fallen into place perfectly—until her mother got involved.

"If you are going to help catch murderers, you must do it the proper way: accompanied by an unmarried, middle-aged woman!" Mrs. Steele insisted.

She would not hear of Beatrice going to London unchaperoned. Without a guardian, Beatrice could fall in with the wrong crowd, gamble her money away, be shamed in the social columns, and be forced to work as an opera singer in order to pay off her debts. Beatrice could not carry a tune to save her life. The scandal would be extreme.

Luckily, the family's close friend and neighbor Miss Bolton volunteered her services without question. As an aspiring playwright, Miss Bolton had her own dreams to pursue in the city. She and her dog, Bee Bee, were happy to come along. Beatrice was grateful for the company, as well as the comfortable town house Miss Bolton rented for their residence.

What she was not grateful for was Mrs. Steele's steel-like grip on Miss Bolton. Beatrice quickly learned that "chaperone" was merely another word for "spy," for Mrs. Steele had not given up on the hope that her eldest daughter would make a fortuitous match. Though Beatrice had hoped to spend her days solving crimes with Inspector Drake, her first few months in London had been a flurry of social activities meant to find a man. And unfortunately this man would be a husband, not a murderer.

That was how Beatrice found herself at a garden party on an overly warm Tuesday in June, taking her fourth turn around the meager gardens of the Carnation Club. She had spent the afternoon elbow to elbow with eligible ladies and gentlemen. She had sampled the lemon ice, played two rounds of croquet, and commented five times on how quickly the grass seemed to grow in this neighborhood. Now she was struggling not to faint, from both heat and boredom.

"They must water the lawn often," Miss Bolton said for the sixth time. "Speaking of water . . . this punch is terrible."

She and Beatrice were wedged in between four other chaperones and their charges, all shuffling through the moist garden.

"Does it taste bitter?" Beatrice asked at once, her slippers squelching as she halted in the grass. "Someone could have poisoned it with hemlock, or even laurel water—"

"No one has been poisoned, Beatrice," Miss Bolton assured her. "And that is a good thing, so don't look disappointed."

"I merely thought the lethargy brought on by the toxin could explain why everyone here is acting so dull," Beatrice sighed.

"That is due to the heat, and the fact that most people possess passionless personalities," Miss Bolton said. She took another sip of her punch and then pursed her lips nervously. "Though . . . if it *were* poison—"

"Then you should administer brandy to counteract the effects," Beatrice said immediately. "I could fetch you some, just in case—"

"Not necessary!" Miss Bolton removed the lid of her hat, revealing several small bottles stored inside. She selected a vial of brandy, dumped it into her punch glass, and then replaced the hat lid. "Your mother insists that *nothing* shall stop us from participating in this Season, so I came prepared."

There were three assembly rooms in Beatrice's London neighborhood: the Rose, the Tulip, and the Carnation. Each had a summer Season that young ladies and gentlemen could attend. One had to be invited, of course; this was how private clubs provided protection against ne'er-do-wells. When courting, smart gentlemen and ladies always used protection.

Patronesses—married women with an eye for matchmaking—hand-selected the lists of attendees for each Season. This ensured that a young lady could meet just the right sort of man: handsome, genteel, and filthy rich. And likely seeking a wife who preferred playing the pianoforte to pursuing justice.

Beatrice had somehow landed invites to the Tulip and Carnation, but the mysterious, elite Rose Club had not extended such a summons.

"Your mother's instructions were simple," Miss Bolton reiterated. "Participate in the Season, marry a wealthy man, and uphold your family's reputation and subsequent fortune by following a strict code of conduct for the rest of your life."

"Yes, simple," Beatrice said dryly. "But there are so many people here that I can hardly breathe, let alone distinguish myself from the other young ladies in order to find a match."

In Swampshire, Beatrice had felt overscrutinized, her every move watched in a small town in which everyone knew everyone. But now it was as if someone had created a hundred Beatrices and Miss Boltons and dropped them into a garden together, which came with its own challenges. Namely, personal space.

"The Carnation's guest list *is* unwieldy," Miss Bolton agreed as they pushed their way in between two young ladies and their chaperones. "It would be wonderful if you could get an invite to the Rose—"

"They only accept the wealthiest, most elite members of society into their ranks," a chaperone next to Miss Bolton offered helpfully. "The only time all the classes mingle is at Sweetbriar's end-of-summer masquerade."

"Excuse me, this is a private conversation," Miss Bolton said, turning toward the woman. They were nearly cheek to cheek. She then turned back to Beatrice. "What nerve—assuming that we aren't the wealthiest, most elite members of society."

"Well, we aren't," Beatrice said.

"Yes, but she doesn't *know* that," Miss Bolton whispered.

"I thought that we would leave these social games back in Swampshire." Beatrice sighed. "Must we participate in the Season? Don't you ever wish we could just . . . let it all go?"

"I made your mother a promise that I would chaperone you, and I mean to keep that promise," Miss Bolton replied firmly. "The last time I shirked my duties, you nearly died. I won't make that mistake again."

Technically, Miss Bolton was correct in this comment. She had been assigned to chaperone Beatrice on her first case with Inspector Drake. But after Drake questioned Miss Bolton's reliability, she fled, leaving them alone. When Beatrice and Drake were subsequently attacked by the killer, Miss Bolton blamed herself, for she believed abandoning her post had left them vulnerable. After such a close call, she rededicated herself to said post (and to her hats, which ultimately saved the day, since her chapeau's parachute feature had rescued them all from certain death).

But in spite of Miss Bolton's determination, Beatrice knew exactly how to give her dear friend the slip.

"Did you hear that Mr. Percival Nash is somewhere at this party?" she asked casually, and Miss Bolton dropped her arm. Her eyes widened with excitement—and distraction—just as Beatrice had known they would.

"Percival Nash? The star of *Figaro III: Here We Figaro Again*?" Miss Bolton gasped. "I just know he would be perfect as the leading man in my play. He is charismatic, handsome, has incredible breath support . . . and I don't believe the rumors that his hair is fake. If only I could get him to read my script *Altus*—it is a celebration of altos, sung all in Latin. Altos never get a chance to *shine,* you know—"

"Someone said he was by the fountain. You go look, and I shall fetch us more punch," Beatrice told her.

"Make sure it is free of poison," Miss Bolton said distractedly, and then took off. Beatrice ensured that the short woman and her tall hat were out of sight and then rushed in the opposite direction, through a crowd of perspiring garden party attendees.

She felt a stab of guilt as she dodged chaperones and their hopeful charges. She hated lying to Miss Bolton. And truly, Beatrice *should* have been seeking a husband, for the sake of her family. Since her sister Louisa had married the impoverished (though charismatic) Frank, the responsibility of securing a fortune had fallen on Beatrice's shoulders. Yes, there was still Mary, but one couldn't pin too many hopes on Beatrice's youngest sister (nor could you pin any bows to her hair, which was always, strangely, full of dirt).

But Beatrice had come to the city to seek killers, not sweethearts. So she unenthusiastically attended parties, staying just long enough to make her presence known. Then, at the earliest opportunity, she made a hasty departure.

Which is exactly what she did now as she sidestepped a sweating, chatting couple and plunged into the Carnation Club's tall hedges.

Beatrice fell out the other side only slightly the worse for wear. She had a few tears in her white muslin dress but was otherwise unscathed. She straightened her bonnet and turned to complete her escape.

"I, too, find doors overrated." A chipper voice made her jump, and she whirled around to see a man leaning against a tree. He wore his fair hair combed back and was clean-shaven, revealing a strong jawline. A pipe was poised in one hand, halfway toward his full lips.

At first, Beatrice wondered if he was an actor. There were many hanging around the neighborhood, hoping to be discovered—but though this man had the good looks of a performer, he was dressed in an aristocratic ensemble. He held himself with an air of nobility, she observed, and he had no traces of leftover stage makeup on his visage.

This man was a gentleman.

"Sometimes a lady needs to make a creative exit," Beatrice said, feeling a flicker of curiosity.

What was a gentleman doing lingering outside a party alone?

"Indeed," the man agreed. He lifted the pipe to his mouth and inhaled, now looking thoughtful. He exhaled several rings of smoke and added, "It makes her memorable."

"That was not my intention," Beatrice said, her curiosity turning to concern. It was the last thing any detective would want, after all; investigating was easiest when no one paid her any attention. Which had been the case thus far in London.

But now she realized that the street outside the Carnation Club was empty apart from her and this man, and her concern grew.

She considered several possible modes of attack, from kicking the man in the crotch to jamming his pipe down his throat. He lowered his pipe and broke into a warm smile, clearly unaware of her imaginings. Though he looked oddly familiar, they couldn't possibly have met, Beatrice thought. She had been in London for months, but the Season had only just begun, and she had hardly spoken to any eligible men—let alone one as handsome as this.

"I shall *try* to forget you," the man assured her, "though I admit . . . it will be a challenge." And then he actually winked.

At this, Beatrice turned on her heel and strode away. She had learned that one could never trust a gentleman who was excessively charming and handsome. He might be a cold-blooded killer.

She rounded a corner, and the empty street opened up to a wider passageway lined with flowers.

Sweetbriar was named for the wild roses that grew everywhere, their vines twisting along fences and hedges and buildings. The color added warmth to the neighborhood's Gothic architecture: Gray houses with turrets and spires towered over the streets, casting long shadows over gardens, with gargoyles flanking each doorway.* The pleasure garden surrounded the local theater, the Sweet Majestic.

(Unfortunately, the Sweet Majestic was the reason there were so many mimes and amateur actors hanging about; they performed continuous one-person shows in the hopes that a director might pass by and discover their talent.)

Sweetbriar was divided into four sections, and Beatrice was currently in the southeastern corner. It was dubbed the Carnation Quarter, after the social club she had just fled. It was also where Inspector Drake and Beatrice had a small office, which was Beatrice's destination.

Mrs. Steele was under the impression that Beatrice did occasional "secretary work" in this office (accompanied by Miss Bolton, of course). Beatrice knew that her mother only conceded to this because she thought it might keep Beatrice's morbid in-

* The people of Sweetbriar were obsessed with gargoyles, as they thought these stone guardians protected against "the ancient curse of the wolf." Beatrice did not understand this random obsession. *Her* hometown did not contain a single gargoyle, and there had never been any issue with wolves or curses. At least, nothing confirmed.

terests "under control and only discussed behind closed doors." Neither Susan Steele nor Helen Bolton knew that Beatrice snuck away regularly to spend as much time as possible on her morbid interests—and she hoped to keep it that way.

The afternoon was dissolving into early evening, though the heat of the day lingered. In the main square, the street was far from empty: Londoners sat at small tables in front of restaurants, sipping tipples; gentlemen hailed carriages; and couples strolled arm in arm down cobblestone streets. A certain spirit seemed to have arrived with the swell of heat; people had an extra sparkle in their eyes. A joie de vivre, one might say, if one were forced to speak French.

Beatrice watched one group in particular—a swathe of fashionable ladies, out for a stroll. From their chic gowns to their confidence, they radiated a cosmopolitan air that Beatrice envied. Would she ever be like one of those city women, walking with such ease—such belonging?

She was jolted from her musings when a carriage careened past. An arm grabbed her and pulled her back, and she turned to see a tall man. She felt a thrill of excitement when she saw that he was holding a skull—

Until she realized that it was fake, and he was using it as a prop in an impromptu sonnet.

"She paid no mind to carriage or to me, the lass who wore a gown from season last," he began mournfully. "She nearly perished right here in the street—had it not been for one quick-thinking lad—"

"Yes, thank you," Beatrice said, dropping coins into an overturned top hat at the man's feet. "Though you should know that 'last' and 'lad' are really just a slant rhyme, which some say isn't a *real* rhyme—"

"I pulled her far away from certain death, I saved her life right here before your eyes," the man continued loudly. A crowd had gathered to hear the poem, and Beatrice squeezed away from them, not interested in more lines about her close call with the carriage.

But just as she thought she had gotten away from the performer, he appeared in front of her again.

"And how will she repay me, one might ask?" he said loudly. "By passing on my portrait to a cast . . . ing director." With great flourish, the street performer handed Beatrice a piece of parchment. His likeness was sketched above a list of stage credits.

"I don't know any casting directors. I am egregiously unconnected!" Beatrice insisted, but the man had already turned away and launched into a fresh sonnet about the beauty of a passing woman. No doubt it would end with the same poorly worded couplet she had just heard, Beatrice thought as she stuffed the man's portrait into her reticule and took off down the street once more.

London was so different from Swampshire. It was more than the street performers; the city sizzled with heat and energy and . . . a whiff of murder?

No, she realized as she sidestepped a splash of liquid—someone was emptying a chamber pot out a window above.

"Squirrel incoming!" someone else yelled, and the group of well-dressed, cosmopolitan ladies in front of Beatrice ducked.

Beatrice was too slow on the uptake, and the flying rodent came out of nowhere. It smacked her in the face, and she stumbled back.

(The Carnation Quarter was the most affordable part of the neighborhood, as it bore the worst of the squirrel infestation.)

"Watch where you're going," a passerby scolded, pushing past Beatrice impatiently.

She stepped out of the walkway, pressing herself against the cool stone exterior of a shop, until she finally recovered her composure. Even considering her hometown's frequent hailstorms and squelch holes, she had never had so many near-death experiences on one simple stroll.

She was out of breath and flustered by the time she finally reached her destination: a small office with discreet gold letters on the door, spelling out DS INVESTIGATIONS.

The initials made Beatrice's heart lift. Would it ever feel real to see the "S" on the sign and know it stood for "Steele"? Would she ever truly believe that she was one half of an actual detective office in London? Her life in the city was not exactly as she'd pictured it, but this, at least, felt like a dream come true.

She wrenched open the door and stepped inside, where a small room held two desks piled high with letters and notebooks. Shelves stuffed with books lined the walls, and two armchairs faced a pin-striped chaise. In the center of the chairs sat a chessboard atop a mahogany coffee table, a game paused in play. Golden light from the sun filtered inside, casting a glow over the cozy office.

As Beatrice entered, she saw a familiar, tall Indian man wearing a rumpled suit and an eye patch. Though he had a scowl across his scarred face, she knew from the flash in his remaining eye that he was glad to see her. She met his stern look with a smile. For a moment she thought she saw his mouth twitch up at the corners—but then his jaw clenched, and he affected an even sterner look.

"Miss Steele," said Inspector Vivek Drake. "It's about time."

Dear Beatrice,

I trust that you and Miss Bolton have had a fortuitous start to the summer season. Now that the heat has come, so will the parties . . . and the eligible men!

I am glad to hear that you enjoy the London town house. Does it really have such a horrifying gargoyle above the front door, or was that some sort of self-portrait in your last letter? In either case, please do NOT send any more drawings in further correspondence. Use words only to paint a picture of your London life, and spare me the nightmares.

As for business here in Swampshire: Louisa, Frank, and your niece, baby Bee Bee, are doing well, and send their regards. They would visit you in town, but since Frank is destitute apart from his one measly mansion, there is no money for a carriage. Mary asked me to include some sentiment from her, but I forgot what it was. However, please let Miss Bolton know that she is taking excellent care of Fauna Manor; she has looked into the howling incident and concluded there is nothing to worry about.

Your father sent his regards in a separate letter, though I believe he wrote it in invisible ink. I would repeat his message here, but we are not currently speaking, as he exploded the staircase as part of some stupid joke and has offered no ideas for how we shall afford repairs. My nerves, and the banister, may never recover.

But truly we are wonderful, other than the fact that we all grow more impoverished by the day, our bank account drained dry, our spirits broken, unable to access any rooms upstairs . . . this could all change, of course, if you marry well.

Therefore I must remind you, Beatrice, that you are in London to participate in the Season. You must not become distracted by morbid fancies, secretarial duties, or a certain inspector. (Give Mr. Drake my regards, by the way.)

Sweetbriar is a respectable neighborhood, with three wonderful assembly halls. The Carnation and the Tulip have both fostered many advantageous matches, but of course, you must try to get on the list at the Rose. According to the society columns, it counts the wealthiest gentlemen among its members.

Remember that you grow more decrepit and unmarriageable with each passing day. You must try to find a husband before the wrinkles take over. They are distinguished for men but unsightly in women.

I hope you will return to Swampshire the moment you have secured this husband's ~~money~~ hand in marriage.

I miss you, my darling. Sending all my love,

Your mother,

Susan Steele

CHAPTER TWO

A Case

As the door closed, the noise on the street faded. Beatrice and Drake were now alone together in their small office.

Unbeknownst to anyone else, she and Drake were alone regularly now, whenever Beatrice was able to shake Miss Bolton. Though Mrs. Steele would not have approved, she needn't have worried. Drake treated Beatrice with the utmost professionalism, even offering her port and a pipe at the end of particularly long workdays. (Neither of them smoked, but they agreed that it was fitting for detectives to at least possess the prop.)

"Any new cases?" Beatrice asked. She took off her bonnet and shook out her dark curls. The white streak in her hair—gained during a competitive round of whist—had grown a bit thicker after the events of last autumn. Catching a killer was almost as stressful as a boisterous card game.

"Nothing of interest," Drake replied. "Any new beaus?" His

deep voice was touched with a hint of an Indian accent—and contempt.

Inspector Drake disapproved of high society, and could not understand Beatrice's attempts to participate in the Season *and* solve crimes. But Drake was not the one who received constant correspondence from Mrs. Steele, telling tales of her financial misfortune and insisting that a prosperous marriage was the only way to rescue the family. He did not have anyone who relied upon him for monetary support, as Beatrice did: Sadly, his mother had passed long ago, and his wealthy half sister, Alice, was off on a Grand Tour, enjoying her newfound freedom after being locked in an attic for years.

Beatrice, on the other hand, had recurring nightmares of chasing shadowy figures around the city while her sisters, parents, and darling niece huddled in a shack submerged in the Swampshire squelch holes, wasting away. . . .

She tried to perish the thought.

"As a matter of fact, I received three marriage proposals today," she informed Drake, withdrawing a parcel from her reticule.

"Really?" Drake raised an eyebrow.

"No. I suffered through three conversations about paint drying." She set the parcel on his desk.

"What is that?" he asked, eyeing it suspiciously.

"Cake that I stole while everyone was droning on about the paint," Beatrice replied.

"It was unnecessary to bring that all this way," Drake told her. "Supplying me with sweets is not in your job description."

"It's almond," she told him. "Your favorite."

"I never said that was my favorite."

"I am capable of deduction, Inspector." She crossed to the chessboard in the center of the office, considered it a moment, and then moved her queen.

"Going to the queen so early?" Drake said as he unwrapped the cake parcel. "Dangerous."

"Why hold back such a powerful piece?"

"Why indeed," he murmured. "There are a few letters we received from prospective clients," he went on, his tone growing businesslike as Beatrice removed her muslin shawl and hung it by the front door. "Though none seemed promising for— What are you *wearing*?"

"I know, it's last season," Beatrice began apologetically, gesturing to her gown. "Five seasons ago, really—"

"I wouldn't know anything about that," Drake scoffed, indicating his own rumpled suit. "I am talking about the tassels!"

Beatrice looked down at the colorful embellishments sewn around the neckline, sleeves, and skirt of her dress.

"Miss Bolton added them to help me stand out among the other young ladies of the Season," she explained.

"You certainly stand out," Drake said, raising an eyebrow. "Though perhaps not in the way she intended."

"Keep up the commentary and I'll add some on to *your* clothes," Beatrice told him.

"An empty threat, as you can't sew a single stitch," Drake replied.

Beatrice could not argue with this—her attempt at sewing had once gotten a man killed, after all—so instead, she crossed to her desk and began to leaf through a pile of letters. As she riffled through them, she unearthed one in a familiar script and tore it open.

She scanned the contents. Spotting the words "husband" and "eligible," as well as at least two guilt trips, Beatrice deduced the sender immediately.

"My mother sends her regards." She folded it closed and returned it to the desk.

"Is she in good health?" Drake asked. Though he affected a

disinterested tone, Beatrice could tell from the way he watched her, intently, that he genuinely cared. In spite of the fact that Drake had wrongly accused Beatrice's sister Louisa of murder, the Steele family had forgiven him—and even taken a liking to the matter-of-fact inspector. After all, through his accusations, he had unearthed a plethora of secrets and ultimately forced the family closer together.

"She is fine, apart from her usual nerves," Beatrice assured him. "Which are nothing that couldn't be healed by an increase in income . . ." she added under her breath.

She brought her hand to her throat reflexively. She always wore a locket with a sketch of her sister Louisa and niece, baby Bee Bee, inside—a token from home.* (Her niece and Miss Bolton's dog had the same name, which led to some confusion, but as they were both named after Beatrice, she could not complain.) Though Beatrice had wished to come to London, she could not help but miss the family she'd left behind in Swampshire—financial complaints and all.

But her hands felt no cool metal. Instead, they brushed bare skin.

"My locket," Beatrice gasped, panic rising in her throat. "It's gone!"

She looked around, hoping it had merely fallen to the floor of the office—but the little necklace was nowhere to be seen. She pulled out her reticule and began rifling through its contents: an extra hat pin (extra sharp), newspaper clippings, old letters, a bloody handkerchief she had found and thought might be something sinister, until the blood turned out to be lipstick . . . but no locket.

* Beatrice had asked an artist to draw her youngest sister, Mary, as well, but the miniature portrait he created mysteriously disintegrated when placed inside the silver locket.

"Did you walk here alone again?" Drake asked, crossing over to her, his expression darkening. "I have warned you time and time again, this is a city, with pickpockets, thieves, mimes, poets—"

As he spoke, Beatrice reached the bottom of her reticule and withdrew one last item: the poet's portrait.

"Aha!" she cried, waving the parchment in the air. "It must have been him!"

Drake took the portrait and scanned the name and credits listed below the painted headshot. "'Archibald Croome,'" he read. "'Actor, poet, bard, and sonneteer.' Not a very talented one; most of those words mean the same thing."

"I should have known he wasn't saving me just to do a good deed," Beatrice muttered. "It was all a guise for picking my pocket."

"You are accustomed to the slow pace of the countryside, as well as its lack of street performers," Drake told her, tossing aside the portrait. "Things move quicker here. You have to keep up."

"I can keep up," Beatrice said immediately.

She could not be seen as provincial. Not if she wanted to be taken seriously as his partner. But, she thought, her naïveté was apparently obvious to all—even a stranger on the street had recognized it.

Drake motioned for her to come closer, and she obliged. "Poets and pickpockets thrive when you are distracted," he began, his tone annoyingly didactic.

"I'm never distracted," Beatrice began.

"Someone outside is stabbing people with a broadsword!" Drake interrupted.

"Fetch my shield!" Beatrice shrieked. "I knew it was a useful purchase—" She whirled around to look out the window. A group of men with top hats and canes passed by, no medieval weaponry in sight.

When Beatrice turned back to Drake, confused, he held one of her earrings in his hands.

"How did you do that?" She pressed a hand to her now empty lobe.

"Street smarts," Drake repeated. "One must know the way of criminals in order to catch them." He stepped forward and gently put the earring back in her ear, one hand resting on her chin.

She caught his scent, reminiscent of cinnamon and oranges. Drake looked down at her, his hand still holding her chin, and a strange feeling rushed from his fingertips into the pit of her stomach.

Drake's eye met hers.

"Now, next time," he said softly, "you shall be en garde."

"Please, Drake," she whispered, "you know how I feel about French."

He nodded, holding her gaze. Then he finally dropped his hand.

"Now you are *prepared,* then," he said, his brisk tone returning. "I cannot have a partner who is vulnerable in such a way. What if someone stole important case information off your person? Not that we have any important cases . . ."

Beatrice had no reply to this, so she turned and opened the office window. The heat had become too stifling. If only she could relieve her growing insecurities as easily . . .

She returned to her desk and began to sort through a stack of letters.

There had to be *something* for them to solve.

She moved aside a half-full teacup—how long had that been there?—and sliced open the next letter. Holding it up, she read aloud:

"'To DS Investigations. I have contacted Sir Huxley about this matter, and he suggested that I ask the two of you instead. After a dinner party last Sunday, my spectacles went missing.'"

Drake sighed. Beatrice felt his frustration.

Inspector Drake's half sister, Alice, had paid for their office. She had used her family fortune to furnish it, stocked the shelves with research books, and left Drake a stipend for business expenses. Yet though this was much appreciated, it did not guarantee the operation's success. Alice Croaksworth could pay for a lease, a library, and lamps, but she could not change public opinion. And the public of London had chosen Sir Huxley as their foremost inspector.

According to the sketches of Huxley in the newspaper, this gentleman detective was devastatingly handsome, with a full mustache and chiseled features. He flitted around the city with his asp-topped cane, solving all the best crimes. His connections with the upper classes afforded him access anywhere, and his fame was further buoyed by newspaper articles singing his praises. Once, Beatrice had been Huxley's biggest fan—and Inspector Drake had been his partner. But then Drake and Huxley had parted ways, and Beatrice had learned Huxley was a hack who relied on fans like her to send him answers and clues to the crimes he then "solved."

Still. No one else in London knew this, and therefore they turned to Sir Huxley for all intriguing cases. Drake and Beatrice were left chasing cats, dogs, and eyeglasses.

They had to start somewhere, Beatrice supposed.

"Last Sunday," Drake said thoughtfully, leaning back in his chair. "It was very hot that evening. Even worse than today."

"Perhaps he removed his spectacles, due to the heat," Beatrice suggested. "They were probably fogging up." She paused, looking over at Drake just as he spoke.

"We can't know that for sure," he said, at the exact same time she recited the words along with him. He made a noise of irritation in the back of his throat. "Well, it's true," he said.

"I'm going to write back and advise him to check his windowsills," Beatrice said. "I surmise that he opened one for some air, removed his glasses when they fogged up, and left them on the ledge. Though if you have another idea, based on more evidence, I am happy to include that as well . . . ?"

"I concur with the windowsill theory," Drake said stiffly. "But please indicate in your reply that it is just that: a theory."

Beatrice penned a reply, adding Drake's addendum (though in very small writing), then folded up the letter and placed it atop a tall stack of outgoing mail.

"You already replied to the rest of the cases?" Beatrice asked in surprise.

"You haven't been around in a while," Drake replied, straightening his already-tidy desk.

I should be grateful, Beatrice thought. Drake's diligence would keep the business going, even in her absence—and if she and Drake could find a *real* crime, the positive press would be profitable. They'd be able to attract a steady supply of cases, and Beatrice would have an income of her own, without relying on Alice Croaksworth's charity. She could support her family, ensure that baby Bee Bee was well provided for, and avoid a marriage of convenience.

For some reason, at that moment, her mind conjured an image of the fair-haired man who had stood against the tree, smoking his pipe as she pushed through the hedges of the Carnation Club.

A little bell chimed as the door to the office opened, wrenching Beatrice from her thoughts.

A man stepped into DS Investigations. "Good afternoon," he said in a grand voice. "I hope I've come to the right place. I need someone to solve a horribly brutal murder."

"A brutal murder?" Beatrice exclaimed, leaping to her feet. "Yes, you have *certainly* come to the right place."

CALLOUS CRIMES

By Evana Chore

Memories of the London Menace are fresh in the minds of Sweetbriar's residents. Evidently, however, this killer has ceased his reign of terror, with no new attacks reported in months. Even so, the neighborhood is under a new threat. The artists who have found their way into this little corner of London bring with them "self-expression," which many do not realize can kill in a different way: by murdering morals and destroying decorum.

Over the past several months, there has been an increase in artists renting townhomes in the unfortunately affordable Carnation Quarter. Needless to say, their influence has already been felt: Local ladies have adopted flamboyant fashions, no doubt inspired by the costumes they see, and they repeat unbecoming "jokes" picked up from street-corner comics. Mimes and singers present stories of bold, silly characters who seem outlandish now—but what if our young women soon adopt not just the outfits and jokes of artists, but the attitudes as well? One has to wonder: How long will this go on before we Sweetbrarians stand up for ourselves?

Now is the time to demand change, before the neighborhood becomes overtaken by these so-called free spirits. Dally not, citizens. Action must be taken. You will be effective in driving these troublemakers away if you refrain from patronizing any local performances.

Dear Beatrice,

If you are reading this, you have cracked the code and applied heat to the letter to reveal its invisible ink (lemon juice). Huzzah!

I send my regards to both you and Inspector Drake. Louisa tells me that you are hard at work solving cases, whereas your mother assures me that you are attending many social events in order to find a husband. These two activities sound very demanding on your time, and I hope you are leaving space in your schedule for merriment. We must live, laugh, *and* love. I try to do all three at least once a day, as should you.

Sincerely,

Your proud father,

Stephen Steele

PS: Enclosed is a large quantity of firecrackers. Your mother attempted to confiscate them after a bit of an incident. Could you please lend them to Inspector Drake, for safekeeping?

CHAPTER THREE

A Death

The man who had entered their office had a cleft chin, a roguishly charming smile, and auburn hair tied back with a dark green ribbon. He held himself with poise, and Beatrice could tell that he was the kind of person who was accustomed to having everyone's eyes upon him.

But Beatrice also sensed concern beneath the man's confident façade. He kept glancing out the window as if afraid he had been followed. There were beads of sweat upon his brow. And though his clothes were elegant and well tailored, he had misbuttoned his jacket.

"Please, sit," Beatrice told him, ushering the man toward the office chaise. He obliged, while Beatrice and Drake took seats in armchairs across from him. Drake opened his yellow notebook, quill poised to take notes.

DS Investigations had never had a client walk through their

doors with something truly terrible to report. Beatrice hoped this case would be good.

Or, rather, she hoped it would be nasty.

"My name is Percival Nash," the man began.

Drake gasped. Beatrice turned, startled, having never heard him utter such a noise. His eye was wide in shock, and his quill fell from his hand.

"Mr. Nash," Drake repeated, his tone reverent, "forgive us for not recognizing you at once. I have only seen you upon the stage, of course. . . ." He turned to Beatrice. "This man is a renowned opera star," he whispered, as if Percival were not within (very close) earshot.

"I have heard tell," Beatrice assured him. It was true; Percival Nash was a local celebrity. Miss Bolton spoke of him with the same admiration, but Beatrice would have never expected this of Inspector Drake. Normally he was so stoic; she had not imagined he could be starstruck.

"We should offer him something," Drake continued to whisper, flustered. "Coffee? Port? Shall I make a trifle? I don't know how, but I am a quick study. . . ."

"Your continued devotion, as well as coffee, would be enough," Percival cut in.

"Of course," Drake said, shutting his notebook. He scrambled to procure the beverage, while Beatrice turned back to Percival Nash.

"Forgive my partner. Evidently he is . . . a fan," she explained.

"And you are not?" Percival inquired, raising one perfectly shaped eyebrow.

"I have heard of your talents," Beatrice said, "but as I have only recently come to town, I have not yet been to the opera. Of course," she added hastily, "I shall remedy that at once."

"If you assist me, you shall have free admittance for life," Percival assured her as Drake returned with a tray of coffee and almond cake. He nearly dropped the entire thing at Percival's words, and Beatrice had to rush to assist.

"Please, Mr. Nash," Beatrice said, passing out the coffee before Drake ruined the carpet, "tell us about the murder."

Percival took a sip of coffee, holding eye contact through a dramatic pause. Drake looked rapt, but Beatrice felt a spark of annoyance.

Dramatic pauses belonged onstage. When it came to crime, she wanted no delay.

People's lives could depend upon it.

"Sweetbriar was once a beacon of artistic achievement," Percival said finally, setting his coffee cup on its saucer with a small *clink*. "Painters, poets, singers, and actors flocked to its streets to offer their expression. The Sweet Majestic was built, our grand opera theater, and we enjoyed the patronage of the upper classes."

"And . . . there was a murder at the theater?" Beatrice prompted. She had waited long enough for a case. Was she really to wait even *longer*?

"Madam," Percival Nash said, pressing a hand to his heart, "never interrupt an actor in the middle of a monologue."

"Yes, Beatrice, show some respect for the performance," Drake scolded.

"Pardon me. I thought this was a *dialogue*," Beatrice grumbled, but fell silent.

"Now, where was I . . ." Percival affected a formal air once more. "This neighborhood was once a haven for artists. It shall be no more: Some members of the upper class do not appreciate our ideals. Those in power consider us a threat to the status quo. Which is why I believe that I am being framed . . . for murder." He rose to his feet and struck a pose.

"No!" Drake gasped.

"*Whose* murder?" Beatrice pressed, unmoved by the tableau, which had still given her little information. Drake glared at her. "It's rather important," she insisted.

"You are right. And I am glad you asked," Percival replied. "The setting is the Rose." He swept a hand across the office as if he were onstage, a curtain about to rise. "Sweetbriar's most exclusive social club."

"There is no need to act everything out—" Beatrice began, but Drake shushed her, and she sighed.

Percival Nash lifted the table from in front of Beatrice and Drake and placed it in the center of the office. "Imagine a dinner party taking place inside the Rose," he told them. He knelt in front of the table and mimed eating and drinking. "The room would have been alight with merriment and laughter as members discussed the upcoming Season." He laughed, as if someone at the table had told a hilarious joke, but then his face immediately turned serious. "Until one man peeled away from the group: Mr. Walter Shrewsbury."

Though Beatrice was irritated, she had to admit Percival had *it,* whatever *it* was. She could not tear her eyes away from him as he acted out the scene.

"Mr. Shrewsbury retired to the lounge. Perhaps for a cigar." Percival mimed smoking. "Perhaps for a tipple." He picked up his coffee cup and downed the dregs. "He never knew that this was his final drink, before he would shuffle off this mortal coil."

"No!" Drake gasped again.

"Yes," Percival replied dramatically. "Someone crept into the lounge of the Rose Club. . . ." He began to tiptoe, then pantomimed lifting a knife. "They beat Walter Shrewsbury and then stabbed him to death." He jumped to the spot where Walter Shrewsbury would have been, mimed being stabbed in the chest, and then crumpled to the floor.

"Bravo!" Drake yelled, rising to his feet.

Percival Nash stood and sank into a bow. Beatrice clapped along.

"Thank you," Percival said graciously. "It all just comes naturally to me, really. . . ."

"Encore!" Drake said, then quickly amended: "I mean . . . we do not want an encore to murder, of course—"

"What I would like to know," Beatrice cut in, "is how does the murder of this man—Walter Shrewsbury—concern *you,* Mr. Nash?"

Percival stopped bowing and sank back into the seat across from Beatrice and Drake. Now that he was "offstage," his concerned countenance returned. "As this case regards a member of the gentility, the usual inspector was brought in," he explained. "That detective with the enviably handsome mustache."

Drake and Beatrice exchanged a look of displeasure. They could guess who this was.

"Sir Lawrence Huxley," Percival confirmed. "He came to question me about the case. He suspects that I had something to do with it. Can you even imagine? Someone like me, a killer?" He took a fan from inside his jacket, unfurled it, and began to fan himself vigorously, as if overcome by the very idea.

Truly, though Percival could possibly play any part, Beatrice could *not* imagine him as a killer. He wanted to be praised and adored; murdering someone might put a damper on his fans' reverence.

"Huxley is quick to jump to conclusions," Drake said darkly. "If he has fingered you for this crime—"

"That charming detective can finger me all he wants, but I could not bear it if I were arrested!" Percival cried. "I need someone to prove my innocence and find the true killer. It is about more than just my good name," he added, pressing a hand to his chest. "The fate of all artists in Sweetbriar is at risk."

"How so?" Beatrice asked, hoping Percival was not about to launch into another reenactment. He had been captivating, yes, but she wanted *answers*—and she feared that if he got going again, he might actually break out into song.

"If I am arrested, it won't be long before ladies and gentlemen will consider *all* artists dangerous," Percival explained. "I represent the artistic ideal. If I am tarnished, we are all tarnished."

"Who would ever attack the opera?" Drake said, shaking his head in disbelief. "Everyone loves opera!"

Beatrice chuckled, and Percival and Drake both turned to look at her.

"I beg your pardon," she said, trying to regain a straight face. "Of course you are correct." She cleared her throat and went on. "Mr. Nash, I wonder, why did Sir Huxley suspect you in the first place? And do you have an alibi for the evening of the murder? We might easily prove your innocence, if anyone can confirm your whereabouts."

"I know not why Huxley thinks I have anything to do with this death," Percival insisted. "But you must find out the real killer, before he puts me away . . . *forever*."

"He has not arrested you yet," Beatrice pointed out.

"Only because there is no sufficient evidence to do so," Percival replied. "But it is only a matter of time. Huxley will finish his questioning and then make an arrest, whether or not he comes up with proof. You must clear my name before this occurs."

He rose to his feet once more, clearly meaning to leave the office.

"Wait," Beatrice said, also standing. "There is the question of payment."

There was also the question of his alibi, which Beatrice noted that he had not given.

"If you solve such a crime, your reviews shall be raves," Percival assured her. "Rave reviews lead to compensation."

"Well yes, but we must—" Beatrice began, but Drake interrupted her.

"We will take the case."

He and Percival shook hands. Percival turned and held his hand out to Beatrice, but she did not offer hers so quickly.

"If Inspector Drake and I are to investigate this crime, we need access to the Rose," Beatrice told him. "I doubt they will let two investigators waltz through their locked iron gates, especially since Huxley has already been hired."

"Quite right," Percival agreed. "I suggest you secure your place on the list before the Season officially begins. It's one of the only ways inside such a fortress." He took her hand, kissed it gallantly, then crossed to the door. Before leaving, he turned back once more. "Thank you," he said sincerely, pressing a hand to his chest. "You have been a wonderful audience."

With that, he whisked away.

Drake turned to Beatrice. "Can you believe it?" he said, evidently still in awe. "Percival Nash, star of the opera, came to *us* for assistance!"

"Vivek Drake," Beatrice said, shaking her head, "a fan of the theater. I never would have suspected it."

"Opera is not just theater. It is a musical experience," Drake said immediately. "My mother took me regularly in my youth, and I have a deep appreciation for the art form."

"That is all very well," Beatrice allowed, "but because of this 'deep appreciation,' you have just accepted a case for no pay. And one which Sir Huxley has already claimed, at that. How are we to go about such an investigation?"

"We get on the list, as Percival suggested," Drake told her. "By the way, what is 'the list'?"

"The patroness of the Rose will have a register of eligible ladies and gentlemen selected to participate in the Season," Beatrice explained. "One has to be invited in order to attend their events."

"Wonderful. You are part of the Season, so you must be on the list," Drake said, but Beatrice shook her head.

"I am on the list at the Carnation and the Tulip. The Rose is the most exclusive club in town. We will not find our way in quite so easily."

Drake's jaw tensed. "'We'?"

"The last time we investigated separately, you wrongly accused my sister of murder, and I almost married the killer," Beatrice reminded him. "So I would recommend that we stick together this time to ensure none of that happens again."

"'Almost married' is putting it strongly," Drake said tartly.

"He was perfect apart from his killer instincts," she replied. "A lady doesn't always have many options."

"I am certain you will find a better option," Drake said. An odd look came across his face, but it passed as quickly as it had come. "So," he continued, brisk once more, "you will get on the list—"

"And so will you, and therefore we will both be able to investigate. Together."

"In high society," Drake grumbled.

"To clear the name of your favorite opera star," Beatrice told him.

Drake's dilemma was evident in his conflicted expression: He loved solving cases as much as he detested participating in social gatherings. Still, Beatrice was certain that Drake's desire for justice would prevail. And though they would not be paid for this case, Percival was right—good press would help the office. Not to mention that Beatrice would be able to please her mother by participating in the Season, while also doing what she loved most.

Hunting a killer.

She shivered with excitement. It would all be perfect—if they could figure out how to secure an invite into the most exclusive assembly hall in town. She hadn't been motivated before to seek a place on the Rose's list, but now it felt like a worthy goal. . . .

The office clock chimed, interrupting her thoughts, and Beatrice jumped.

"The garden reception! I've been away too long!" she yelped. "Miss Bolton will be sending out a search party!"* Beatrice grabbed her bonnet and retied it haphazardly, then flung her muslin shawl over her shoulders.

"We just got hired to solve a murder. You're going to leave, before we even have a plan in place?" Drake stared at her incredulously.

"If we are to somehow get on the list at the Rose, my reputation must be spotless," Beatrice told him. "Unexplained disappearances tend to tarnish one's good name."

Drake looked irritated but held out his arm. "At least let me escort you back. You've already been robbed once today. Who knows what might happen if you go back out there alone."

"I am fine," Beatrice assured him, but she took his arm nonetheless. Truthfully, she could not handle dealing with any more performers today, and Drake had mastered the Londoner's "stay away" stare.

Together, Drake and Beatrice stepped out into the busy street. The sounds and smells of the city immediately flooded her senses, but this time, Beatrice breathed it all in with relish.

They were officially, *finally,* on a case.

* Miss Bolton was wont to create search parties; in Swampshire she had often started them to find Mary, who seemed to disappear exactly once a month. This always lined up with the full moon, which was helpful in illuminating the search party's path.

Dear Beatrice,

I hope that your latest outing at the Carnation Club was a success. Your father subscribed to *The London Babbler* due to its "impeccable cartoons," so I have been keeping up with the society columns therein. Strangely, they have yet to mention your name as a stunning new young lady on the social scene. I trust you shall soon be featured?

Time is of the essence. I do not want to worry you, dear Beatrice, and your darling sister Louisa asked me not to write—but I must inform you of the latest. A particularly difficult hailstorm ripped through Swampshire last night, and Frank and Louisa's tiny mansion was damaged. They are staying with your father and me for the time being, but there is little money for repairs, and repairs they shall need. Their roof, I fear, is as dented as that custard pie you once tried to bake. (Which reminds me: Remember that for you, the way to a man's heart is *not* through his stomach, unless you procure the sweets elsewhere.)

If only you could ~~trick~~ catch the eye of a wealthy gentleman there in London, he could take care of all our problems. For a man with such a fortune, our little repairs would be a mere drop in the proverbial bucket!

I look forward to receiving your wedding invitation as soon as possible. Your future husband should feel free to enclose banknotes along with it.

All my love,

Your mother,

Susan Steele

BULLETIN SERVICES FROM THE NEIGHBORHOOD ASSOCIATION OF GENTLEMEN SWEETBRIARIANS

(BS from NAGS)

In light of the death of our beloved member Walter Shrewsbury, this summer's Season at the Rose is hereby POSTPONED.

We have discussed the matter at length. Cancellation was considered; the murder of a stand-up gentleman in our community suggests that this community is changing . . . for the worse. Yet ultimately, this is why we must forge ahead. Sweetbriar needs shining examples of gentility now more than ever. The Season at the Rose is a chance to demonstrate true refinement and what it can achieve.

Therefore we shall see all those on the list at the (somewhat later) start.

Cheers!

CHAPTER FOUR

A Cover

"Each assembly room has a patroness, who determines which young ladies and gentlemen are permitted to attend their Season," Beatrice told Drake as they made their way down the street. Their shadows grew long on the walkway as the sun sank lower into the horizon. The teacups in the cafés they passed had been replaced with crystal cordial glasses, and passersby were now clad in evening dress.

"So in order to get on the list, one would have to impress the patroness of the Rose," Beatrice went on as Drake expertly guided her out of the way of a spray of mud from a passing carriage.

"Then do that," he told her matter-of-factly. "Impress the patroness, I mean."

"I wish it were that simple," she murmured. "I don't even know who she is, let alone what might dazzle her. Unless she likes clumsy dancing or frightening artwork, I have few options. . . ."

"You have quick wit and fine eyes," Drake said, and then added hastily, "and an ability to push your way in anywhere."

"I don't know whether to be offended or flattered," she replied.

"A lady can do both simultaneously, I expect." Drake steered her through the neighborhood's pleasure garden maze and came out the other side without ever meeting a dead end. His knowledge of London was impressive. Though Beatrice had studied maps of Sweetbriar extensively, these maps did not show the shortcuts only locals knew.

But she soon realized that Drake's path had not led back to Miss Bolton and the Carnation garden party. Instead, Beatrice found herself looking up at an imposing building.

It was the Rose.

Like most buildings in Sweetbriar, the Rose was a Gothic structure, with two gargoyles on either side of the front door. The garden was a tangle of pink flowers, which crept their way onto the iron gate, winding around its heavy bars.

"See," Beatrice told Drake, indicating the gate. "Impenetrable, unless we are invited in."

"A person *might* scale it," Drake suggested.

"Not without puncturing flesh," Beatrice replied, pointing to sharp spires lining the top of the gate.

"Is this a fortress or an assembly hall?" Drake muttered.

Are they really that different? Beatrice thought. She had always imagined London as a huge city where all sorts of people could consort. Yet so far, she had found it disappointingly cordoned off, so many places off-limits. She thought of Percival Nash's observations, the rising panic about the impact of different classes and types of people mingling. What was the point in leaving her small town just to be confined once more?

She stared in between the gate's iron bars at the stone building before them. Even the tall windows of the Rose were closed, their drapes drawn shut, which was a disappointment—Beatrice adored peering into windows. Clearly, those who weren't invited inside would not get so much as a peek beyond the exterior.

There were hoofbeats in the distance. Beatrice and Drake turned to see a black carriage careening toward the club. It was obvious that the carriage was headed to the Rose—and judging by its speed, the occupants had no hesitation about their place inside those gates.

The idea came into Beatrice's mind before she had a moment to second-guess. She stepped away from Drake and toward the road, just as the carriage shot through a puddle of mud. The wheels spattered liquid everywhere, and Beatrice was doused from head to toe in the spray. She let out a scream, which she knew would attract onlookers. No one could resist a frenzy. Sure enough, several people stopped to stare at the scene Beatrice had orchestrated. They whispered, shocked at the sight of a young lady in a gown from five seasons ago now completely drenched in mud.

"Beatrice, what are you *doing*?" Drake shouted, grabbing her by the shoulders. "Didn't you see that the carriage was headed straight for the mud? Didn't you mentally chart its trajectory? You must always mentally chart the trajectory!"

Drake's mother had perished in a carriage accident, and ever since, he had harbored a fear of the vehicles. Beatrice felt a rush of guilt for causing him such concern.

"I have a plan. Trust me," she assured him, staring into his green eye. He knit his brows together in confusion but finally dropped his hands from her shoulders. She turned back to the carriage.

Had it been a foolish hunch? Would the occupants simply continue on their way? Her throat tightened in panic—but then, blessedly, the carriage screeched to a halt.

Just as she had hoped.

The door banged open, and a woman descended onto the street. She looked around until she saw Beatrice and crossed to her, hand pressed against her chest.

"My dear," the woman said, "are you quite all right?"

Though her voice was dreamlike and breathy, the woman's dark, catlike eyes appraised Beatrice with shrewdness. She had silver hair that was intriguingly held in place with a pearl hat pin. Wisps of hair had escaped, lending the woman a windswept look.

She seemed about the same age as Miss Bolton, who would have envied the mysterious lady's chic wardrobe: Her plum-colored overcoat had silver trim that matched her hair, and jewels sparkled in her ears and around her neck. Wealthy, clearly. Elite.

And if there was one thing Beatrice knew about the elite, it was that they valued appearances. A drive-by mud spray would be a terrible look for this woman. Now she owed Beatrice penance.

"She is stunned into silence, poor thing," the woman purred. She waved a handkerchief in front of Beatrice's eyes as if trying to wake her from a dream. "Excuse me? Miss? I said, *are you all right*?"

Beatrice blinked and then affected the grand voice that Percival Nash had used earlier in the office. "I was almost *suffocated* by this mud," she announced, and then pretended to swoon.

Thankfully, Mrs. Steele had forced her to practice this move many times, in the event that Beatrice needed to place herself in distress so as to attract a handsome gentleman. As it turned out, the faint feint could also be used in an investigation. Drake caught her, clearly perplexed by such technique.

"I'm a delicate young lady who has just arrived in this city," Beatrice went on. "I cannot think how terrible it would have been had I died here in this puddle before finding the perfect gentleman with whom to share my life."

Drake gently righted Beatrice, still looking confused, but the woman's lips curled into a knowing smile.

"Well, well, well," she murmured. "How intriguing. A lady who knows what she wants . . . and has a plan to get it."

A man stepped out of the carriage.

Though the woman was tall, the man with her was even taller, with broad shoulders and a strapping form. He wore an affable expression that tempered his imposing physique.

"My love," he said, "we are going to be late." He did not seem to notice Beatrice, his eyes passing over her. The snub was clear, and effective: At once, Beatrice felt invisible.

"We have a situation," the woman told him, gesturing at Beatrice, her motion lifting the snub.

The man finally glanced at her as if seeing the "situation" for the first time, though Beatrice could not think how he had missed it. A crowd had gathered, and Beatrice stood in the center, covered in mud-drenched tassels. She was a sight.

"Oh, my," the man said with a chuckle. His eyes crinkled at the edges, giving his face a boyish look that further contrasted his serious salt-and-pepper hair and towering height. "I know young ladies like to gossip, but this is a whole new level in getting the dirt."

Before Beatrice could reply, another man—this one portly, with long, bushy sideburns—pushed his way through the crowd.

"Horace! Are you unscathed?" He began to check the tall man as if searching for injuries. "We have already lost Walter; we cannot lose you!"

He must be speaking of Walter Shrewsbury, Beatrice thought, her curiosity prickling at these words. Were these two men friends of the murder victim? Did they know something that could prove helpful in the investigation?

"I am fine," the tall man assured Sideburns. Though he still wore a pleasant expression on his face, Beatrice noted that he took a step back, as if unconsciously distancing himself.

Sideburns did not seem to notice. He took a step forward. "I saw everything," he told the tall man. "It was all *her* fault!" he added in a wheedling, nasal voice as he pointed at Beatrice.

"I'll thank you to watch your tone," Drake said, stepping between Sideburns and Beatrice.

"I shall take care of this, Horace," Sideburns said, ignoring Drake as he turned back to the tall man. "You have more important things to do than argue with street urchins. Namely, the agenda for our next NAGS meeting. Perhaps we might add a discussion about women's proximity to carriages and its potential regulation?"

"Nags? What is that? Or . . . those?" Inspector Drake inquired, watching the man with clear dislike.

"The Neighborhood Association of Gentlemen Sweetbriarians, obviously," Sideburns replied, evidently shocked that Drake did not already know of them. "Don't you read our neighborhood bulletins?"

"No," Drake said.

"We have been entrusted with maintaining the aesthetics, morals, and quality of life of our neighborhood," Sideburns explained.

"Entrusted by whom?" Drake asked, raising an eyebrow.

"Ourselves." Sideburns squared his shoulders. "This man right here is Mr. Horace Vane, one of the esteemed founders of NAGS," he said, gesturing reverently to the tall man, who was now glancing at a pocket watch. "Mr. Vane and his friends Cecil Nightingale and Walter Shrewsbury—may Walter rest in peace—saved our neighborhood by starting the association. Can you even imagine what this place would be like without gentlemen like them—and myself, of course—imposing important rules and regulations?"

"Yes," Drake replied.

"The NAGS make sure shrubs are well shaped, buildings are sturdy, and performances are pleasing. We promote decorum and beauty," Sideburns went on, not hearing him.

"I believe it was Shakespeare who said, 'Beauty is bought by judgement of the eye,'" Beatrice said, finally getting a word in.

"We do not allow Shakespeare in this neighborhood. Too many double entendres," Sideburns informed her.

"Are you speaking of censorship?" she inquired, trying to sound casual. This NAGS group clearly wanted control over everything, including access to the arts. Could they be the ones attempting to frame Percival Nash for Walter Shrewsbury's death?

"My husband supports the artistic community here in Sweetbriar," the silver-haired woman said firmly.

"As long as they are proper," Sideburns added.

"And contain only single entendres," the woman said dryly, withdrawing a long cigar from her reticule. She stuck it between her teeth. "Now, has anyone got a light?"

Did she mean to smoke the cigar outside? Beatrice wondered. London women were so *daring*.

"Ah, my dear," the tall man chuckled, taking the cigar from her mouth. "She is right, of course, that the culture here is what makes our neighborhood great. My wife has long been a trendsetter," he told Drake. "An unofficial adviser to the NAGS. We always take her insight into account."

Confusing, Beatrice thought.

"And you have always been a pillar of the community," Sideburns told the tall man, taking two steps forward for every one step the others retreated. "Gentlemen and artists alike should thank you for your contributions, and be inspired by your achievements, and copy your wardrobe choices—"

"Thank you for your kind words and your concern, Gregory," the tall man interrupted.

"I am so glad I could be the first on the scene to assure your safety," Sideburns—or, rather, Gregory—replied immediately. "I had arrived early to speak with you, actually. Since Walter has passed, I thought there might be room on the hunting trip for me to—"

"I can take things from here," the tall man interrupted.

"Of course, of course," Gregory gushed. He shot one last admiring glance at the tall man, and one last glare at Beatrice, before shuffling off toward the iron gates of the Rose.

The tall man and his silver-haired wife exchanged a significant look, and then they both turned back to Beatrice.

"Excuse all of that," the tall man said. "Now. To the sticky—or rather, muddy—situation at hand. Naturally, we must pay for your wife's gown. I trust this will be enough?" He withdrew banknotes from his pocket and offered them to Drake, who looked from the banknotes to Beatrice.

She could read his inquiry in his gaze: *What do you want me to do?*

Follow my lead, she shot back with her eyes.

"This was a one-of-a-kind creation, selected by my chaperone for my very first Season, as I am unmarried and eligible," Beatrice told the tall man, purposefully speaking loudly, so the small crowd who had gathered would hear. "It cannot be replaced."

"Oh, dear. One-of-a-kind . . . very foolish. One should always have a backup. But I hope she can find something comparable with this payment? My wife and I could not bear to cause any problems for your . . . sweetheart," the man continued, still only addressing Drake, banknotes still outstretched. "Let me grease your palm so that you may clean hers."

"There is no need for wordplay," Drake said, still not accepting the money. Once more he looked to Beatrice for further direction.

"I *would* love to purchase something new," Beatrice said, raising her voice even louder. Could this man not hear her? "If I might wear it to the Rose."

"Young girls are always dreaming," the man said to Drake with another chuckle. He pressed the banknotes into Drake's palm in a smooth motion, as if he were merely shaking his hand. As if everything had been decided, without any need for Beatrice's input. "My advice: Keep her grounded, so she doesn't float away on fantasy."

He smiled, winked, and turned back to the carriage.

But the silver-haired woman lingered. She continued to watch Beatrice, her head cocked to one side.

She almost seemed . . . disappointed, Beatrice thought. It was as if she had wanted more of a challenge.

That was it, Beatrice thought excitedly. All was not lost: If it was a fight she wanted, it was a fight she would get.

"Oh, no," she said, swooning again. She grabbed for Drake, who dutifully held out a hand to support her in spite of his bewilderment. "The carriage has done more than spray me—I am injured!"

"Yes," the silver-haired woman said, taking a step forward. "I feared that!" Her catlike eyes glimmered. "But if you are injured, you must see a doctor. You would be in no state to attend any balls. . . ." She paused, waiting for a reply.

No, not a reply, Beatrice thought—a rebuttal.

"Sometimes these issues in ladies are not physical," Beatrice told her. "They are matters of the heart. Perhaps I feel this way because I am heartbroken over my exclusion from the Rose, meaning that a ball would be the very balm for these pangs of disappointment."

"I am confused," Drake said, looking from the silver-haired woman to Beatrice. "Do you need to see a doctor, or—"

But Beatrice shot him a look, and he broke off.

"The club's list has already been created," the silver-haired woman said smoothly. "How could we justify such a late addition?"

"It is never too late for charity," Beatrice told her. "Everyone would admire your goodwill, recommending a young lady who would be cured through an invitation. You would be saving my life."

"What is your name?" the woman said, peering down her long nose at Beatrice. It was as if they had passed the first level in a test. Now Beatrice had to complete the next.

"Beatrice Steele, ma'am."

"Who are the Steeles? Where do they come from?"

"Swampshire." Beatrice took a fan from her reticule and waved it around, tried to look delicate. This proved difficult, as the ensuing breeze merely splattered the mud on her visage.

"I have never heard of it," the woman said.

"It is small but very proper," Beatrice assured her.

"Your age?"

"A lady never tells," Beatrice replied. This seemed to be the correct answer, as the woman went on with her rapid-fire questioning.

"And your father? What is his profession?"

"I beg your pardon," Beatrice said, feigning offense. "My father is a gentleman. He does not have a *job.*" Unless you counted constructing elaborate fake death scenes in the parlor, and this had hardly proved profitable.

"So." The woman tilted her head to the side, studying Beatrice with her dark, astute eyes. "Beatrice Steele of Swampshire would like to be presented as one of the Rose's debutantes. She wishes to find a husband among our ranks of eligible gentlemen. But to this I must ask one final question: Why is a proper lady like yourself out in the street with this man you admit is not your husband—unchaperoned?" Her sharp eyes fell on Drake, who stiffened.

"I do not know him," Beatrice said immediately. "I was out for a walk—with my chaperone, naturally—but we became separated. This kind stranger was trying to help me when your carriage came along and nearly killed us both."

"Charity supersedes decorum," Drake added, and Beatrice shot him an approving look.

"What a story," the woman murmured. For a moment she was quiet, mulling it all over, and then a smile crept across her lips. "I deem that it shall have a happy ending. You must join us for the Season. Miss Beatrice Steele . . . you just made my list."

Her list? Beatrice's pulse began to pound as she realized: This woman was not just any socialite.

She was the patroness of the Rose herself.

"Along with your rescuer, of course," the woman continued, indicating Drake. "I *have* carefully curated my list, keeping an even number of ladies and gentlemen, and it would not do to ruin such plans. He must be your escort, when you are presented." She adjusted her gloves, now businesslike. "I shall send over a full schedule of the Season's events to your place of residence, Miss Steele. The first event was postponed to tomorrow evening, so you are joining just in time. I look forward to seeing you two there—with a chaperone, this time," she added, her dark eyes sparkling.

She turned back to her jet-black carriage. The tall man stepped out to usher her inside, and she whispered something to him. He looked at Drake, and then, as if seeing her for the first time, he turned his gaze to Beatrice.

He smiled, but though the man had that boyish grin, a certain charm, and a friendly demeanor, Beatrice could see that his smile did not reach his eyes.

She did not like him. She had no real reason—unless one counted that he had ignored her during their entire encounter.

"What was *that*?" Drake demanded once the couple and their jet-black carriage had taken off and disappeared through the iron gates of the Rose. The crowd that had gathered began to dissipate, no longer interested now that the conflict had abated.

"That was a brilliant plot to investigate the death of Walter Shrewsbury!" Beatrice whisper-yelled, still thrilled with herself. "We now have full access to the Rose."

"As . . . debutantes," Drake said, the word sour upon his lips.

"Who knows, Inspector," Beatrice said, taking his arm once more, feeling as if she were floating on air, "you might catch a killer *and* a sweetheart."

"I don't want a sweetheart, I want *you*. I mean," Drake said, now flustered, "I want to *investigate* with you."

"And I want the same," Beatrice assured him, her face growing hot. Would this weather ever relent?

"Then I suppose we have a plan," Drake said, squaring his shoulders as if steeling himself for the horrors of the ensuing investigation (or, more likely, the horrors of the Season).

"We will clear Percival Nash's name and catch the real killer," Beatrice assured him. "Then DS Investigations will become the toast of the town, and we shall never have to scrounge for cases again."

"I would warn against such optimism," Drake sighed, "but I know better. I was right when I said you would find your way in anywhere. Whoever tries to stop you seems to find themselves defeated—and swiftly."

"It is not a *game,* Inspector Drake," Beatrice assured him, "though if it were, I would be winning."

"Which is why I am grateful to be on your side," he replied.

They walked back in the direction of the Carnation, both unable to stop grins from spreading across their faces. It was swelteringly hot, and they were covered in mud, but in that moment, neither Beatrice nor Drake would have had it any other way.

Their investigation had begun.

THE LONDON BABBLER

Riveting Ribbons

By Elle Equiano

Another summer Season is in full swing, my darlings, which means it is time for all us young ladies to select new ribbons. Whereas satin was the material of the spring, linen is for summer! Wear a nice, thin ribbon under your bust, or spruce up a bonnet with a bright color for a festive touch.

In addition to a ribbon, you might consider purchasing a brooch. Though it seems the London Menace has disappeared, a lady should always be prepared to defend herself with its sharp point. One never knows if another murderer is around the corner.

Miss Equiano—

I love the idea of linen for summer. Groundbreaking! However, I have concerns about the conclusion of your piece. As I have told you many times, "Riveting Ribbons" is meant to be a light column for ladies, NOT a discussion of crime. THE LONDON BABBLER has many who already report on this, in addition to the weekly piece from Huxley himself, "Restoring Order." Please stick to your own topic!

—*Your editor*

THE LONDON BABBLER

Curious Crimes

By Evana Chore

Sir Huxley is on the case: London's favorite gentleman detective has taken several local artists into questioning, in connection with the murder of Mr. Walter Shrewsbury.

Sources report that Huxley suspects a certain popular actor, though no arrest has been made—yet.

Fans of the detective waited outside his office last week, eager for any news in the case. Among these were members of the so-called Huxley Appreciation Society, a group of young ladies obsessed with Huxley and his cases.

"We are grateful that London has such a wonderful inspector to keep our streets safe," gushed Lavinia Lee, president of the HAS.

Young ladies are encouraged to admire Sir Huxley, but this reporter has to wonder: Has the admiration gone too far? If Miss Lee carries on, a veritable mistress of murder, she will have no room in her life for a husband.

It is best for young ladies to appreciate Sir Huxley privately, and save fervor for its proper place (and theirs): the home.

Dear Mrs. Steele,

Happy, happy news! Your daughter Beatrice has been chosen as one of this year's debutantes at—perhaps you should sit down before reading this—the Rose!!!

We were attending an event at the Carnation when she received the invite. I am still a bit confused as to exactly *how* it all happened. I actually thought Beatrice had been kidnapped by the Specter of Sweetbriar (a local ghost who is known to recite poetry in a very spine-chilling manner), and I was quite hysterical about it. But as it turns out, she disappeared from the party because she was speaking with the patroness of the Rose, who extended the invitation. Beatrice also fell into mud, apparently? I did not think there were squelch holes here in London; Swampshire seems to follow us everywhere. But now she shall be presented at the most elite assembly room in London! I knew the tassels would work their magic!

I have consulted other chaperones and determined that the patroness of the Rose is a respectable woman with intriguing silver hair named Mrs. Diana Vane. She and her husband, Mr. Horace Vane, are well-known in Sweetbriar society. They frequent the theater, they sponsored the local pleasure garden, and they even own the deed to the Rose's assembly hall itself. (They are blessed with no children of their own, else I would have tried to set Beatrice up with any eligible sons.)

The Season begins tomorrow evening with an opening reception, and there is a ball nearly every night to follow. Though I know you are desperate for her to make a quick match, I must say: Beatrice deserves someone who truly appreciates her, and whom she loves in return. We do not want a repeat of last autumn. Therefore if I suspect any man is trying to murder instead of marry her, I will object to the match! I am prepared as chaperone to put my foot down.

On that note (murder, I mean), I know you have been concerned about Beatrice's morbid tendencies. I assure you, there is nothing to fear. Beatrice thinks only pure thoughts about securing a husband. Now that she has gained entrance to the Rose, crime is the last thing on her mind.

Sincerely,

The best chaperone of all time, if I may blow my own trumpet,

Helen Bolton

CHAPTER FIVE

A Wardrobe

Beatrice awoke to late-morning light as Miss Bolton tossed open her bedroom drapes.

"WE MUST GO SHOPPING!" she cried, her voice too loud for the moments between sleep and waking.

"Tea first," Beatrice mumbled, blinking the edges of a dream from her mind—something about a man with a cigar, warm hands on her face, and the scent of cinnamon and oranges. . . .

"Tonight is the opening reception at the Rose, and then a slew of balls," Miss Bolton was saying. "Not to mention the end-of-summer masquerade, which shall be here before we know it . . . there is no time for tea!"

Normally, Beatrice would have dreaded so many social obligations, but thanks to Walter Shrewsbury's death, she was actually looking forward to a summer of dances, drinking, and whist. After all, each ball was an opportunity to question members of the Rose Club about the murder. In her mind's eye, she could imagine Walter Shrewsbury, face beaten and bruised, a knife plunged into his chest. So much blood. And she, Beatrice, would be the one—along with Drake, of course—to nab the vicious killer. . . .

"There is one problem we must address," Miss Bolton went on. For a moment Beatrice felt a chill—did Miss Bolton know about the murder? Was she suspicious? But then Miss Bolton brandished the Rose's schedule, pointing at a note printed at the top. It read: *Formal Wear Required for All Events. Gentlemen—one suit shall suffice. Ladies—absolutely no outfit repeating.*

"I have formal wear," Beatrice assured her, relieved that it was merely a question of clothing, but Miss Bolton shook her head.

"Beatrice, you don't even own *one* hat of interest, and now your best muslin has been irreparably damaged. I still don't understand how that occurred. . . . Normally Mary is the one whose wardrobe is in such disrepair." She went to Beatrice's wardrobe and began to rifle through gowns. She pulled several garments from the wardrobe and threw them in a heap on the bed as she rejected each one. "No, no, no . . . none of this will do. . . . We must get you an entirely new wardrobe. You have balls to attend—and, did I mention, a *masquerade*? Your ink-stained, tattered garments might have passed muster at the Carnation, but you are a true socialite now. You need to look like one. Thankfully, I can be of assistance, for if there's one thing I know, it's fashion." She patted her hat (which appeared to be knitted from cat fur).

"I like my clothes," Beatrice said, throwing back her covers. She took a brown evening gown from Miss Bolton's hands. "This is very easy to run in," she explained.

"You shouldn't be running away from anyone," Miss Bolton said, exasperated.

"I'm running *toward* them," Beatrice replied. "To catch them. In a romantic sense," she added hastily.

"I suppose it will do for tonight," Miss Bolton said, looking at the drab garment with distaste. "But we must shop for new clothing posthaste."

"Miss Bolton," Beatrice said quietly, her face feeling warm, "the fact is that I do not have the money for a new wardrobe."

Beatrice had always rolled her eyes at her mother's money-making marriage schemes, but now that she was on her own in a city, she had a newfound understanding of Mrs. Steele's financial desires. London may have been a land of opportunity—but that opportunity came at a price. Since Percival Nash had given no deposit for Drake and Beatrice's services, Beatrice remained dependent upon Alice Croaksworth and Miss Bolton to line her pockets. And to pay for said pockets.

She yearned for money of her own, though she would not use it for clothes—the moment Beatrice earned anything from DS Investigations, she was determined to send it straight back to Swampshire for her family's home repairs.

The frustration was almost enough to make her desire a wealthy husband. But as much as Mrs. Steele pushed this matter, Beatrice had to think: Would he not simply be one more person upon whom she would have to rely for charity?

"I have more than enough to purchase your wardrobe, Beatrice," Miss Bolton said kindly. Beatrice opened her mouth, but Miss Bolton cut her off. "Don't protest. It is my pleasure to select the perfect gowns for your Season. Consider it an investment in your future."

Beatrice let her protestations die on her tongue, feeling both grateful and a bit concerned as to what Miss Bolton's idea of the "perfect gowns" might entail. She did not want to look a gift horse in the mouth, but the fact that Miss Bolton owned a life-like horse hat gave her pause. Still, it was true that the Rose Club was much more formal than anywhere Beatrice had ever been, and if she wanted to gain the trust of its members for the sake of her investigation, she would have to look the part. It *was* an investment in her future—though not the one Miss Bolton and Mrs. Steele imagined for her.

"Thank you," Beatrice said finally. "I don't know what I would do without you, Miss Bolton."

"You would survive. But you would have a very dull wardrobe," Miss Bolton replied. She withdrew a teacup from her cat-fur hat and handed it to Beatrice. Somehow, it was full of piping-hot tea, plus one whisker. "Drink up and get dressed. We must get to the shops immediately."

When Beatrice and Miss Bolton emerged from their town house, it was already hot, the sun blazing down on crowds taking their morning turns.

Carriage and walking trails encircled the Sweet Majestic, which was located in the center of the neighborhood. Most residents of Sweetbriar took a stroll or ride first thing in the morning, to see and be seen. Already, well-dressed women and their chaperones made the rounds, completing laps of the walkway, hopeful expressions on their faces each time a handsome gentleman tipped his hat. Beatrice noted that she and Miss Bolton were the only women wearing hats; the ladies of London carried parasols to shield against the sun.

A second reason for the fashion choice was clear soon enough: A few flying squirrels burst from a tree, and they bounced off a nearby lady's parasol. Beatrice and Miss Bolton were terribly vulnerable. They cowered as they walked, trying to avoid any sky rodents.

"I have never been greeted by so many people," Miss Bolton told Beatrice after four gentlemen in a row tipped their hats to the pair of them in spite of their unfashionable appearances. "Word must have gotten around that you were invited to the Rose Club. I cannot wait to rub it in everyone's faces—subtly, of course, as befits a top-tier chaperone. . . ." She looked around.

"Now, the dress shop is somewhere this way, but I have forgotten how to get there. . . ."

A voice spoke up. "Perhaps you could use a knowledgeable escort?" Beatrice and Miss Bolton turned to see a man approach them, his grin showing off deep dimples. "I am also excellent at fending off the squirrels."

It was the blond man from outside the Carnation, Beatrice realized. He had no cigar today, just a walking cane and top hat, and he politely tipped his brim at them.

"Why, yes, that would be wonderful," Miss Bolton said excitedly. She pushed Beatrice toward the man. "You must get used to this, now that you are one of the Rose's blooms," she whispered. "That is what they call their debutantes. All of the wealthy gentlemen will be interested to know more about you. But never fear, I shall always be just behind you, ensuring that they do nothing untoward."

Beatrice was more concerned that *she* would do something untoward, such as kick this man in the shins. She did not trust a lurker, and certainly not one who seemed unnecessarily cloaked in mystery, but she could not be rude and risk social ruin. So she begrudgingly took the man's arm and allowed him to guide her once more around the Sweetbriar walkway, Miss Bolton shuffling quickly behind them in order to keep up on her short legs.

Whereas Inspector Drake was very tall and towered over Beatrice, the blond gentleman was closer to her height. They fit together easily, walking arm in arm, and she could not help noticing his musky cologne. He even *smelled* expensive.

"Lovely day, isn't it?" the man said pleasantly.

"I find it a bit hot," Beatrice replied.

"Heat *can* cause agitation," he allowed.

"And agitation can drive people to do unspeakable things," Beatrice said, trying not to sound too enthralled by this prospect.

"Then the heat may be good for business, at least," the man said.

Beatrice turned to look at him so quickly that she nearly strained her neck.

"You must forgive me, but I was curious after our encounter outside the Carnation, and henceforth conducted a bit of research," he said with a grin. "Why didn't you mention you were in the world of investigating?"

Beatrice felt her face flush. "Well . . . it's not something I advertise," she sputtered. "How did you—"

"I am very well-connected," the man assured her, and Beatrice could not tell if he was being wry or serious. Before she could ask, he continued, "Perhaps you might tell me what cases you are working on, at the moment? I find your profession very interesting."

"Most people find it full of morbid creeps," Beatrice said, shocked at the man's forward nature—and forward thinking.

Though socialites in London were obviously intrigued by crime—any paper featuring Sir Huxley flew off newsstands, after all—a lady detective was still a novelty. Women in the city could be *fans* of the mustachioed, dashing Huxley, not try to *become* him.

"I am not most people," the man said with a wink. This time, Beatrice found the gesture . . . *charming*?

She must get ahold of herself.

He led her around a corner, where the walking path aligned with the entrance to the pleasure garden's hedge maze.

"I know how much you like hedges," he said conversationally. "Shall we attempt the pleasure garden's maze? We might find a dead end, which would provide the perfect nook in which to discuss crime."

"My chaperone and I are due at the dress shop," she said, actually feeling a little disappointed. He had painted an intriguing picture of an afternoon together.

"Very well, Miss Steele," the man said. "Continue straight, and the shop will be on your left." He tipped his hat as he took his leave, murmuring, "I hope we meet again."

"What an attractive man," Miss Bolton said, rushing forward to take Beatrice's arm in the man's stead. "Is he well endowed? Financially, I mean; it doesn't take a modiste to see he dresses to the left. . . . If we can determine a subtle way to find out his salary, and the sum proves acceptable, he would make a charming husband."

"Goodness, Miss Bolton!" Beatrice said, realizing. "I did not even get his name."

"Well, a lady cannot *ask* a gentleman his name," Miss Bolton said, offended by the very notion. "He must offer it himself."

"I certainly hope I learn it soon, else our wedding shall be awkward," Beatrice replied dryly. She was not convinced that she needed to rush after a proposal—

Yet she had to admit that she was intrigued by the unnamed man in spite of herself.

His directions proved correct, and they soon located the bustling dress shop. The shopkeeper had Beatrice stand on a platform in front of a large mirror and took her measurements while Miss Bolton rooted furiously through piles of ribbons and fabric in the shop. She kept rushing over to hold swatches up to Beatrice's face and then murmuring, "No, no . . . that will never do . . . not nearly enough *sparkle*. . . ."

In the mirror's reflection, Beatrice watched as two fashionable young women entered the store, a bell on the door chiming as they strolled inside.

One of the ladies had dark brown skin and dark eyes framed by long lashes. Curls peeked out of the edge of a gray silk turban, and she wore a quizzing glass on a chain around her neck. She lifted the glass up to one of her eyes to examine a ribbon, pursed her lips, and then put the ribbon away. Evidently it was not satisfactory, Beatrice thought, wondering how a person would even know such things.

From the young lady's attire—as well as the confident air with which she carried herself—Beatrice could tell that she was a member of high society.

"... which is why I'm certain that Sir Huxley will solve the murder," the second woman was saying. This young lady had a swanlike neck, a pale complexion, and white-blond hair piled atop her head in a complicated chignon. Her gray eyes were large and unblinking, emphasized by dark circles underneath them. She wore dainty spectacles perched on her nose. Whereas the first woman was quiet as she inspected ribbons, the second spoke in an unbroken stream of chatter.

At the mention of Sir Huxley, Beatrice's ears prickled. She continued to watch in the mirror's reflection as the two women browsed fabric.

"The only thing which perplexes me is that the Rose's Season is going to continue, in spite of a member's death," the bespectacled young woman said enthusiastically. "Naturally I'm pleased. Pleased about the continuation of the Season, not the death," she clarified. "I know you were at last year's Season, but this shall be my first, so it would have been a great disappointment had it been canceled. I never thought *I* would receive an invite to such a prestigious assembly hall!"

Beatrice felt a rush of interest. These ladies were debutantes at the Rose, like herself—and they were discussing Walter Shrewsbury. She focused in on their conversation, straining so as not to miss a word.

"Stoicism is very fashionable right now, so perhaps the decision to move on in spite of the tragedy makes sense," the bespectacled woman went on.

"We need the Season now more than ever," the first woman replied. "To keep up morale and demonstrate the staunchness of the marriage mart."

Was that a note of sarcasm that Beatrice detected?

Confident *and* contemptuous. She liked this woman already.

"Did anything like this happen last Season?" the bespectacled lady pressed.

"Last Season, the London Menace was terrorizing the city, but it seems he is out and a new killer is in," the woman with the quizzing glass replied. "Even with such intrigue, I expect this year to be just as dull as the last. None of the gentlemen ever want to discuss these matters; all they talk about is the weather, the size of the last fish they caught, and how much carriage traffic they encountered on their way to the ball."

"How dull," the bespectacled woman gasped.

"Indeed. And not a single question shall be thrown your way, to be sure." The first woman locked eyes with Beatrice through the mirror, clearly drawn by a feeling that someone was watching her. Beatrice flushed.

She had two younger sisters, but apart from them, she had rarely interacted with other young ladies.* The only woman her age in Swampshire, Caroline Wynn, had turned out to be a con artist in disguise. Needless to say, she and Beatrice had never formed a bosom friendship. (Though they had shared an enthralling sword fight.)

The appearance of the two young ladies in the dress shop, who shared such an easy confidence, sparked a yearning for companionship that Beatrice had never felt so strongly.

The bell of the front door chimed again, and both Beatrice

* Beatrice rarely interacted with her youngest sister either; Mary liked long, solitary walks in the forest, and preferred the company of other animals as opposed to human women.

and the dressmaker turned to see a man with distinct sideburns enter the shop. It was Gregory, Beatrice realized—the portly man who had inserted himself into the carriage incident outside the Rose.

"Ugh, not again," the dressmaker muttered, speaking Beatrice's own thought aloud.

"Madam Gest, a moment, please?" Gregory said, beckoning the dressmaker over. She sighed.

"Excuse me," she told Beatrice, setting aside her measuring materials and crossing over to Gregory. "How may I help you, sir?" she asked in a falsely bright tone.

"I am a member of the Neighborhood Association of Gentlemen Sweetbriarians," he began.

"I know. We have met many times," she interrupted, the bright tone already giving way to annoyance. "Is there a problem?"

"You were informed that your fabrics are too bright, your bodices cut too low, and your sleeves too short," Gregory informed her, his voice loud and, Beatrice thought, uniquely pestiferous. "It savors strongly of dandyism—something we NAGS oppose."

"This is the fashion of today," the dressmaker replied, taking a step back.

"And the NAGS want it gone by tomorrow," Gregory said, taking a step forward.

The lady with the quizzing glass and the bespectacled young woman both paused their perusal of fabrics, watching the interaction.

Did they agree with Gregory? Beatrice wondered.

"The ladies like bright colors. And my silhouettes allow them freer movement," the dressmaker was saying. "And since they're the ones *wearing* the garments, not you—"

"This is not a discussion, *madam.*" Gregory sniffed. "You were told to adjust your designs. As I see from the gowns in the window, you are still peddling rejected wares. You will dispose of them, else we will have to take further action."

"I cannot throw out my work! It is my livelihood!" The dressmaker's voice turned pleading.

"No one wants to buy *that,*" Gregory snapped, gesturing to a particularly bright pink gown that was displayed in the front window.

"I do!"

For a moment Beatrice was confused. Three voices had rung out, one of them hers. She realized that both she and the two other young ladies in the shop had all spoken the same interjection at once.

Gregory looked from the woman with the quizzing glass to the bespectacled woman, his eyes finally landing on Beatrice. He turned back to the dressmaker.

"Amend your gowns, Madam Gest, or you can expect to receive further correspondence from my organization," he told her. "And I suggest using greater discernment in your clientele. Outspoken women like *that*"—he nodded toward Beatrice—"and members of Huxley's Hussies," he said, now indicating the bespectacled woman, who reddened, "will hardly give you an air of respectability." He licked his fingers and smoothed his sideburns, then flounced away.

Defeated, the dressmaker began to remove the pink gown from the window.

"Package that up, darling," the woman with the quizzing glass instructed. "I meant what I said; I wish to purchase the garment."

"The NAGS have deemed it indecorous, miss," the dressmaker said sadly. "I fear if you wear this, you will be ruined."

"Then it is worth double," the woman told her, withdrawing a large stack of banknotes from her reticule and passing them over. "Scandal makes for the best stories, don't you think?"

If one could afford it, Beatrice thought—and clearly, this lady could. The dressmaker took the notes with gratitude and then began to pack up the garment from the window. Before Beatrice could understand what had occurred, the two young women were approaching her.

"You have good taste," the first woman said, tipping her head to the side. "I don't believe I have seen you around Sweetbriar before."

"I am new to London," Beatrice told her. "Beatrice Steele," she added, feeling suddenly nervous.

She wanted to say the right thing to these ladies, and not because of the investigation. For purely personal reasons, she desperately wanted them to like her.

"Lavinia Lee," the second, bespectacled woman said brightly. "So pleased to make your acquaintance." She sank into a little curtsy.

Close up, Beatrice could see that Lavinia wore a choker with a cameo dangling from its chain. It stood out against her pale, swanlike neck. The cameo featured the painted figure of a man, and from the shape of the figure's mustache, Beatrice could tell it was a depiction of Sir Huxley.

"Do you like it?" Lavinia asked, clearly noticing Beatrice's gaze on her choker. "I painted it myself. I am the president and founder of the Huxley Appreciation Society," she explained. "Are you a fan? We'd love to have you at one of our meetings!"

Beatrice was struck with an odd feeling. Not long ago, she would have given anything to belong to the Huxley Appreciation Society and mingle with other young ladies who admired the detective as much as she had. But now Beatrice could not imagine being satisfied as simply a fan, after having tasted the excitement of solving a crime herself.

"Thank you for the invitation," she said finally. "It is very kind."

"This is Elle Equiano," Lavinia said, now indicating the woman with the quizzing glass and gray turban. "She writes for the *Babbler*. You may have read her column, 'Riveting Ribbons.' It's simply fantastic. It has helped me select *so* many ribbons, and even a pair of gloves!"

"You flatter me, darling," Miss Equiano said, waving a hand modestly.

"I don't know why that man thinks he would know fashion better than you," Lavinia went on, clearly referencing Gregory.

"Because it isn't about fashion," Elle replied.

"It's about control," Beatrice agreed.

"Precisely," Elle said, her dark eyes now gleaming with interest. "Now, *that* would be an interesting column: an exposé about the NAGS."

"You should write that," Beatrice said, a bit too quickly—but wouldn't that be exactly what she needed for her current investigation?

"Alas, I am restricted to ribbons because my editor thinks it unbecoming for a lady to write about any interesting topics," Elle replied. Though her tone was light, her eyes were serious; Beatrice could tell that this was a point of contention.

"Or talk about them, it would seem," Lavinia said, adjusting her spectacles. "If that gentleman with the horrendous sideburns is a member of NAGS, he is a member of the Rose—all of the men in that organization belong to the best assembly hall, of course—and he called me Huxley's hussy. I have not even been presented as a debutante yet, and my reputation is already tarnished!"

"I thought everyone in London was obsessed with Huxley," Beatrice said, confused. "Why are you criticized for supporting him?"

"It's best to keep that obsession behind closed doors," Elle explained. "Especially this Season . . ."

"Is there something I should know? I am also participating in the Season. I'm actually a bloom at the Rose," Beatrice said, trying to sound casual and merely curious, as if she hadn't been eavesdropping from the moment they entered the shop.

"Oh! What fun! So are we!" Lavinia said eagerly, clapping her hands, momentarily distracted from her public shaming. But Elle simply smiled and raised her eyebrow, as if she knew there was more Beatrice wanted to ask.

"Are you saying this Season will be different because of . . . Walter Shrewsbury's death?" Beatrice asked quietly.

For a moment she was terrified that Elle and Lavinia would leave the shop immediately, offended at such a bold and disturbing question. After all, they had just been talking about the dangers of discussing tawdry subjects in public.

But instead they leaned in, both clearly intrigued. As Beatrice had hoped and suspected, the two young ladies were kindred morbid spirits.

"I wonder," she whispered, "if you have any idea who might have killed him."

"He didn't have any *direct* enemies, per se," Lavinia whispered back, "but Mr. Shrewsbury was a powerful man. And powerful men are often targets. Think of Huxley's seventy-first case—"

"A Duke in Danger," Beatrice recalled.

"Exactly! I knew you were a fan!" Lavinia said excitedly.

"Walter Shrewsbury was a founding member of the NAGS, along with Mr. Cecil Nightingale and Mr. Horace Vane," Elle told her. "Those three have a great influence over Sweetbriar, as you just saw. They have been cracking down as of late, sending their errand boy Gregory all over town to deliver edicts. They think artists have gotten a little too brazen in their work, and that we ladies have gotten too free in our dress and speech and interests." She snorted. "Apparently we cannot even wear bright colors anymore."

"And I am certain that they planted a story about my club in the paper to hurt my reputation and dissuade our gatherings," Lavinia added. "No doubt one of them saw my society meeting for tea and overheard a bloody conversation. And I mean 'bloody' literally," she explained. "We were discussing a stabbing. But we are fascinated with the pursuit of justice, not the act of committing a crime."

"Believe me when I tell you that I understand completely," Beatrice assured her.

"I am sure the NAGS have made enemies with their current efforts," Elle said. "And now that one of their own has been murdered, I fear they will begin to impose even stricter rules for us all." She sighed. "They're frightful spoilsports, if you ask me."

It all aligned with Percival's fears, Beatrice thought. Wealthy gentlemen did not care for the way society was changing and blamed the arts. Yet Horace and Diana Vane claimed the NAGS *supported* local culture. Once again she was struck by the contradiction.

"I shall probably be kicked out of the Season at once, considering all of these rules," Beatrice murmured, somewhat to herself, but Elle Equiano immediately shook her head.

"Of course you won't, darling. We shall help you. Won't we, Lavinia?"

"Yes," Lavinia said, nodding eagerly.

"You must become our special project, Miss Steele," Elle said, and Beatrice felt both nervous and exhilarated at the young woman's sudden look of anticipation. "A murder, a heat wave, and a new friend . . . Perhaps this Season will turn out to be fun after all." Her lips curled into a mischievous grin.

The dressmaker reappeared with the pink gown, now packaged up in a box. Elle took it and then turned back. "Until next time, just remember," she told Beatrice, "be careful with whom you discuss murder."

With that bit of advice—or was it a warning?—the two ladies exited the shop with a swish of silk.

Beatrice watched them fold into a crowd on the street outside.

She was struck with a sudden vision of herself, clad in an elegant ensemble, going into dress shops with Elle and Lavinia. Discussing the latest intrigue and defying any petty gentlemen they encountered.

Could this cosmopolitan dream actually become reality?

"Beatrice, did you hear me?"

Beatrice blinked and then looked down to see Miss Bolton standing next to her. "I said, what do you think about this one?" She held up a bolt of blue fabric, so bright that Beatrice resisted the urge to shield her eyes. Evidently Miss Bolton had been so caught up in shopping that she had missed the entire encounter that had just occurred.

"That might be more your shade, not mine," Beatrice said politely. An idea forming, she went on. "Perhaps you should be measured for a new wardrobe yourself, Miss Bolton. After all, you are my chaperone, so you will be attending many events, too. You wouldn't want to be seen in last season's garb."

"Oh, I don't need anything new," Miss Bolton began to protest, but Beatrice interrupted.

"I have heard people call you a trendsetter. You wouldn't want to let them down, would you?"

"I suppose I've never really thought of it like that," Miss Bolton said, looking at the dressmaker. "Could you fit me in?" Without waiting for a reply, she helped Beatrice off the dressmaker's podium and stepped up herself. "Beatrice, you don't mind waiting?"

"Of course not," Beatrice assured her. "I could browse ribbons for hours."

The moment Miss Bolton looked away, raising her arms to be measured, Beatrice slipped out of the shop.

This would likely be her last chance to speak with Drake before they were presented at the Rose, and she wanted to make sure they were prepared for the evening.

But more truthfully, her head was spinning with everything Elle and Lavinia had just said, and Beatrice wanted to hear Drake's calm, logical take.

The dress shop was thankfully close to DS Investigations, and Beatrice pushed her way through the door.

"I have to tell you all about— Good heavens!"

Inspector Drake was standing in the middle of the office, wearing only trousers. Beatrice whirled around, her face burning, but she had already seen his broad, bare chest.

"Miss Steele," Drake said, sounding flustered. "I did not expect you today. Miss Bolton sent a note, saying you were to be fitted for a new wardrobe. . . ." He cleared his throat. "I am decent."

Beatrice slowly turned around. Drake now wore a loose white shirt, and she tried not to glance down at the sliver of chest that was revealed by its open neck. He was *barely* decent, and surprisingly muscular—the observation made her lightheaded, for some reason.

"I thought I would take the afternoon to do the same," Drake went on, gesturing to a pile of suit jackets strewn across his desk. Beatrice could see now that he was halfway through trying on formal wear.

"And . . . you couldn't do that at the tailor's?" she asked, her voice coming out weirdly hoarse.

"I can't afford a tailor," he said stiffly. "Percival Nash sent these over from the theater's costume department for me to borrow so I will fit in among the gentlemen at the Rose." He pulled on one of the jackets. "I did not expect to see you. You're rarely here."

"I am here right now," Beatrice shot back. She gestured to the jacket he had pulled on. "That one is nice. I'd suggest you wear it for our presentation." Her cheeks felt hot.

"Thank you," Drake said stiffly. "I suppose I will."

He avoided her gaze as he took it off, back in only a thin white shirt once more, and he tossed the jacket aside.

"So . . . why *are* you here?" he asked.

She explained her encounter with Gregory, Elle Equiano, and Lavinia Lee. Drake began to pace the room, listening as Beatrice informed him of the tidbits she had gleaned. She tried to focus her gaze on their chessboard, though her eyes kept wandering to the opening of his loose shirt.

"So the NAGS will be imposing stricter rules, whatever that means," he said, his brow furrowing as he considered Beatrice's words. "This could apply to actors as well as ladies. Percival mentioned the tension between artists and gentlemen."

"Yes," Beatrice said, "our first goal at the Rose should be to establish relationships and gain trust. The more we understand the inner workings of this club, the closer we shall be to catching the killer. After all, as Lavinia said, all of the members of the NAGS are members of the Rose. They are the gentlemen at the top of society here in Sweetbriar."

"Yes . . ." Drake stopped pacing and looked at her, his jaw tense. "Are you sure you're ready for this?"

"What do you mean?" Beatrice exclaimed, turning from the chessboard to meet his gaze. "Of course I am. This is all I have ever wanted!"

"That is the problem," Drake told her. "You think you can do it all. As in, be an inspector *and* a debutante. But I must urge you to put this case ahead of any social goals."

"My position as a debutante is purely a ploy to appease my mother, and a way to get access to suspects for questioning," Beatrice assured him.

"So you are not using this as an opportunity to secure an engagement?" Drake pressed.

"What do you want me to say? That I am committed to becoming a spinster?" Beatrice asked, growing irritated. What business was this of Drake's?

"I am merely trying to glean your interest level in the eligible gentlemen we shall meet. It might affect the investigation," Drake insisted.

"It is very low, unless they show bloodthirsty tendencies. I trust your 'interest level' in the ladies we meet shall be the same?" Beatrice shot back.

Drake pursed his lips.

"I am glad we cleared that up," he said finally.

"If you *do* take an interest in someone, though, let me know. I am happy to play matchmaker," Beatrice said, unable to resist taunting him. He deserved it, after behaving in such a galling manner.

"You will do nothing of the sort. I have seen someone swayed by the promise of high society and the allure of a flirtatious glance," Drake said sternly, though he still looked flushed. "Neither of us must fall to this fate," he added.

"You're talking about Sir Huxley," Beatrice said, now understanding the reason for Drake's ire: He had worked with the gentleman detective, until Huxley had let a murder suspect go free because he had thought himself in love with her. "We are nothing like that fraud," she assured him.

"The London Season is a whirlwind of parties, promises, and power," Drake said, still seemingly unconvinced. "It might be more than you can handle."

He leaned toward her, and her heart began to pound in anticipation—but he was merely reaching over to pick up his knight. He knocked her rook aside, placing the knight in its new square on the chessboard.

"It won't be," Beatrice told him firmly. "If we solve this case, we will establish ourselves as worthy investigators. Cases will pour in—as will cash." She started toward the door, then turned back. "But if you truly do not want to find a sweetheart, I'd suggest you keep your clothes on from now on. Otherwise you shall drive the debutantes mad."

She had said the words so *he* would be the one to blush, but as she took her leave of the office, she found that her own cheeks were still warm.

THE ARTISTS' QUARTERLY

Sculpture Gallery Has Opened—and Closed

A new gallery opened on Friday, displaying works of local women artists such as the celebrated sisters Lady Budrovich and Lady Budrovich.

Readers likely recall that the Ladies Budrovich are known for their squirrel-inspired sculptures, fashionable pieces which fetch hefty figures at auction.

Unfortunately this gallery also closed on Friday, due to a fire.

Authorities ruled the flames an accident. This will mark the sixth gallery in Sweetbriar to open this year, as well as the sixth to close. Readers will remember the other galleries as lost to another fire, a flood, a building collapse, and two cases of mysterious critter infestations. Similar events have sadly plagued the local music hall and drawing studio.

Those seeking culture can still find it at the Sweet Majestic. A new production of *Figaro* is under way just in time for the summer months, with Percival Nash set to reprise his role as Figaro. Tickets, fans, and squirrel shields may be purchased at the theater beginning Wednesday.

Dearest Members of the Rose:

You are cordially invited to attend this
Season's unveiling of debutantes!

In spite of the tragedy which has concerned our community of late, we are committed to our most successful Season yet, showcasing the Rose's strength and resilience even in the face of a setback such as murder. Indeed, such a situation makes this Season even more important.

Schedule of the Evening

Presentation of Debutantes

Refreshment and Social Hour

And a special surprise to follow,
arranged by Mrs. Diana Vane!
We look forward to your willing attendance at this mandatory event and your tacit compliance with all of the usual rules and regulations, as well as any additional ones we may come up with between now and then.

Sincerely,

The Neighborhood Association of Gentlemen
Sweetbriarians (NAGS)

CHAPTER SIX

A Debut

Beatrice thought she had seen opulence. After all, Swampshire had once been home to the infamous Stabmort Park, a mansion with dozens of rooms and a turret (before it burned to a crisp). But she felt, now, that Stabmort was a swamp in comparison with the splendor of the Rose: Beyond the iron gates was a sprawling garden, ornate pillars flanking the grand front staircase to the club, and not one but *six* turrets.

Inside, it was even more lavish. Busts of former members lined the room, as well as statues of various Greek gods and goddesses. Everything was made of white marble, from the walls to the floors, as if all the color had been drained from the room. That is, except for the roses. They were everywhere, their vines tangled around the bases of statues, clinging to the walls, the air heavy with the scent of their perfume.

Somewhere within those walls, Walter Shrewsbury had been murdered. Perhaps his killer was even in attendance tonight.

The evening marked the beginning of the Rose Club's Season, and Beatrice and Drake's official debut among the ladies and gentlemen seeking to make advantageous matches. But more important, it was their first chance to speak with members of the Rose who may have seen or heard anything about the recent death behind the mansion's closed doors. Beatrice was tense with anticipation, a feeling she could tell Drake shared from how tightly his jaw was clenched.

She followed him into the center of the receiving room, where a footman held out a tray of crystal glasses. Drake took two. He passed one to Beatrice and then one to Miss Bolton, who trailed behind her.

"To think, both you and Beatrice have been invited to the top social club in Sweetbriar!" Miss Bolton gushed as she took the glass. "Even though Beatrice is poor and unconnected, and you are a workingman who was fired from his previous crime-solving position and therefore publicly disgraced!"

"Thank you for that reminder," Drake said dryly.

Miss Bolton wore a thick velvet hat, in spite of the summer heat ("Fashion does not take a break for the summer, Beatrice!"), and it dampened her hearing enough that Beatrice was able to lean toward Drake for a private word.

"We should find out who knew Mr. Shrewsbury best and start our questioning with them," she suggested. "I could ask the ladies and you, the gentlemen—"

"Where *are* all the gentlemen?" Drake inquired, glancing around.

They were surrounded by swathes of women only, Beatrice realized. There were no eligible bachelors to be seen.

The question of their absence was answered promptly, when a harried-looking attendant appeared and beckoned to Inspector Drake.

"Gentlemen must wait in the ballroom," she said frantically.

Drake looked back at Beatrice as the attendant ushered him down a hallway, his expression pained.

Beatrice stared back, her gaze an attempt to communicate the plan.

Don't think of how much you hate society events. Think of solving the murder at hand.

His look back seemed to say, *If I am forced to dance, there shall be a second murder. . . .*

Beatrice shot him a last look before she and Miss Bolton turned toward the women gathered in the atrium.

There were about twelve ladies there, with their chaperones, including Beatrice and Miss Bolton. The ladies were dressed in evening gowns, nervous expressions upon their faces. Beatrice was certain that her own expression mirrored this anticipation. For the first time since she had moved to London, she felt she fit in with her peers—at least in this one regard.

She spotted two familiar faces among the crowd, and relief welled up within her. Beatrice pushed her way over toward the two young ladies from the dress shop.

Miss Lavinia Lee and Miss Elle Equiano were clad in fine evening wear: Lavinia's spectacles shone, perfectly polished, and she wore a sapphire-blue gown. Her white-blond hair was pinned back, showing off painted earrings. As Beatrice grew close, she was unsurprised to see that they were miniature portraits of the handsome, mustachioed Sir Huxley. It seemed that the negative comments in the society columns had done little to quell Lavinia's public appreciation for the gentleman detective.

For her part, Elle Equiano seemed to be the only debutante who was not nervous. In fact, she looked bored, her expression contrasting with her exciting ensemble. She wore the bright pink gown from the dressmaker's window, paired with a matching headpiece, which shimmered in the candlelight.

As the new wardrobe had not yet arrived from the dressmaker, Beatrice was being presented in her plain brown dress, made even more drab in comparison with her peers' lively ensembles. At least she had a colorful sash of tassels, which Miss Bolton had insisted upon.

Beatrice squared her shoulders, trying to affect a confidence she did not feel. "Good evening," she said, and both Lavinia and Elle turned to appraise her.

"Miss Steele," Elle said, her bored expression giving way to delight. "We were wondering where you were."

"I was hoping to find you both," Beatrice confessed. "I could do with any advice for the evening."

"Indeed, my darling," Elle said, beckoning her closer into their fold. "We were just discussing curtsies. We are meant to perform one as we are presented."

"I seriously doubt anyone would consider one of my curtsies a performance," Beatrice said, nerves rising. "Unless they like tragedies. Or, I suppose, comedies."

"No one will laugh at you tonight," Elle assured her. "Not even if you tell a joke on purpose; trust me, I've tried, and these society types never get it. Just nod, smile, and keep your dance card full. Oh, and don't show an ankle during your curtsy, else you may start a riot."

"I heard," Lavinia said, lowering her voice conspiratorially, "that last year, one of the debutantes did not secure *any* dances at the first ball, and she was so embarrassed that she hid in the kissing closet."

"That was me, darling," Elle said, flipping her hair. "And I wasn't embarrassed; I had ten pages left in a Gothic and simply *had* to finish it!"

"How do I secure dances?" Beatrice blurted. "What is a kissing closet? How do I ensure my ankles don't cause a riot? And," she continued, her alarm hitting her throat and forcing her voice up an octave, "what do I do if there *is* a riot and I cannot hide my enthusiasm for pandemonium?"

Several other debutantes and their chaperones looked over, and Beatrice could hear titters as they whispered judgmentally. This only added to her distress. If she did not behave correctly tonight, she risked losing access to the places, suspects, and gossip pivotal to solving the case at hand. Thus she was very, very concerned about the ankle situation.

Mercifully, Elle and Lavinia pushed in closer to Beatrice, shielding her from the curious looks of those who had overheard her outburst.

"Do not fret," Elle said evenly. "First of all, a kissing closet is simply a nickname for a ballroom's small coat chamber."

"Because some people use it for other purposes," Lavinia explained in a whisper. "Not here, of course," she hastened to add. "The gentlemen of the Rose are very respectable."

"And you curtsy once your name is called," Elle went on. "It's simple, really, just don't expose any skin. Or move too quickly. Or dip too low, or not low enough . . ."

"There should be some sort of guide which enumerates all of this," Beatrice said, still feeling overwhelmed. In her hometown, women had been able to consult *The Lady's Guide to Swampshire* for questions of etiquette. But here in London, there seemed to be so many unspoken rules that everyone but her knew. How could she focus on a murder investigation when she could not solve the puzzle that was the basic rules of decorum in London?

"Don't fixate on the ankles, darling," Elle told her, waving a hand. "Unless yours are particularly alluring . . ."

"My mother always called them 'sturdy,'" Beatrice said.

"Then you have nothing to worry about!" Lavinia said happily.

Miss Bolton reappeared.

"There you are, Beatrice," she said, looking flustered. "Come, come . . . everything is about to begin. . . ."

She grabbed Beatrice's wrist and tugged her through a cluster of debutantes and chaperones, toward the ballroom's doors.

"I have determined the course of the evening from the other chaperones," she said excitedly. "It seems that each young lady will be presented in front of current members of the Rose, who are all waiting in there." She indicated the doors to the ballroom. "When your name is called, you will step forward, curtsy, take the arm of your escort, and wave to the crowd."

"The . . . crowd?" Beatrice felt a sudden twist in her stomach.

She had imagined an informal evening of introductions, during which she might gather information about Walter Shrewsbury's death. No one had said anything about standing in front of a bunch of judgmental strangers.

She had never liked being the center of attention; her sister Louisa had always held everyone's gaze. Rightly so, for Louisa was athletic, beautiful, and sweet.* Beatrice was likely to say the wrong thing or make an unladylike remark—it was best that as few people as possible overheard such talk.

"You will be fine," Miss Bolton said, giving Beatrice's arm a kindly squeeze. Once in a while, the peculiar woman seemed as if she could read Beatrice's mind, and tonight Beatrice was grateful for the reassurance.

Even if she worried that it was misplaced.

The doors to the ballroom opened, and there was a flurry of movement as all the debutantes and chaperones turned.

"It's her," Miss Bolton said excitedly. "Mrs. Diana Vane!"

* Mary was also athletic—her bite had an almost canine strength to it—and though she was often overlooked, her bark could attract attention when necessary.

Indeed, it was the tall, silver-haired woman from the carriage—the Rose's patroness. A hush fell over the crowd at her appearance.

She wore a deep-red gown—"Amaranthus, what a daring hue!" Miss Bolton whispered—and her silver hair was swept atop her head, held in place once more with a long hat pin. As Mrs. Vane drew a piece of parchment from her bodice, Beatrice noticed a beautiful ring on her fourth finger. It was studded with garnets, and they caught the light, gleaming.

Almost like blood.

"My blooms," Mrs. Vane said wistfully, breaking the anticipatory silence. She unfolded the parchment and began to read: "'By participating in this Season, you are joining a long and important tradition. This tradition upholds the values of dignity, gentility, and leadership in our community. There are those who might criticize the exclusivity of the Rose, but as you have all been selected, you understand that preferential acceptance is necessary to ensure continued adherence to these values. So on behalf of myself and the other members of the Rose, we welcome you, and we look forward to one day entrusting this club—and its ideals—to this next generation.'"

There was a smattering of applause and Mrs. Vane smiled.

"She is so chic," Miss Bolton murmured.

Yes, Beatrice thought, it was obvious why Mrs. Vane held the position of patroness. She stood out, even in a crowd of fashionable women.

What was it that made her so alluring? Beatrice wondered. Her outfit and jewelry were tasteful, yes, but it was more than that. She led the most exclusive assembly hall in London yet claimed to support artists far below her in social status. The woman was a walking contradiction.

Even her voice represented this inconsistency; it was dreamy, but her words were rote, read from a paper that she surreptitiously crumpled and dropped to the floor.

It was most unusual. Had someone forced her to say such pointed remarks about tradition, and thus she'd crumpled them up in protest? And why even bother saying such things at all, Beatrice wondered as she stared at the paper on the ground. Everyone already knew that the Rose was exclusive, and no one here wished it otherwise.

After all, *they* had been chosen.

It seemed that Mrs. Vane was finished with her piece, for she had now produced a scroll. She unfurled it and then turned toward the ballroom.

"Miss Breanna Carey," she announced, reading from the scroll. A tall blond lady stepped forward, straightened her posture, and then walked through the double doors. Applause sounded from the other room, making butterflies rise in Beatrice's stomach.

But at least Drake would be waiting for her. Tall, scowling Drake, stern but steady. Perhaps he already had leads for them to follow and suspects to question. These thoughts calmed her immediately. Her heartbeat slowed to a normal pace as she stepped forward with the other blooms in anticipation of her own name being called from the scroll.

Beatrice straightened her gown, as if smoothing out the skirt would somehow change the plain fabric into silk.

"Miss Elle Equiano," Mrs. Vane continued.

Elle stepped forward. She turned back and caught Beatrice's eye, struck a little pose as if to say, *Nothing to it,* and then allowed Mrs. Vane to usher her through the doors.

"The other chaperones were all talking about her," Miss Bolton whispered in Beatrice's ear. "Evidently it is her third Season. She is very rich and well sought after—*perfect* penmanship—but no one has secured her hand. She is considered too clever for her own good . . . you may have read her column in the *Babbler*."

"'Riveting Ribbons,'" Beatrice finished. "Yes, I heard something about that. . . ."

Too clever for her own good. Beatrice had heard such judgments before. But why should Elle have to change herself to fit a suitor's preference? She did not need to marry for money. If she wished to marry for love, diminishing herself to gain affection would hardly indicate true romance.

To marry for love. What a concept, Beatrice thought. She had never considered it for herself, as it had never been an option considering her family's dire economic straits. But if she truly did establish herself as a worthy inspector, with an income, it might actually prove possible.

Beatrice blinked the thoughts away. If she spent the evening daydreaming about love, she would never find the killer.

She refocused on the ladies entering the ballroom, each stepping inside after her name was announced, trailed by her chaperone. She could not see beyond the doors but could tell there were many people inside, judging by the thunderous sound of the applause after every entrance. But she refused to let concern creep back into her thoughts.

Drake was there on the other side of the door, waiting for her. They would perform the necessary rituals and then turn their full attention to the case at hand.

"Miss Beatrice Steele," Mrs. Vane called, and Beatrice felt herself go hot with anticipation.

"Go, go, go!" Miss Bolton whispered, and shoved her toward the door.

Beatrice stepped into the ballroom and immediately froze.

There was a huge crowd of people, all staring at her.

She gave a perfunctory curtsy sans ankle and turned to her left, reaching out for Drake. But to Beatrice's horror, there was no one. She looked to her right, but still, she was utterly alone.

Whereas the other debutantes stood in front of the crowd of Rose Club members, all draped on the arm of their escorts, their chaperones standing proudly behind the couples, Beatrice was companionless.

Where was Drake?

Someone rushed up to Mrs. Vane and whispered into her ear, and her eyes widened.

"It appears that Miss Steele's escort cannot be located," she told the crowd. There were a few murmurs of confusion, and Beatrice heard someone snicker.

For the first time in her life, she thought she might actually faint, unlike all the times she had pretended to do so in order to get out of a difficult situation. Beatrice stood in front of a judgmental crowd, wearing an old, unfashionable gown, her ineptitude laid bare for all to see. She couldn't help but pinch her arm. Was this a nightmare? Would she wake up back in Swampshire and find that she had never even moved to London at all? Would that be a relief?

She felt someone's arm loop through hers and turned to see a blond man smiling at her. With some surprise—but mostly relief—Beatrice realized that it was the gentleman from the Carnation Club's hedges.

"It's you," she said, and the man smiled, revealing his dimples.

"Yes, Miss Steele. I saw a damsel in distress and had to act," he said. "Come, this way."

He led Beatrice toward the crowd, and the clapping resumed.

"Wonderful. Beatrice has been saved by the man who consistently saves us all," Mrs. Vane announced. "Sir Lawrence Huxley."

THE LONDON BABBLER

Breaking News

Local heartthrob and crime solver Sir Lawrence Huxley was spotted yesterday in Brovender's Lounge, sporting a clean-shaven face. That's right, Hussies, Huxley's signature mustache is gone—and he looks more handsome than ever.

Why the change? Well, London's gentleman detective is seeking something other than a culprit these days, and the *Babbler* has the exclusive: He plans to participate in this year's Season at the Rose.

When asked what type of lady he hopes to meet, Huxley remained terribly tight-lipped.

"Every woman has a chance with me," he assured reporters after a few drinks at Brovender's. "For now, at least, there is plenty of Lawrence Huxley to go around."

CHAPTER SEVEN

A Secret

Once the last of the ladies had been introduced and stood among the Rose Club members, Mrs. Vane closed the doors to the ballroom.

Beatrice was half mortified, half furious. Drake had abandoned her, and now she stood next to Sir Huxley, of all people. She could barely believe it.

In newspaper sketches, Huxley was always portrayed wearing a top hat, with an emphasis on his full mustache. She hadn't recognized him without the facial hair, but there was also a charisma about him that a simple sketch could not have captured. This was a man overflowing with charm and confidence—a man who knew that all eyes were upon him, and liked it. Just like Percival Nash.

Standing beside Huxley, Beatrice could feel everyone's gaze upon her, too, but she wasn't enjoying it nearly as much as he seemed to be. She knew others would be wondering: What was a shabbily dressed lady with a small-town air doing with the most famous man in London?

As she tried to avoid the curious stares, she noticed a familiar face.

Percival Nash stood next to Diana Vane, wearing a fanciful costume, his auburn ponytail and green ribbon gleaming in the candlelight as if Beatrice had conjured him from her thoughts just seconds before. What was he doing here? she wondered. He was under suspicion of murdering a member of the Rose; it made little sense that he would be welcomed beyond its doors. After all, though he had not been arrested, he had also not been cleared.

"Welcome, all. Now that our debutantes have been formally introduced, allow me to walk you through the evening at hand," Mrs. Vane said. This time her voice was freer, unbound by pre-written statements. "Rose members, please get to know the young ladies and gentlemen of this year's Season. Drinks and refreshments shall be served—I recommend the wine for a memorable evening, and our signature Sweetbriar punch for a forgettable one," she said, then paused, as if waiting for a laugh. She was met with silence—Elle had been right about the lack of humor among the group, Beatrice thought—but Diana Vane took it in stride as she continued. "Once you have become acquainted, we have a special indulgence: By my invitation, the great Percival Nash shall be performing a small preview of the Sweetbriar's summer opera, the latest installment of *Figaro*."

She gestured to Percival next to her, and he beamed and dropped into a bow. So *that* was why he was here: to perform. Murmurs swept through the crowd at the announcement—it seemed Beatrice had not been the only one wondering about the actor's presence. Heads turned, and Beatrice traced everyone's gaze.

They were looking at Horace Vane—Diana's husband. The

man Beatrice had met in the fateful carriage incident stood a head taller than most of the crowd, his salt-and-pepper hair striking in the ballroom's glow. For a moment he seemed to hesitate, and then he lifted his hands and began to clap. Diana broke into a smile, and Percival Nash bowed as the rest of the room joined in with the applause.

"Thank you, thank you," Percival said, putting a hand on his heart. "If anyone seeks an autograph, I shall be in the conservatory, completing my vocal . . . *warm-ups*!" He sang the last word, and the crowd broke into a fresh round of applause. A footman appeared and ushered him from the ballroom. Percival blew kisses to his audience along the way.

At Beatrice's side, she felt Sir Huxley tense.

"How could Horace allow this?" he muttered.

She was wondering the same thing. It seemed a public show of support. Did Mr. Vane believe in Percival Nash's innocence? Perhaps she had misjudged him.

Once Percival had left, the crowd collapsed into conversation with one another, and Beatrice turned to Sir Huxley.

"Thank you for your assistance," she began, "though you might have mentioned your identity in any of our previous encounters."

"And miss the look upon your face when you learned it tonight? Not a chance," he said with a roguish grin. "But," he added, growing earnest, "it was you who assisted me. As a last-minute addition to the Season, I thought I would be alone this evening, so you can imagine my relief when I spotted another unaccompanied soul. I feel much more at ease now that you have graced me with your company."

He was very smooth, Beatrice thought. He gazed at her intently, as if she were the only woman in the room.

For years, she had followed Sir Huxley's cases in the London papers. Though she knew now that he was a fraud, the passion of a girlhood crush did not wear off so easily. She *must* resist the flattery, she told herself. *Remember who this man is.*

"You're welcome," she said finally, trying to match Huxley's confident tone. "However, I must not monopolize your attention; surely many here wish to converse with you. Perhaps we could make the rounds?"

With the niceties out of the way, she was eager to speak with Mr. Vane. She had questions.

Thankfully, Sir Huxley offered his arm without delay. He led her straight to Mr. Vane, who was now in conversation with another gentleman.

Was this a coincidence, Beatrice wondered, or was Huxley pulling at the same threads she wished to follow? Either way, she planned to capitalize on his celebrity. People would talk to Huxley—and Beatrice would listen.

"Miss Beatrice Steele of Swampshire," Sir Huxley said, "may I present Mr. Horace Vane and Mr. Cecil Nightingale?"

"How do you do," Beatrice said, dropping into yet another awkward curtsy. "Mr. Vane, we met before—"

"Do not take offense, Hux," Mr. Vane said at once, ignoring Beatrice. He angled his body, blocking her so he could speak only to Sir Huxley.

". . . my prime suspect," she heard Huxley mutter. The gentleman detective was obviously irritated, and Mr. Vane put a hand on his shoulder. He murmured something in reply, his words frustratingly unintelligible.

They were arguing about Percival, clearly—yet Beatrice would not be privy to whatever information was being exchanged. Properly shut out, she was forced to turn to the other man.

"Miss Beatrice Steele," Cecil Nightingale said, taking her hand in his sweaty palm. "What a little doll you are. Where did Diana Vane find you? You are so gloriously *provincial*!"

He was short and muscular, with a face too small for his large head. Beatrice withdrew her hand at once, already annoyed at the man's cloying tone.

But she now recalled that Gregory had mentioned a Cecil Nightingale during the carriage incident.

Mr. Vane and his friends Cecil Nightingale and Walter Shrewsbury—may Walter rest in peace—saved our neighborhood by starting the association.

This man, Beatrice realized, was the third founding member of the mysterious NAGS, the group that seemed to control culture in Sweetbriar.

"I wanted to ask—" she began, a thousand questions on the tip of her tongue, but at that moment Mr. Vane and Sir Huxley turned back to the circle.

Mr. Vane smiled, and Sir Huxley looked resolute; whatever words they had exchanged had evidently appeased the gentleman detective as to Percival Nash's presence.

If only Beatrice knew what those words had been.

"Sir Huxley is joining us for our shooting party on the Glorious Twelfth," Mr. Vane informed Cecil Nightingale. "Always a relief when all of this is over and we can get on with the *real* season—hunting and fishing, that is. You should have seen the size of the trout I caught last year—"

"Horace, not in front of the lady," Mr. Nightingale warned. "She will be worried about the little fishies!" he added, smiling indulgently at Beatrice.

"If she is cavorting about with Sir Huxley, she has likely heard worse," Mr. Vane said lightly. "Now, I shall excuse myself; I must make the rounds. May you catch the prey you seek," he added, flashing a boyish grin at Sir Huxley. With that—and no acknowledgment toward Beatrice—Mr. Vane swept away.

"That Horace," Sir Huxley chuckled. "He loves his wordplay."

Beatrice felt both disappointed and irritated. She was hardly *cavorting about* with Huxley, and she was no prey to be ensnared. She might have gained access to the Rose—but its occupants were proving even more impenetrable. How was she to find answers if she could not even ask questions?

"Mr. Nightingale," she said, determined to get *some* question past the literal and proverbial gates, "are you excited to hear the opera preview? What do you think of Percival Nash?"

"Oh, little pet," Cecil Nightingale said, taking up a saccharine tone once more, "you are too young to know how it used to be. In the halcyon days, actors stayed onstage where they belonged. They didn't mingle with respectable society."

Well. At least Mr. Nightingale deigned to talk to her, Beatrice thought.

"One could say that all the world's a stage," Miss Bolton cut in, appearing at Beatrice's side. Beatrice moved over to allow Miss Bolton—and her unwieldy hat—to join the circle.

"Please, no Shakespeare," Mr. Nightingale admonished her. "We NAGS do not approve of him and his filthy turns of phrase. It's not fit for little ladies like yourselves."

"Oh, I have read—and written—much filthier works," Miss Bolton assured him. "Odes to inexpressibles and the like—if I may recite a few lines—"

"Figaro is even worse than that!" Cecil Nightingale exclaimed. "He is a character who acts above his station. *Very* indecorous. We often discuss whether his story should be permitted to continue. . . ."

So the fate of Figaro *did* hang in the balance. Would Mr. Vane tip the scale? Beatrice wondered. He seemed to support Percival, judging by his public applause just moments earlier.

"Back in my day, such a story would never have been told," Mr. Nightingale went on. "You are too young to remember that, my dear," he added, and—as Beatrice had dreaded—he patted her head.

"But Figaro is based upon Brighella, a character from Italian commedia dell'arte," Miss Bolton piped up. "Variations of this personality have been seen onstage for hundreds of years!"

Thank heavens for Miss Bolton. If not for her chaperone's interjection, Beatrice might have accidentally headbutted the saccharine Cecil Nightingale.

"Oh, poppet, this is England! Not Italy," Mr. Nightingale replied.

"That explains why we haven't been able to find the Colosseum. We were *so* confused," Beatrice said dryly.

"Women are terrible with geography," Mr. Nightingale said, shaking his head. He withdrew a hideous yellow handkerchief and used it to dab at the perspiration on his brow. Night had fallen, but the air remained stifling, and considering how many people were crowded into the candlelit room, it was unlikely to change. Though Beatrice had almost nothing in common with Mr. Nightingale, she couldn't deny that she was also uncomfortable.

"Perhaps the performance will be a welcome distraction from the heat," Sir Huxley said, clearly trying to change the subject to something neutral.

"And with Mr. Nash in the spotlight, it will be easier to keep an eye on him," Beatrice added, unwilling to talk about the dreaded weather yet again.

"True," Sir Huxley agreed immediately. Then he pursed his lips, as if he should not have spoken. His quick reaction confirmed her thoughts: Huxley still suspected Percival Nash, in spite of whatever Mr. Vane had said. He cast a sidelong look at Beatrice, who smiled back innocently.

Huxley shook his head but turned back to Mr. Nightingale.

"Any word on installing a dipping pool in place of the rose garden? Seems like it would be quite refreshing on a night like this."

Beatrice was disappointed by another change in conversation, until she saw Cecil Nightingale flush crimson at these words.

"Mrs. Vane suggested the dipping pool," he said quickly, "but Mr. Vane refused. The rose garden was part of the building's original construction. A pool is a modern contraption, and a garden is tradition. One cannot simply change tradition."

"Why not?" Beatrice inquired. She had a feeling they were no longer speaking of gardens and pools but was not entirely sure *what* Mr. Nightingale meant.

Before Mr. Nightingale could reply, someone pushed their way into the circle.

"Forgive my intrusion," Lavinia Lee said, "but I must offer my regards to Sir Huxley." She dropped into a deep, reverent curtsy. "I did not think it possible, but you look even more handsome without the mustache, if I may be so bold. Oh," she inhaled, "that *was* too bold, wasn't it? Do forgive me—"

"Miss . . . Lavinia Lee, is it?"

"You know me?" Her eyes sparkled behind her spectacles.

"How could I forget the president of the Huxley Appreciation Society?" Huxley said graciously. "You and your members send the most wonderful fan mail. And the knitted tapestry for my birthday? A genial touch!"

"Should such a sweet little head really be filled with thoughts of the macabre?" Mr. Nightingale asked, shocked.

"I am not being so offensive as to try to *solve* the crimes," Lavinia responded quickly, clearly growing nervous under Mr. Nightingale's judgmental gaze. "There are many women who support Sir Huxley's pursuit of justice and we express our admiration most appropriately, through conversation and cross-stitch."

"She is right. I am one of them," Beatrice said, unable to stop herself. She could not leave her new friend undefended.

"You are?" Sir Huxley asked, now turning to Beatrice, raising one eyebrow, clearly intrigued.

"Yes. Apart from the cross-stitch. My samplers are infamous, I'm afraid," she informed him.

"I suspected you might be here, Sir Huxley, based on the clues," Lavinia continued, as if she could hold this in no longer.

"Clues?" Beatrice asked, the word piquing her interest.

"His last column was titled 'Restoring Order for Summer Entertainment,'" Lavinia explained excitedly. "The first letters in that headline spell 'Rose.' There were ninety-four words in that column. Nine plus four equals thirteen. 'M' is the thirteenth letter of the alphabet." She raised her eyebrows significantly, but Beatrice could only stare back in confusion. Lavinia went on, with the tone of explaining something to someone very stupid. "'M' for 'marriage.' Therefore, it's *obvious*: Huxley seeks marriage at the Rose!"

"Goodness me," Miss Bolton said. "I fear I have been reading the paper all wrong."

Beatrice expected Huxley to share her own incredulous expression, but when she glanced back at him, he was beaming.

"You cracked my code!" he said, delighted. "I confess that Mr. Vane's wordplay inspired me; I thought I might have a little fun with my latest article."

"I have read every single one of your articles," Lavinia gushed. She began to recount his latest case, in which he had rescued a young woman from a swindler disguised as a mime. As they spoke, Beatrice watched Cecil Nightingale, who had gone quiet.

She expected his face to remain twisted in disapproval at a "little lady" discussing such grim topics, but instead he became pensive, apparently deep in thought.

He put a hand in his pocket, and Beatrice heard a crinkle. Mr. Nightingale winced.

It was a subtle movement and could have meant nothing—but the tiny change in his expression caught her attention.

What was in his pocket that caused such stress?

"It *is* a bit hot in here," she said, making her voice sound weak. "Perhaps I should sit down. . . ." She pretended to sway.

"You poor, fragile thing," Mr. Nightingale said, reaching out his arms to take hold of her. "This is exactly why ladies should not speak of such heinous matters. We must protect their innocent ears!"

"This is all my fault," Sir Huxley said apologetically. "Women are constantly fainting in my presence."

"Perhaps wearing less cologne could help," Miss Bolton suggested.

"It's understandable, Miss Steele," Lavinia said kindly. "I feel lightheaded, too, being in proximity to such a sweet-smelling hero."

"Yes, I must excuse myself," Beatrice said feebly, clutching Mr. Nightingale tightly. "The excitement of the evening is simply too great for a delicate, provincial flower like myself." She tried to keep her face straight as she uttered the ridiculous words.

"I will fetch smelling salts," Mr. Nightingale told her. "I always keep them on hand; my wife—may she rest in peace—was always fainting. She could hardly get two minutes into conversation with me without being forced to retreat to her chambers for hours, with only books to keep her entertained, poor thing—"

"You are so kind, but I will be fine. Please, pardon me," Beatrice insisted. She disentangled herself from his grasp and pushed through the crowd before anyone could stop her, and before Miss Bolton could catch up with her.

She was just on her way out of the ballroom when she collided with Elle Equiano, on her way back in.

"Miss Steele? What's wrong?"

"I might ask you the same thing," Beatrice said. Elle looked distinctly frazzled. The young woman gestured to the waist of her pink gown, where a dark stain was spreading.

"It's nothing I didn't expect . . . that Gregory man 'accidentally' spilled his punch," she sighed. "A show of his disapproval for the garment, I'm sure. I tried to blot it in the powder room, but I fear I've only made it worse."

Beatrice untied her tasseled sash and placed it around Elle. "There," she said, "now you can hardly see it."

"You are a gem," Elle exclaimed. "In exchange, I shall cover for you while you do whatever you were about to sneak off to do."

"I'm not . . ." Beatrice began, but at Elle's knowing look, she broke off. "Thank you," she said earnestly, and then slipped out of the ballroom, grateful for a newfound ally. Who needed Drake, she thought with a pang of defiance.

Once alone in the entrance hall, Beatrice stepped behind a marble statue and unclenched her fist. Curled up inside was a piece of paper that she had plucked from Mr. Nightingale's pocket.

At least Inspector Drake's lessons in street smarts had come in handy.

In flowery handwriting, a message was written across the page:

Confess, or die. You decide.

The edges of the ink were rippled, as if the paper had gotten wet and then dried. Below the words, there was a detailed sketch of a moth, with a line through its thorax, as if it were pinned to the page.

Excitement flooded her body.

"How could you bring him here?"

A voice startled Beatrice, and she ducked lower behind the marble statue.

As Cecil Nightingale had noted, she *was* a "little lady,"

height-wise—which came in handy, when one's short stature meant that one could easily hide behind a sculpture so as to eavesdrop.

From behind a marble bust of the goddess Angerona, Beatrice watched as Horace and Diana Vane came into view. It was Mr. Vane who had spoken, and his wife whirled around to face him.

"You said that if you could write my opening words, I could plan tonight's entertainment," she replied, twirling a cigar in her fingers.

"Yes, but I did not think you would invite a murder suspect beyond our gates!" Mr. Vane said, his voice strained. "Sir Huxley was furious. I appeased him as best I could, but he will take it as a slight. You know that."

"Percival is innocent, Horace. *You* know that," Mrs. Vane insisted.

"Of course I do," Mr. Vane said, his voice softening. He took Mrs. Vane's hand in his. "But Sir Huxley suspects him, and it's a bad look to undercut such a renowned inspector by inviting Percival to perform this evening. Surely you understand."

"It is precisely *why* I invited him here tonight. We set an important example, Horace. If we maintain support for the artists, the others will follow our lead," Mrs. Vane shot back. "I always appreciate how you speak up for them at the NAGS meetings. If it weren't for us, their very existence would be in danger. Cecil would get rid of *Figaro* tomorrow if he could. Gregory would dress everyone in gray. Walter—may he rest in peace—practically wanted to outlaw music."

"I know," Mr. Vane sighed.

"You must continue to sway them all to our point of view," Mrs. Vane said firmly. "Look at how everyone waited for your reaction, before applauding for Percival earlier this evening. Your leadership makes a difference. A pun today could save a sonnet tomorrow."

"The pun is mightier than the sonnet," Mr. Vane said, his eyes darkening. "It is more difficult to condense wit into a mere word than to draw it out into sixteen tedious lines—"

"Yes, yes," Mrs. Vane said placatingly. "Just promise me you will support Percival."

The darkness cleared, and Mr. Vane pressed his lips to his wife's palm. "As always, I am with you."

As he kissed her hand, he smoothly removed the cigar from her grip. Beatrice watched as Mr. Vane slipped it into his own pocket.

Diana did not seem to notice. She smiled up at her husband, satisfied, and then let him pull her back toward the ballroom.

Beatrice waited until they disappeared and then emerged from behind the marble statue, reeling from what she had heard.

The atrium was open to the second story of the Rose, and just as Mr. and Mrs. Vane disappeared, someone else appeared high above. A tall, dark-haired, eye-patch-wearing figure, slipping into one of the second-floor rooms.

Beatrice tucked the note into her bodice and then took off to trail the figure.

She had much to tell Inspector Drake—but first, he had some explaining to do.

THE ARTISTS' QUARTERLY

Classifieds

MIME SEEKING MIME for a two-person act. Inquire (nonverbally) at the corner of Maple and Chirpingham.

ACTOR WANTED for exciting and unconventional role. Must be tall, dark, handsome, and willing to alter appearance for the sake of the integrity of the work. Please send inquiries to Miss Evana Chore at *The London Babbler.*

JUGGLING BALLS available, cheap. Wife claims that I shall never get the hang of it, so "why prolong this embarrassment." Bachelors may apply to Mr. Julius Greiner, former juggler, 67 Mill Road.

CHAPTER EIGHT

A Closet

"How dare you abandon me to investigate by yourself," Beatrice said, following Drake into a room and slamming the door behind her.

She took in the chamber she had just entered. It had scarlet carpet, leather club chairs, and wood paneling. Candlelight illuminated a bookshelf at the back wall, stuffed with dusty tomes and cluttered with antiques. In the middle of all of it, notebook in hand, was Inspector Drake, looking as guilty as if he had committed a murder himself. He immediately rearranged his features to cover the expression.

"I thought we would divide and conquer," he said.

"And *I* thought we agreed that never ends well," Beatrice replied, crossing her arms.

"I saw an opportunity to slip away and explore," he told her.

"You saw Huxley and left me to deal with him myself," Beatrice said, correcting him. She would not tell Drake that she had been dealing with the gentleman detective more than he knew. She also would not confess that Drake's abandonment stung, for reasons beyond just the investigation.

She had imagined the moment of being introduced into the Rose Club and then turning to see Drake beside her, his arm outstretched, ready to escort her into a ballroom of debutantes. And *then* they would have slipped away—*together*—to investigate a bloody crime.

Was that really too much to ask?

"Where are we?" she said finally, trying to push away her confusing feelings as she glanced around the room.

"This is the Rose's lounge," Drake replied at once, obviously relieved to have momentarily escaped her scolding.

"How do you know?"

"I studied the Rose's original blueprints," Drake told her. "One must always study the blueprints. For example, did you know that the rose garden just outside was not part of this building's original design? It was added about twenty years ago."

"You should inform Mr. Vane," Beatrice said, considering this piece of information. "Evidently he did not want to install a dipping pool there, because he thought the garden was traditional. Perhaps he might change his mind if he knew the truth, and we could all be in a pool right now, instead of melting from this heat."

"You spoke with Mr. Vane?" Drake asked sharply. "That was quick work. What did he say? Do you think him a potential suspect?"

"He and his wife apparently believe that Percival Nash is innocent," Beatrice said.

"But . . . you suspect Mr. Vane's motives," Drake said.

"I suspect *something* is off," she confessed. "If Horace Vane is the head of the NAGS, and he supports the arts, why does everything seem so . . . tense?"

"You have . . . a gut feeling," Drake said with a mixture of interest and disapproval.

He was resistant to her hunches, she knew, preferring hard evidence over unfounded suspicion. But Beatrice had learned: The feelings that people instilled in others, their gestures and their words, *were* a type of evidence.

"I met the other founder of NAGS," she went on. "Mr. Cecil Nightingale. He revealed an obvious disapproval of the arts, just as Percival Nash warned."

"This was precisely how you wanted to begin the investigation—fraternizing with club members. So it all worked out," Drake told her.

"Mr. Nightingale treated me like a child, and Mr. Vane speaks only to men," Beatrice informed him, not ready to let Drake off the hook so easily. "We might have gleaned more information if you had been there. Instead, Huxley had the honor of driving the discussion."

Guilt flashed across Drake's face, but he forged ahead. "I found something of interest. Do you want to see it, or continue to berate me?"

"A lady can do both simultaneously," Beatrice said, stepping forward.

The lounge smelled of hot wax and something metallic. As Beatrice came to stand next to Drake, in front of an armchair, she looked down at the scarlet rug, which bore a dark stain.

"Dried blood," she murmured. "This is where Walter Shrewsbury died." Perhaps Beatrice was now standing precisely where the murderer had stood, she thought with a shiver.

Drake handed her a crumpled piece of paper. "I found this under the bookshelf. No doubt Huxley missed it in his initial review of the crime scene; he was never thorough when surveying evidence."

Beatrice smoothed out the paper and then gasped.

"What?" Drake asked sharply.

"I just stole this off Cecil Nightingale," she told him, withdrawing the note from her bodice. "He was concealing it in his pocket. Look."

She held the two notes side by side.

They were identical: *Confess, or die. You decide.* Below the words, a moth with a pin through it. Whereas the paper Beatrice had stolen from Mr. Nightingale felt stiff, as if it had gotten wet and then dried, the note Drake had found was smooth. Fresh. Perhaps it meant nothing, Beatrice thought—but she noted it nonetheless.

"If Walter Shrewsbury received this message and then died, and now Cecil Nightingale has an identical letter . . ." She looked up at Drake.

"Mr. Nightingale may be in grave danger," he finished, his eye darkening.

A sound echoed from the other side of the door. Beatrice and Drake froze.

It was clearly the sound of a scuffle. And it was close by.

"This way," Drake said, opening the door and pulling Beatrice toward the noise. She went eagerly, following him down the hallway.

The banging noises grew louder as they ran past a row of closed doors. It sounded as though someone was running into a wall.

Or being shoved into it, violently.

"In here," Beatrice told Drake, and pushed open a set of double doors.

They led to a ballroom, identical to the one downstairs—but slightly smaller. It had the same dance floor, its perimeter lined with marble statues and silk chairs where ball guests could rest between waltzes. Unlit chandeliers dripped from above, crystals sparkling in the moonlight streaming through the ballroom's floor-to-ceiling windows.

And in the center of the ballroom was a gentleman, crumpled in a heap on the floor.

"See if he's alive. Check for breath," Drake said immediately, flinging something into Beatrice's hand. "I will see if the attacker is still here."

He rushed around the room, pushing aside curtains, while Beatrice knelt next to the body on the floor. She looked down at what Drake had given her, to find a silver spoon in her palm.

It had belonged to Drake's father, a philandering gentleman named Croaksworth who had abandoned both Drake and his late mother, Nitara. Etched onto its handle was a Scottish terrier, the adopted crest of the Croaksworth clan. Though Drake's parents were both gone now, Beatrice had discovered his lineage using the spoon as a clue, helping him connect with a half sister and gain answers to long-held questions.

Now she went to hold the spoon up to the man's nostrils. If his breath fogged up the silver, it meant that he was still alive.

But as she pushed his limbs aside to get to his face, she gasped.

The gentleman's face had been bashed in until it was unrecognizable. Even for a seasoned crime reader such as herself, the sight was pure horror. It actually made one miss the tidiness of poison.

With shaking hands, Beatrice held the spoon to where the victim's nose had been. When she withdrew it, she saw what she dreaded.

No fog. No breath.

She looked down at his torso, and now she could see that a knife protruded from his chest. He had been beaten and stabbed—to death.

Drake hurried back to her, his face set.

"No one is here," he said angrily. "We must have *just* missed them. If only we had been seconds earlier—"

"Then he might have survived," Beatrice said, holding up

the spoon. "It seems, Inspector Drake, that we are once more in the middle of a ballroom with a corpse, with a murderer on the loose."

"I certainly hope this isn't *exactly* like our first case," Drake said as he took the spoon back. "After all, if we attempt to do the same thing twice, we will end up on top of a crumbling mansion, nearly burned alive."

"And it would be annoyingly repetitive," Beatrice added.

They both turned back to the body. Beatrice let out a gasp as she noticed something she had missed while distracted by the carnage. She leaned over and pulled a familiar, ugly yellow handkerchief from the man's jacket pocket.

"Drake," she breathed, "it is just as we feared: This is Cecil Nightingale."

"How can you possibly recognize that face?" Drake shuddered.

"I didn't. This is his handkerchief," Beatrice said, holding up the yellow rag. "I was just speaking with him moments ago and noted its unbecoming color. Just moments ago," she repeated to herself.

One never got used to this sort of thing, she thought. It was a shock to see a man walking around, speaking—however condescendingly—and then to stumble upon his corpse such a short time later. The tragedy was not lost upon her, but she knew she could not wallow in it. Letting sadness consume her was of no use in a murder investigation, not to mention that it was decidedly un-English. To catch a killer, one had to carry on.

"The notes both men received were not explicitly blackmail letters," Drake said thoughtfully. "They were more . . . warnings."

"Death warnings," Beatrice agreed. She looked beyond Cecil's battered visage to where his jacket and shirtsleeve had lifted up, his arm splayed at an odd angle. She felt a chill when her gaze fell upon something unusual. "Inspector," she said excitedly, "look."

Inked on Cecil's wrist was a detailed tattoo of a moth.

She and Drake leaned forward, their heads nearly touching as they stooped to examine the tattoo more closely.

"Is it strange for a gentleman to have this?" Beatrice asked, hoping the question did not make her sound provincial. Perhaps tattoos were all the rage in London—but Drake nodded.

"It is unusual. I have seen such art on navy men, and sometimes on particularly adventurous painters—"

"But it seems out of place for a gentleman who was known to dislike the arts to have such a marking," Beatrice finished. Drake nodded.

"The ink is faded," he noted, pointing at the blurred edges of the tattoo. "This indicates that it was done years ago."

"A youthful dalliance," Beatrice murmured, "which led to death . . ."

"Speculation," Drake coughed, but she ignored him.

Though he was right, and the ink *was* faded, she could still see how intricate the artwork was. The shading on the wings made it seem as if the insect were about to fly off the dead man's wrist. She and Drake simultaneously held up the notes they had each found, comparing the drawing of the moth to the tattoo.

It was identical, apart from one detail: the pin, cutting through the moth's body.

Just like the knife now piercing Mr. Cecil Nightingale.

"'Confess, or die,'" Beatrice read from the note. "Both Walter Shrewsbury and Cecil Nightingale evidently chose the latter. The question is: What secret is important enough to take to the grave?"

"No, the question is, why would the killer change murder weapons during an attack?" Drake told her. He pointed to Mr.

Nightingale's face. "These wounds would have been fatal, making the knife literal overkill."

"Not to mention that a death from blows seems spontaneous, whereas a knife wound indicates premeditation," Beatrice added. "Unless it was a knife the perpetrator always carried."

Drake walked to the perimeter of the ballroom and began to push curtains back and peer behind marble pedestals.

"I thought you said the killer was gone." Beatrice rose to her feet in excitement.

"They are. But they may have left something behind. The blows to the face have white markings in the wounds. Dust, perhaps . . ."

Beatrice forced herself to look back at Cecil's bloody visage. She could see now that Drake was right: There was a powdery dust present in his wounds.

"This could indicate that a weapon was used, which left behind residue. Of course that is just a hunch . . ." Drake muttered. "Aha!"

Beatrice rushed over to where he stood, next to a high marble pedestal.

"There was something here," Drake said excitedly, pointing to the top of the pedestal. "See how the gap in the dust reveals it?"

"I can't exactly see," Beatrice told him, rising to her tiptoes. She was much shorter than Drake, and her eyeline did not reach the top of the pedestal. "Lift me up."

"You can take my word for it," Drake assured her.

"I want to see!" Beatrice said firmly. "I know you can lift me. I have seen your muscular . . ." *Dash it all.* She had not meant to say that aloud. "Your muscular . . . well, physique."

"Oh. Er . . . yes." Drake cleared his throat. He stepped closer to her and seemed to steel himself, his hands still at his sides.

"Sometime tonight would be useful," Beatrice told him.

He let out a noise of irritation but relented.

Normally it would have been unheard of for a man to place his hands upon a lady's waist in such a way, unless as part of a dance, but this was just business.

As Drake hoisted her up, Beatrice caught sight of the top of the marble pedestal. In the dust was an octagonal imprint, where an object had once been placed. But now it was gone.

"It has an unusual shape," she murmured. "What do you think it was? A statue? A vase? It must have been chipped—look at this indentation." She touched her finger to the dust and held it up, examining the white powder left there. "The dust looks just like the residue left in the wound. When the attacker used this statue, it left its mark."

"Just as I suspected," Drake told her.

He gently lowered her to the ground. For a moment, his hands were still on her waist, and Beatrice turned to face him.

Drake immediately dropped his hands and took a step backward.

"It's impossible to know what the item was without further evidence," he said stiffly, avoiding her gaze. "But there is a *possibility* that it was used to bludgeon Mr. Nightingale's face."

"And it suggests that the killer was tall, as they would have had to reach the item," Beatrice added, feeling a little lightheaded. It was excitement due to the case at hand, she was sure.

"Taller than you, at least. That does not rule out many people," Drake pointed out.

At that moment, voices sounded in the hallway. Footsteps echoed closer and closer.

"Someone's coming," Beatrice hissed, her body going cold with panic. "Quick—the kissing closet!"

"The *what*?" Drake said, but Beatrice did not have time to explain. She pulled Drake through a narrow door just as someone entered the second ballroom.

THE ARTISTS' QUARTERLY

No More Cheap Seats at the Sweet Majestic

With the summer will arrive the newest installment of *Figaro,* starring the beloved Percival Nash. But citizens with lower incomes may find tickets out of reach this year.

The Neighborhood Association of Gentlemen Sweetbriarians (NAGS) has voted to eradicate affordable seating: The inexpensive "pit" will no longer be a haven for those paying a penny to ogle an aria; it has been filled and flattened.

"This decision was difficult, but will allow for a better view in the orchestra seating," said Gregory Dunne, spokesman for the NAGS. "Previous patrons of the pit can enjoy inexpensive street performances, instead. There, your tomato-throwing is welcome."

"I never threw no tomatoes," Miss Crenshaw, frequent pit patron, told reporters. "I would never disrespect Mr. Nash like that. The NAGS just don't want the likes of us maids in their fancy theater. They're the only ones I want to flatten with fruit!"

The NAGS gave no rebuttal to this claim.

CHAPTER NINE

A Discovery

Beatrice closed the door just as someone else entered the ballroom.

The so-called kissing closet was filled with coats and jackets, shawls, and empty hooks. Drake stooped in the back of the space, half-obscured by cloaks, while Beatrice stood at the front, staring through a crack between the door and the wall. She tried to focus on what was happening in the room, but she was distracted.

She felt overly aware of Drake's proximity to her in such a small space. The unsteadiness she was experiencing around him of late was disconcerting, but she was beginning to understand the cause.

Beatrice had been brought up in a strict environment in Swampshire, where men and women were not to fraternize unchaperoned. Though she knew, logically, that their relationship was professional, her body was rebelling as if she were doing something scandalous. She merely needed to adapt, and eventually, her mind and heart would align; it was perfectly permissible to be alone with a *business partner* in a kissing closet.

No, she mentally corrected herself—a *coatroom*.

Drake pushed aside the cloaks and leaned forward so he could also see through the crack. At once Beatrice smelled oranges and cinnamon, the scent enveloping her like an embrace.

She forced herself to turn her focus to the person who had just entered the room.

It was the man with bushy, overgrown sideburns whom she had met next to the Vanes' carriage and in the dress shop. Gregory something; she had never gotten his surname.

"Cecil? Are you in here? The performers are about to begin the preview of *Figaro*. Horace wants us there to—"

Gregory froze as he saw the body crumpled on the floor, and then he rushed to it. He plucked the ugly yellow handkerchief from beside the corpse and gasped, seemingly coming to the same conclusion Beatrice had as to the dead body's identity.

"Cecil, no . . ." He began to shake Mr. Nightingale by the shoulders. "Cecil, my boy, wake up!"

But Cecil Nightingale would never wake up, Beatrice thought, and he would never see another opera. Like Walter Shrewsbury, he was gone.

And his killer was still at large.

Beatrice's spine prickled as the door creaked open again and a second man entered: Horace Vane, tall and confident, his affable smile crinkling the edges of his dark eyes.

"Mr. Nash, are you in here?" he called as he strode into the room. "The performance was meant to begin— *What is the meaning of this?*" He had finally registered Gregory in the center of the room, hovering over the corpse.

"It's Cecil," Gregory said hoarsely. "He's . . . I think he's dead."

As Beatrice watched the men side by side—Horace Vane

towering over the shorter, stockier Gregory—she wondered if Gregory had modeled his sideburns after Mr. Vane's. While they flattered Horace Vane with his large and striking features, the sideburns only overtook Gregory's mousy visage. He had become more sideburn than man.

"Yes," Mr. Vane said, glancing at the body, his expression inscrutable. "He is deceased—in just the same way as Walter."

His words sent a prickle down Beatrice's spine. Whereas Gregory had said he *thought* Cecil Nightingale was dead, and had just shaken the man violently to make sure, Mr. Vane seemed certain without any further investigation. His pronouncement was too flippant, too quick.

As if it were predetermined.

Did Horace Vane know that Cecil Nightingale would die tonight? Or, Beatrice wondered with a shiver, did he do the deed himself? There was sweat upon his brow, but this did not necessarily mean he had been involved in the scuffle—it was, after all, swelteringly hot.

"Now both of your closest companions are gone. I am so sorry, Horace," Gregory whispered, standing on his tiptoes to grip Mr. Vane's shoulder. "You trusted them completely—the three of you transformed our community with the institution of the NAGS. No doubt you are thinking, *Can I even go on without them? Who will I turn to? Could someone else become my best friend?* I assure you, there are others who can be just as loyal. Just as worthy of your amity. For example . . . me."

Whatever bond existed between Walter Shrewsbury, Cecil Nightingale, and Horace Vane, it did not include Mr. Gregory Sideburns, thought Beatrice. He might have been some sort of messenger for the NAGS, but he was clearly not "one of them." As someone who often felt on the outside looking in, Beatrice recognized his yearning. She could only hope she was not quite so annoying.

"Thank you for your concern, Gregory," Mr. Vane said, turning ever so slightly so Gregory's hand shook loose. "Now, if I could have silence for a moment, to consider what should be done . . ."

"Yes, of course. I also appreciate silence. It is so helpful, when one is committed to one's thoughts—silence is golden, I always say—" Gregory gasped, interrupting himself. "Horace, you don't think it has anything to do with . . ." He pushed back his jacket sleeve and pointed at his wrist. Beatrice noted that it was bare. Unlike Mr. Nightingale, Gregory had no moth tattoo.

Did that mean, she wondered with a shiver of excitement, that Mr. Vane *did* have one? Did Gregory know of the blackmail notes?

She turned to Drake, who stood behind her, watching through the crack in the door above her head. They exchanged looks, and she knew he was wondering the same thing.

"I know exactly what this is about," Mr. Vane said, squaring his shoulders. "The artists of Sweetbriar are defying restriction. They are retaliating against it. I told Sir Huxley exactly who to look at in Walter's death, and I was right. He has killed again."

"You mean to say that the murderer is—" Gregory began.

"Percival Nash," Mr. Vane confirmed.

Aha, Beatrice thought with grim satisfaction. She *knew it.*

Horace Vane had applauded for Percival Nash and assured his wife that he supported her and the arts—but behind her back, he was Percival's accuser. Beatrice had known something was off, that someone was lying—and now the culprit stood before her, unmasked. Those who played with their words, she had learned, were not to be trusted.

"You came in here looking for Percival!" Gregory recalled, anxiously smoothing his sideburns. "Am I to understand that he was unaccounted for while Cecil was being murdered? That ponytailed *fiend*! His vocal warm-ups consisted of *murder*!"

"Yes, he was not in the conservatory, so I went searching," Mr. Vane confirmed. "Diana invited him here tonight against my wishes . . . and now a man is dead."

"She should never be entrusted to arrange an evening again," Gregory said immediately, but Mr. Vane looked up at him, his expression fierce.

"It is Percival Nash who is at fault here, not my innocent, impressionable wife. This is exactly why we must protect women from people like Nash. Sweetbriar will never be safe so long as these *artists* roam our streets."

"Of course, of course," Gregory said quickly. "I agree completely."

Beatrice and Drake exchanged yet another look. It was frustrating that they could not discuss these revelations at the moment, but Beatrice could guess her partner's thoughts, just as he often knew hers.

It was too easy to blame Percival Nash. She knew Drake, like her, still maintained Nash's innocence. True, he had been unaccounted for in the case of both murders, but this hardly proved his guilt. After all, why would he have hired Beatrice and Drake to investigate if he were committing the murders himself? Surely a criminal would want *fewer* detectives around, not more.

Mr. Vane and Gregory halted their conversation as the door opened once more. This time, it was Sir Lawrence Huxley who strode into the room.

"Has anyone seen Miss Steele? The dark-haired lady with the cheerful gap in her front teeth . . . intriguing little white streak in her curls . . . She was by my side, but then I turned back and she was gone—" Sir Huxley broke off, just as the other men had done, the moment he entered and saw Cecil Nightingale's body splayed out on the floor. "No!" He inhaled sharply. "The killer has returned."

"I am so sorry, Sir Huxley, but we now require your services for *two* murders," Mr. Vane told him gravely.

"Do not fear," Sir Huxley assured him. "No matter how many murders occur, I shall be here to solve them all."

"I should hope there won't be *more,*" Gregory sputtered, but Huxley ignored him.

"You still suspect Nash?" he asked Mr. Vane, who nodded grimly.

"He was not in the conservatory. I went looking for him. Evidently he reprised his role . . . as a *killer.*"

"Very good, sir," Gregory told Mr. Vane. "Wit in the face of tragedy is admirable."

Sir Huxley began to pace around the corpse, taking note of the scene. He leaned down, gripped the hilt protruding from Mr. Nightingale's chest, and pulled the knife out with a sickening squelch. Sir Huxley lifted the weapon to examine it in the moonlight, its silver blade slick with scarlet. "'Property of the Sweet Majestic,'" he read aloud.

Gregory gasped. "A knife from the theater!"

Beatrice drew back in shock. They had not seen *this.* As she recoiled, she collided with something. Drake inhaled sharply, and she turned to see that she had made direct contact with his nose.

"I'm sorry," she half whispered, half mouthed. "I didn't know you were so close—" That is, she had determinedly tried to ignore it, and done too good of a job.

He held up a finger to his lips, frantic, and she was horrified to see that his nose was gushing blood.

"Did you hear that?" Sir Huxley said at once. He was uncharacteristically observant that evening, much to Beatrice's chagrin.

Gregory gasped. "You don't think the murderer is still *in* here? I will fight him! I would never leave you undefended, Horace.

Of course, I know you can defend yourself. You are *so* strong. But I will fight by your side . . . or rather, slightly behind you. . . ."

"We should secure the area," Sir Huxley informed Mr. Vane. The tall man nodded but stayed in one place as the gentleman detective began to pace the ballroom. He shook the heavy drapes at the window. "No one here," he murmured. "Now, the closet . . ."

Through the crack, Beatrice watched as Sir Huxley spun on his heel and walked directly to where she and Drake were concealed.

"Yes, yes, that is good thinking," Gregory agreed. Still, neither he nor Horace Vane made any move to assist in the search. "*I* was just going to suggest that. Closets are always filled with all sorts of secrets . . . not mine, of course, I keep a very tidy house; my servants do not receive any days off, to ensure that it is always spotless—"

Beatrice and Drake looked at each other in a panic as Sir Huxley approached the little coatroom. The possibility of what was about to occur flashed across Beatrice's imagination.

Sir Huxley would open the closet door to find Beatrice and Drake, and instantly assume that they had committed the murder. After all, what else would they be doing, hiding in a closet in the room where a corpse was crumpled on the floor? He would arrest them on sight. The newspapers would report that they were killers—and probably make up some story that they were lovers, due to the fact that they were unchaperoned in a closet together. Beatrice would be sentenced to death, her mother would die of shame, and Louisa's daughter—Beatrice's darling niece—would have to live her life with the reputation that she was related to a murderer, philanderess, and worst of all, eavesdropper.

The closet door creaked open, and Sir Huxley peered inside. Just as he did, Beatrice pushed Drake as far back as he could go into the closet, so he was swallowed up by a mess of coats and shawls.

Her own discovery was inevitable. But maybe, just maybe, she could conceal Drake in shadow. In spite of *his* earlier betrayal, *she* was loyal. She hoped it would not come to it, but if she was discovered and arrested, Drake could continue their investigation, find the real killer, and prove her innocence.

It all happened quickly: Drake stumbled backward into shadow, Huxley wrenched open the door, and his eyes fell upon Beatrice, seemingly alone.

A look of surprise flashed across his face. He inhaled—but then exhaled, as if deciding something.

"Empty," he said. And then, to Beatrice's shock, he shut the door.

"The murderer has gone, but never fear," Sir Huxley told Mr. Vane and Gregory, striding over to where they still stood in the center of the ballroom. "I shall find the criminal who committed this crime and apprehend them in as dashing a manner as possible."

"I am certain that you will," Mr. Vane replied. "It may be time to draw the curtains on these performers once and for all," he added, almost to himself.

The words sent a chill down Beatrice's spine.

"Yes," Gregory agreed immediately. "These artists, with their creative ideas and pleasing voices, are trying to upend our entire society! They'll turn our wives against us next by teaching them to *express* themselves!"

"Pardon me," Sir Huxley said, confused, "I didn't know you were married, Mr. Dunne."

"I'm not," Gregory said tartly, "and I never shall be, if such utter chaos persists."

"A great loss for eligible ladies, I'm sure," Sir Huxley replied. His eyes flicked to the closet, where Beatrice watched through the crack. She held her breath. But he put his hands on Mr. Vane's and Gregory's shoulders, steering them toward the ballroom doors. "Might I suggest you refrain from inviting any more suspects beyond your doors?" he said as they walked. "And perhaps more security at the front gates . . . I can recommend reliable guards from the ranks of the Bow Street Runners. . . . In the meantime, obviously I will continue my dogged pursuit of the killer. . . ." He closed the door firmly behind them.

For a moment Beatrice and Drake waited in silence. Beatrice half expected Sir Huxley to burst back inside and cry out, with a flourish, that he wouldn't let them get away that easy. She thought he would expose them, arrest them . . . *something*.

She looked at Drake, who had emerged from the back of the closet. His eye was wide, and he held a hand to his injured nose. Beatrice took a handkerchief from her reticule and stepped toward him.

"It'll stain it," he whispered, shaking his head.

"As a detective, I am destined to have bloodstained handkerchiefs," she assured him. She pushed aside his hand and gently pressed the fabric to his nose. He winced but let her stem the bleeding. It was not so bad, but Beatrice lingered there, looking up at him. His eye met hers.

They stood there for a moment, the air thick between them as they waited.

But Huxley never returned.

Finally, Beatrice pushed open the closet. She and Drake stepped out into the empty ballroom.

"That knife is not from the Sweet Majestic," Drake told her immediately, still holding the handkerchief to his nose so the words came out slightly muffled.

"How do you know that?" Beatrice asked.

"They would never use a sharpened weapon in the theater," Drake explained, lowering the handkerchief. "Actors use prop knives, which retract upon stabbing, for the safety of the performers. That wound," he said, now using the bloody handkerchief to point to Gregory's bloody back, "is not from a prop knife."

"You think someone took a real weapon and had the name of the theater engraved upon it?" Beatrice knitted her brows together, wondering. "Why would they do such a thing?"

"To frame Percival Nash," Drake said grimly. "He was right to come to us. Considering what we just heard, I am now certain that Percival—and perhaps all the artists in this town—are in grave danger."

"Drake," Beatrice said, her chest tight with concern, "Huxley saw me. I'm sure of it. Why didn't he say anything? Why is he letting me go?"

"There is only one thing Huxley likes more than unearned adoration," Drake told her, his eye darkening. "People owing him favors."

"So now . . . I am in his debt?" Beatrice said, understanding.

"Exactly," Drake agreed.

"Then we must catch the killer," Beatrice told him, her concern dropping to her stomach and solidifying there, "before Huxley comes to cash in."

BULLETIN SERVICES FROM THE NEIGHBORHOOD ASSOCIATION OF GENTLEMEN SWEETBRIARIANS

(BS from NAGS)

Following the tragic murder of Cecil Nightingale, effective immediately, all artists are prohibited from visiting local assembly halls.

Furthermore, no art of any kind may be publicly performed or consumed without permit.

Those requesting a permit may apply to the Neighborhood Association of Gentlemen Sweetbriarians. Any street performer, gallery owner, or salon without NAGS approval will be disbanded, and perpetrators will be apprehended.

We thank you for your compliance and assure you that it is for the good of our neighborhood. Those who are denied a permit—you will always have Paris. We suggest moving there posthaste.

Dearest Mary,

Thank you for your report on Fauna Manor. I am pleased to hear that all my pets are doing well, and that you have taken care of the bat problem. Those nighttime creatures were tormenting my aviary—however did you manage to drive them away? I thought I had tried everything!

Beatrice began the Season at the Rose last night. Unfortunately, there was a teensy little murder, so the evening was cut short. How odd that this seems to happen so often at the events Beatrice attends! But there is no need to tell your mother about this—we were assured that the gentleman detective here in London, Sir Huxley, is on the case. This week's balls shall proceed as planned, and everything will be sorted soon. Naturally I am concerned about the implications of this murder: that the Rose will henceforth be haunted. I've already told you all about the neighborhood ghost, the one-handed Specter of Sweetbriar. But he merely recites poetry about a lost love, and his lost appendage, and otherwise leaves people alone. I had a sighting of him myself! "She moves upon a cloud, my lady fair . . ." Sonnets are the most chilling of the poetic structures, but I suppose I must accept that hauntings—and iambic pentameter—are simply a part of London.

As you can imagine, after such excitement, Beatrice and I shall rest all day today. She has decided to stay in her room, and I am in my quarters working on my play. Being a chaperone is very demanding, and it is so nice that we can have quiet times like this. I can count on the fact that she is safe and secure in her personal chambers.

Give my best to all of my darling pets.

Your bosom friend,

Helen Bolton

Darling Beatrice,

I am positively trembling in anticipation. You must write to me soon to tell me all about your presentation as a debutante at the Rose. I always dreamed this day would happen for you. I feared you might be too morbid, and your ankles too sturdy, for such an honor. But thank goodness for long hems and people who are unable to decipher your creepy quips! You have made it on the social scene, and you are so close to securing the hand of a wealthy man!

As you get to know the gentlemen at the Rose, do think of your family. You might be tempted to accept a proposal from someone who has, say, five thousand a year. But though this sounds like a reasonable sum, when divided among all of us it will not go far. Therefore I recommend that you aim as high as possible when it comes to your beloved's income.

Perhaps I think too much of money. Perhaps I would not do so, were I permitted to earn or inherit it myself, and thus provide for our family without relying on wealthy men to bestow the honor upon us according to their whims. Ah! There's no point in being so fanciful. That could never happen.

Of course, I do not want you to be *so* unhappy, my dear Beatrice. Once you have whittled down your options to the most well-endowed men (in regard to their fortunes), you may make your final selection based on the one you like the most (based on other endowments). Perhaps the blond gentleman

Miss Bolton mentioned who "looks *very* becoming in breeches"?

Please send me descriptions of all your suitors post-haste, as well as their yearly payouts.

Your doting mother,

Susan Steele

CHAPTER TEN

An Article

Beatrice did not want to lie to Miss Bolton, but she was certain that a good chaperone would not allow her charge to spend every free moment looking for clues in not one but two murder cases. Therefore she ensured that Miss Bolton was in for the day, hard at work on her "magnum opus" (much of which was in Latin, and therefore inscrutable), and assured Miss Bolton that she would be resting for the afternoon. Then Beatrice slipped out the front door.

Now that she was one of the Rose Club's blooms, people seemed to take notice of her more than before. This was a liability, for if someone recognized her unaccompanied on the streets of Sweetbriar, her reputation would certainly suffer. Therefore Beatrice had come up with what she considered an ingenious disguise.

She had pieced together an outfit from some of Miss Bolton's castoffs, as well as fabric found in an old trunk. Beatrice now wore a black gown, a tall hat, and dark lace draped over her face. To any passerby on the street, she appeared as a woman in mourning, and thus she could move about without arousing suspicion.

It was the best ensemble she had ever put together.

She arrived at DS Investigations in record time. Instead of flinging open the door as usual, she knocked, then waited long enough to allow Drake to make himself presentable.

"I'm coming in," she said, pushing open the door cautiously—but she was surprised to find the office empty.

Drake was nearly always there during the day, or in his apartment directly above it, but the curtains upstairs were drawn and the office, still.

At first, Beatrice felt unsure of what to do or where to go. She did not want to return to Miss Bolton's town house, but she could hardly go off and investigate without Drake. Not after she had scolded him so many times for doing the same thing to her.

Unless, she thought with rising irritation, that was exactly where he was: investigating without her.

Where else would Drake have gone? He had no other hobbies that she knew of, apart from attending the opera, evidently—and there would be no performances in the middle of the day. His only family was his half sister, Alice, who was away on her Grand Tour. Drake had never spoken of any friends or sweethearts he might call upon. Not that they had discussed his personal life, Beatrice thought, a strange irritation rising at the idea of Drake with a sweetheart. No doubt because she disliked being kept in the dark, she reasoned.

She slammed the office door shut and took off down the street, folding into a crowd of Londoners along the main strip of Sweetbriar.

Drake never took carriages, so he had to be somewhere within walking distance of DS Investigations. Therefore Beatrice decided: She would track him down.

In her disguise, she was unnoticed as she waded through crowds of ladies and gentlemen fanning themselves in the sweltering summer heat. The one downside to her ensemble was the perspiration that welled under the veil. She had never mastered the genteel art of not sweating.

Beatrice passed a butcher, two bakers, three dress shops, fifteen ribbon stores, and a butcher. She ultimately took a table at a café that faced the street. Though it was terribly Parisian, Beatrice knew that drinking *en plein air* would allow her to observe passersby—one of whom she hoped would be Drake.

She ordered tea but left the hot beverage untouched as she peered through lace at the hustle and bustle of Londoners making their way down the street.

". . . But I don't *want* to watch Archibald Croome's evening soliloquy about the one-handed Specter of Sweetbriar," a red-haired woman whined to a man at the table next to her. "I want to go to the Sweet Majestic and see a *real* show."

Beatrice tried to be inconspicuous as she eavesdropped on the conversation.

"As if I possess enough ponies for passes to a performance," the man scoffed.

"If you loved me, you'd shell out for a ticket," the woman insisted.

"The pit's gone, Miss Cleary," the man told her. "The cheapest ticket at the Sweet Majestic would wipe out my savings, and then we'd have nothing left for our wedding. Is that what you want?"

"No. Obviously I want to have the wedding *and* go to the opera!" Miss Cleary insisted.

They broke out into an argument. Evidently, Beatrice thought, the NAGS's decision to eliminate the theater's pit was already affecting opera attendees. She had read about it in the *Babbler*:

With the cheap seats eradicated, only the wealthy could afford to see shows.

But, she thought, the performers would also be affected. Cheap as those seats might have been, a ticket sale was a ticket sale. Now the Sweet Majestic would sell fewer passes to plays. Was this what Horace Vane meant by drawing the curtains *once and for all*?

The bickering couple's squabble had somehow melted into declarations of love, so Beatrice turned her attention to the party on her other side—two gentlemen, speaking in low voices.

". . . and he died without clarifying if we are in support of inexpressibles," one of the men at the table was saying.

"Obviously Cecil Nightingale would not have permitted such attire. He was a traditionalist," the man sitting with him replied. "Therefore the Carnation, Tulip, and Rose will all maintain our usual dress code."

Beatrice's ears prickled at the mention of Cecil Nightingale. She did not recognize the two gentlemen, but judging by their well-tailored ensembles and the lavish dishes upon their table, they had money. And their discussion led her to think that they were members of the notorious NAGS.

"Gregory thinks that Walter's and Cecil's deaths indicate a turn against all of us," the first man said.

"Gregory believes whatever Horace Vane tells him," the second man scoffed.

"Well, Horace *would* know. He is aware of everything and everyone in Sweetbriar," the first man insisted.

"Horace Vane cares only about his wife," the second man said.

They began to speak more about inexpressibles, which Beatrice knew (from Miss Bolton's poems) were very tight breeches that left little to the imagination.

Horace Vane cares only about his wife. Diana seemed to believe that she and her husband were aligned in their commitment to their role as patrons of Sweetbriar's artistic community. But if Mr. Vane *truly* cared about her, he would truly support the arts, Beatrice thought. Instead, he lied to Diana's face and went behind her back.

She considered what she knew: Walter Shrewsbury, Cecil Nightingale, and Horace Vane had been friends since their school days. Perhaps this was when they had gotten matching tattoos. Could it be, Beatrice wondered, that Mr. Gregory "Sideburns" Dunne was so jealous of Horace Vane's friendship with Cecil and Walter that he had murdered his competition? It seemed a bit desperate, but without Mr. Shrewsbury or Mr. Nightingale, Mr. Vane *had* been forced to converse with the irritating Gregory Dunne.

And then there was Percival Nash. By virtue of his position as a local artist, Percival Nash had a motive to wish the NAGS harm. But surely he wouldn't wish them *dead* . . .

Perhaps the killer was some other artist, Beatrice thought. Percival was not the only star in Sweetbriar. Horace Vane and Sir Huxley might have been right in their suspicions but had simply pointed the finger at the wrong actor.

She was lost in thought until her eyes fell upon a familiar tall figure inside a store across the street.

Drake.

Beatrice tossed payment onto the table for her untouched tea and rushed toward the shop.

Swampshire had only one general store, which sold everything from grains to gowns. London, on the other hand, had a plethora of specialty boutiques. When Beatrice stepped into the one before her, she felt weak-kneed with awe.

It was like something out of a dream. There were books everywhere, lining the walls on shelves, piled high in displays, and in the hands of patrons flipping through pages.

One particular pile of books sat stacked underneath a sign that read: DISTURBING NOVELS OF CRIME AND INTRIGUE. NOT FOR THE FAINTHEARTED.

Beatrice forced herself to pass the beautiful display—she would return to it, she resolved—and made a beeline for Drake.

He had disappeared into the back of the store and was half-hidden by a shelf. He held a newspaper, which he nearly dropped in surprise as she approached.

"How dare you," she growled.

"I am sorry, madam," he said, looking at her mourning ensemble.

"You should be," she snapped, pushing back her veil.

"Beatrice?" Drake's eye widened.

"I went to the office to find you, but you weren't there."

"This store has an archival collection of *The London Babbler*," Drake explained. "I have been combing through them all morning, searching for any mention of Walter Shrewsbury, Cecil Nightingale, or the Rose. I thought it might provide further information for the case, since we have little to go on at the moment apart from Huxley's ridiculous notion that Percival Nash is the killer."

"So you are investigating without me *again*."

Drake scoffed. "Miss Steele, I am not intentionally cutting you out of anything. But you must admit that you possess time-consuming social obligations. What do you expect me to do? Stare blankly at the wall until you are available?" He lowered his voice. "Two men are dead. Time is of the essence."

"You could have sent me a note or stopped by the town house to fetch me before coming here. I had no social obligations today," she insisted.

"And would Miss Bolton have permitted you to do such a thing?" Drake asked pointedly.

To this, Beatrice had no reply.

She had imagined London as a place where a lady could do what she liked—but Drake was right. Beatrice was still bound by her old nemesis decorum; she had to wear a ridiculous disguise to even leave the house today. Why, though, would he not work within her restrictions? Or help her bypass them? Did Drake not value her partnership enough to make such efforts?

Trying to push away these particular concerns, she snatched the newspaper Drake was holding.

"Careful!" he yelped.

It was a very old edition of *The London Babbler,* its pages soft from age. Drake had turned to the society section, and Beatrice skimmed the article he had been perusing.

> New Club Courts Success
>
> Mrs. DV cut a fashionable figure last night when she introduced her debutantes.

"This is about Diana Vane," Beatrice surmised. She read on, intrigued to learn more about the past of the mysterious silver-haired patroness.

> This marks DV's first Season as patroness at the Rose, an assembly hall quickly becoming notable for its exclusivity and mystery.
>
> Few know what goes on behind the Rose's imposing iron gates, but everyone wants the chance to find out. Mr. and Mrs. V met during a Season there, and their marriage is a model of success which other young ladies and gentlemen might emulate.
>
> Though Mrs. V is young for a patroness, her appointment makes sense: She and Mr. V purchased the Rose early in their marriage and have been instrumental in guiding its rise. Without the fashion-

able Mrs. V, or the wealthy Mr. V, the Rose would be just another wildflower along the path. Yet under their guidance, it has bloomed into the rarest blossom in the garden.

With Mr. V's fortune and good name—as well as his ties to Mr. CN and Mr. WS, two other well-bred gentlemen—this reporter is certain that the Rose will continue to flourish.

Yet what of Mrs. V? She had her own fortune before marrying Mr. V, that is true, but those who keep up to date on the society papers may recall that she made quite a splash when she first entered the social scene. Salons, cigars, and a rumored dalliance with a poet . . . oh my!

One must admit, Mrs. V has an eye for fashion and design, as evidenced by the interior of the Rose. Those who are lucky enough to glimpse it will note its Grecian design, a stylish tribute to ancient mythology. And her clothes never disappoint; Mrs. V is always the best-dressed at any ball.

If this were not enough to recommend her, everyone has only to look to Mr. V. He wholeheartedly supports his wife, though she has a past reputation as a bluestocking. Readers can rest assured that her hose have been bleached by an advantageous marriage—even if she is still seen sneaking a cigar now and again.

"What is a bluestocking?" Beatrice asked, once she had finished reading.

"It is a nickname for learned ladies," Drake explained. "Women who support the arts, education, and the like. They sometimes host salons to discuss their interests."

"I wish I could go to one of those instead of all these balls!" Beatrice exclaimed.

"As you can imagine, some gentlemen do not approve of such gatherings," Drake informed her.

"Hm." She considered. "So Mrs. Vane has always been involved with the artistic community. And she had a suitor before marrying Mr. Vane. . . . A poet, no less . . ."

This would surely have been a scandal—if it were true. Society pages often printed rumors, Beatrice knew.

But still. The idea was intriguing.

"There is something else that is interesting," Drake told her. He turned the paper over, where an advertisement had been printed.

"'Mrs. V's Selection,'" Beatrice read aloud. "'Recommended by Mrs. V herself, this sculpture—by sisters Lady Budrovich and Lady Budrovich—elevates any sitting room, lounge, or parlor.'"

Below the description was a drawing of a statue featuring a squirrel. Its base was octagonal—just like the shape left behind in the dust at the Rose.

"The murder weapon!" Beatrice gasped.

"Not necessarily," Drake said, "but yes, this *could* be the sculpture which was used to smash Walter Shrewsbury's face."

"Death by squirrel. How tragic," Beatrice said sadly.

"Yes, but more important, how expensive," Drake told her. "I have seen these types of sculptures before. They are worth a great deal."

"You think that the killer decided to steal the statue and sell it," Beatrice surmised.

"It is a theory, but we have little to go off at the moment, so it is worth investigating," Drake said, nodding. "I know of a nearby pawnshop. If my theory is correct, we may find the murder weapon there. We could go now."

"I am honored to have received an invitation," Beatrice told him curtly.

He rolled his eye but gave no further remarks.

Before they left the bookstore, Beatrice stopped at the cashier. She had Drake use office funds to purchase the old edition of the *Babbler* (and a few books from the disturbing display—for research purposes, of course).

There was something about the story of Mr. and Mrs. Vane that made her feel uneasy. She did not know what, yet—but she was determined to find out.

My dear—

I heard a concerning rumor this morning that the gargoyle shop in town did not receive a permit from NAGS. I have made my opinion on the permit system clear, but I must advocate for this shop in particular. Their stonework is superb, and without such artisans, we shall have to travel far for gargoyle repair, else risk losing the sculptures which give our neighborhood such a unique look. Please, would you put in a good word for this business with your fellow NAGS?

Yours,

Diana

My love—

I have been steadfast in my opposition of the permit system. Still, you must understand that I am merely one member of NAGS. The others may outvote me, even if I advocate for the arts, as you know I do.

Of course I will speak up for the gargoyle shop. I could not fathom Sweetbriar without its signature guardians. I shall be home late; with such a debate ahead of me, I expect to be stonewalled like the very statues I defend.

Yours,

Horace

CHAPTER ELEVEN

A Sculpture

It seemed that the pawnshop was beyond the bounds of Sweetbriar, for Drake led Beatrice down street after street, into an area of London she had not yet seen. The farther they got from their neighborhood, the less well-kept the buildings were, Beatrice noted.

There were flyers pasted along fences for low-bet billiards and cheap gin. Clusters of squirrels chittered in the trees, and Beatrice and Drake sidestepped at least twelve mimes, each pulling on an invisible rope more desperately than the last.

"It is not in a part of town meant for genteel ladies," Drake explained. "If you wish to turn back—"

"Of course not," Beatrice said.

But the path grew rocky and overgrown as they pressed on. The buildings along the street no longer resembled structures; some were merely heaps of collapsed brick. Drake helped Beatrice over a large boulder that blocked their way, looking concerned as she scrambled down, trying not to catch her skirts on its jagged edges.

"One would think that gentlemen would be more concerned about rebuilding local infrastructure instead of undermining the opera," Drake remarked.

Beatrice had nearly reached solid ground when she stumbled on the edge of the boulder. She fell into Drake, her face landing into his very solid chest. He put his hands on her shoulders to steady her.

"Thank you," she said, looking up at him.

"Do try to be more careful," he said with concern, then cleared his throat and kept on walking. Beatrice nearly had to jog to keep up with him—until he stopped, abruptly, and she collided with his very solid back.

"*You* should be more careful," she yelped, but Drake stepped aside, and she saw why he had halted.

In front of them was a rushing stream, which divided their path. It was just wide enough, and looked deep enough, that they could not wade across.

It seemed that there had once been a bridge there, but now it was just a heap of rubble. Drake turned back to Beatrice.

"I will have to jump it. You can wait here, and I will be back presently—"

"What? You cannot go without me!" Beatrice cried.

"This bridge is unsafe," Drake said firmly.

Beatrice pursed her lips, thinking. "I have an idea," she told him, "but you aren't going to like it."

"Miss Steele . . ." Drake began with a heavy sigh, but Beatrice spoke in a rush.

"Louisa and I used to do this when we were girls. When we needed to jump over squelch holes."

"I try not to think about that particular element of your hometown," Drake said with a shudder, clearly remembering when he had almost been swallowed by one of Swampshire's legendary muddy pits. "I dislike depths almost as much as I hate heights."

Beatrice put her hand on Drake's shoulder. "You must crouch down and lace your hands together. I will place my foot there, and you will stand, using the momentum to hurtle me into the air."

"What?!" Drake looked horrified as Beatrice pushed him into a crouching position. "Miss Steele, I *really* do not think—"

"Just trust me," Beatrice told him.

Drake stared from her to the broken bridge. Finally he sighed in defeat and crouched down.

"On the count of three," Beatrice said, before he could change his mind. She put one boot into his interlaced hands, and placed her own hands on his broad shoulders. "One, two . . ."

On three, Drake stood and gave her a shove into the air. It wasn't the most graceful launch ever completed, but it did the trick: Beatrice went sailing over the stream and landed on the other side.

"Are you all right?" Drake called, his voice taut with concern.

"Wonderful," Beatrice assured him. "My ankles may not be attractive, but they *are* sturdy."

Drake got a running start and jumped over the stream to join her. He was much taller, and therefore able to rely on long legs to complete the leap. They got back on the path at once, both catching their breath as they walked.

After a time, Drake spoke.

"You have fine ankles," he said pensively.

Beatrice turned to him, trying to formulate some sort of response to such a random remark, but they came upon a narrow alley and he exclaimed, "This is it!"

Drake led Beatrice in front of a nondescript door. Above it was a tiny wooden sign that read simply, PAWN.

"This looks like just the place to sell something nefarious, doesn't it?" Beatrice said excitedly as she pushed the door open.

Drake followed her into a small, dark room crowded with marble busts, bronze lamps, and porcelain vases.

They could hardly move, else they risked bumping an item and breaking it. Beatrice could not afford to replace any of the merchandise here, so she walked with caution. There were beveled mirrors, sculptures, and intricate paintings in golden frames. Silk-covered chaises were pushed against cabinets displaying jewels that likely cost more than Miss Bolton's entire town house.

The items all seemed touched by sadness. Beatrice could not help wondering about the story behind each necklace, each mirror—no doubt the previous owners had been desperate and forced to make their way to the very edge of town to part with treasured artifacts. She could relate; her mother had sometimes sold items from their home when unexpected expenses exceeded her father's income. Like any lady of few means, Beatrice knew not to get too attached to any piece of furniture or accessory. She tried not to think of what her family might have to part with if she was not able to send money to them soon.

"Good afternoon." A tall man emerged from behind a bookcase of ancient-looking tomes. Beatrice and Drake both jumped.

He looked as if he had never seen the sun, with skin pale as his white hair. His eyes were sunken, and he towered over them, a skeletal waif in a faded silk suit. Both he and the outfit seemed at least two hundred years old.

"Dudley O'Dowde, at your service. Buying or selling?" he asked. His voice was surprisingly chipper, with an Irish lilt. A creaking whisper would have better fit his appearance, Beatrice thought.

"We are looking for an item—" Drake began, and Mr. O'Dowde's gaunt face lit up.

"Buying, then! I have just the piece for you." He began to wade through a cluster of armchairs before Drake could stop him.

Beatrice and Drake were forced to follow. They found Mr. O'Dowde by a small writing desk.

"This beautiful piece is imported from Italy. Rumor has it that if one writes a love letter while sitting here, the receiver will fall head over heels," he explained, running a bony hand over the warped wood. "Can you not imagine how many lasses you might enchant? Can you not imagine how your sweethearts would be banging down your door, eager to ease your lonely soul?"

"I would rather not imagine such a thing," Drake replied. "What I am searching for is—"

"Now, for you," Mr. O'Dowde cut in, turning to Beatrice. "I know exactly what you need."

He turned away and waded through the shop again. Once more, Beatrice and Drake were forced to follow. Mr. O'Dowde stopped at a box filled with rings.

"Mourning jewelry, for the widow," he said, gesturing grandly to the rings. "Perhaps you might select a skull, to remind yourself of the inevitability of death. Memento mori. Or perhaps this one, which contains the tooth of a night wolf, said to heal any wound—even heartbreak—"

"She does not need that," Drake assured Mr. O'Dowde.

"I do need a new locket, actually." Beatrice considered. "But first, do you have any weapons which could fit into a reticule?"

"Ooh! Indeed, I have a series of miniature swords," Mr. O'Dowde told her. "It isn't the size of the blade which matters, but what one *does* with it—"

"We are looking for this," Drake said firmly. He held up the sketch of the squirrel sculpture.

"Why didn't you say so?" Mr. O'Dowde cried. "It is a Budrovich sculpture you seek. One moment." He turned on his foot and disappeared into the back of the shop. He returned with a hefty white statue, which he placed before them.

The piece was marble, with an octagonal base that seemed the same size as the silhouette left behind in the Rose Club's ballroom. Atop the octagon was a sculpture of a squirrel.

It was identical to the newspaper sketch.

Beatrice peered at the base; sure enough, there was a tiny chip in one corner that perfectly matched the shape left behind in the dust. This had to be the statue taken from the second ballroom at the Rose.

But most damningly, the top of the squirrel was covered in a dark substance. Beatrice leaned in to smell it and immediately got a whiff of a metallic scent. She turned toward Drake. The veil may have obscured her face, but by the look in his eye, she could tell he agreed with her unspoken analysis: The squirrel was covered in Cecil Nightingale's blood.

"It's pure marble," Mr. O'Dowde was saying, "so it's very heavy. And worth a good deal. You can tell by the inscription at the bottom that it is a Budrovich sister original. Isn't it a lovely piece?"

"Not really," Drake replied, staring at the blood.

"Perhaps you would like to see something else. I have a *gorgeous* armchair—you'll go *mad* for it—literally, the previous owner was sent to Bedlam—"

"Do you remember who sold this piece to you?" Beatrice interrupted, before Mr. O'Dowde could run off again.

"This was a recent acquisition, so it is fresh in the mind," Mr. O'Dowde told her, "but I would have remembered the seller anyhow. Her name is Miss Felicity Lore."

Drake gasped.

"Let me guess," Beatrice said; she had only heard him make such a noise one other time. "She is an opera singer?"

"Yes, a soprano," Mr. O'Dowde confirmed.

"Sir. She is not just a soprano. She is *the* soprano," Drake said, correcting him. "I have never gotten a chance to see her onstage myself, but of course I have read many descriptions of her soaring arias and incomparable beauty in *Opera Daily*!"

"She can't be *that* wonderful," Beatrice said, a bit irritated by Drake's reverent tone. "*I've* never heard of her."

"She has never performed here in Sweetbriar," Drake replied.

"She will soon!" Mr. O'Dowde assured him. "She is appearing in the next installment of *Figaro,* at the Sweet Majestic!"

"Tell me this is not a jest!" Drake cried. "I cannot believe it! Miss Steele, we *must* go," he said eagerly. "Felicity Lore, here in Sweetbriar . . . one cannot even comprehend it!"

"I think we *should* definitely go see her," Beatrice agreed, "seeing as she was in possession of a *murder weapon.*" With a grunt, she picked up the squirrel statue and waved it in front of Drake. His face fell.

"It must be some misunderstanding," he said, shaking his head. "I am certain that Felicity Lore couldn't have had anything to do with a"—he lowered his voice to a whisper, as if he could not even bring himself to say it—"*murder.*"

"I should hope not!" Mr. O'Dowde piped up. "If she were, the Sweet Majestic's permit could be revoked!"

"Permit?" Drake asked, knitting his brows together in confusion.

"It is a new edict from the NAGS," Mr. O'Dowde explained. "All artists must apply for a permit in order to perform or practice their craft." He sighed. "It never used to be like this. When I was a boy, Sweetbriar was a haven for London artists. It was filled with salons, music halls, galleries . . . there were beautiful statues like these for sale in every shop, romantic sonnets filling the air, mimes and street performers everywhere you turned—"

"That is still the case," Beatrice said, "with the mimes, at least."

"But it is different," Mr. O'Dowde insisted. "Now only acts

approved by NAGS can be performed. I am certain we shall see a decline in expression. Particularly expression which offends the upper classes. You know—stories of servants rising in the ranks, portraits of disgruntled cooks poisoning supper, parodies of beloved classic literature—"

"Or Figaro," Drake said gravely. "After all, he is a conniving servant who subverts evil plots from the upper classes. Also, he is French."

"It seems that does not go over well," Beatrice mused, "with high society." She looked up at Drake. "So these gentlemen abhor art, and they might try to take down Figaro. A character who is portrayed by Percival Nash."

She could see why Sir Huxley suspected the actor in the first place.

"But," Beatrice mused aloud, "surely a simple permit cannot stop art."

"What about a fire, or a flood?" Mr. O'Dowde asked, his pale eyes wide. "Or a suspicious infestation of squirrels?"

"What are you talking about?" Beatrice asked, confused.

"The NAGS will stop artists, one way or another," Mr. O'Dowde said gravely. "Let us hope that Miss Lore has nothing to do with a murder. Right now, the Sweet Majestic is nearly all we have left." He shook his head, his bright countenance returning. "Anyhow. Would you like to see my collection of hair wreaths?"

"Absolutely not," Drake replied.

"Thank you for your time, sir," Beatrice told Mr. O'Dowde. "You have been very helpful. We will recommend your store to all our friends." She whirled around, eager to leave. The shop was stuffy, and she wanted to be alone with Drake so they could more openly discuss these new revelations.

But as she turned, her foot caught on something on the floor. She reached out to steady herself, and her hand nearly collided with a large vase, which began to wobble dangerously, causing Mr. O'Dowde to gasp.

"Madam! Mind the porcelain, please!"

Drake caught the vase with one hand just before it could fall to the ground, and Beatrice's arm with the other.

"My apologies," Beatrice said. She looked around to make sure she hadn't caused any more damage and found what had caused her to trip.

There was a seam in the wooden floor of the shop, an uneven bump that had led to the tumble. As Beatrice peered at it more closely, she could make out the outline of a trapdoor.

Mr. O'Dowde had more than just antiques in this shop, she thought with a thrill. What was beyond that door?

But that was a mystery for another time, she thought; they had gleaned the information they needed. She hastened from the pawnshop before she could knock over anything else.

As she reached the front door, she could hear Drake following close behind. They exited, slamming the door behind them.

There was an unfortunate tinkling sound of breaking glass.

"Walk quickly," Drake instructed. "If one breaks it, one buys it."

They raced down the alley from whence they had come, cleared the stream with a second launch (not quite as clumsy as the first), and continued on, only slowing down when they had arrived back in Sweetbriar.

"We must go to the opera tonight," Drake said once they had caught their respective breaths, "and speak with Miss Lore." She couldn't tell if he was breathless from the idea or their quick escape. "Though affordable tickets are no longer available, perhaps we can try to get in touch with Percival before the show. . . ."

"I agree," Beatrice told him, "but it will have to wait until tomorrow."

"What? Why?" Drake demanded.

"We have a ball at the Rose tonight," Beatrice reminded him.

"Well, we shall have to skip all that society nonsense. We have a lead to follow," Drake insisted.

"You know that the Rose's blooms are expected to attend every event. We can't miss it, else we could lose our spots on the list, and therefore our access. Lest you forget, 'all that society nonsense' is how we were able to investigate the scene of the crime."

"Yes. A scene that we had to hand over to Huxley," Drake shot back.

"Relationships matter, Drake," Beatrice said sharply. "We must ingratiate ourselves with the members of the Rose so we can gain their trust and they will answer our questions. That is how you find a killer."

"That is how *you* find a killer," Drake pointed out. "*I* prefer facts and evidence, which are leading us to the opera, not to inane small talk and silly dances."

While Beatrice agreed with him about the futility of these tiresome customs, she was growing frustrated over his refusal to see the sense in her approach. She took a step forward. "I know you are accustomed to doing things your way, but you have a partner now. We have to discuss these matters."

Drake gave no reply, instead staring at her as if he was holding something back.

Beatrice's heart fell.

They *were* partners, that was true—but was Drake regretting that? His silence left too much room for her doubts to fester.

"Fine," she said finally, her voice coming out clipped and unnatural. "Tonight, I will be at the Rose. I hope you shall be there, too, as our attendance is expected. Any absence could cause suspicion. You recall what I said before about unexplained disappearances tarnishing one's good name?"

"Yes, I remember all too well your dedication to society," Drake said stiffly.

"While you might not care about public opinion, I should remind you that the future success of our business rides, at least in part, on the respect of others in society," Beatrice shot back. "That is, if you still want this *partnership* at all."

With that, she broke away from him, heading back toward Miss Bolton's town house.

She hoped she was making the right decision. In a city with so many choices, and so many different voices advising her one way or another, it was becoming difficult to tell.

Dearest Members of the Rose:

You are cordially invited to the first dance of the Season!

In spite of the (latest) tragedy which has befallen our community, we must remember the values upon which this assembly hall was established: tradition, staunchness, and dancing. Therefore, the ball shall proceed as planned, featuring melodic compositions and musicians that have satisfied permit requirements.
Also: We have received several inquiries regarding the dress code. Gentlemen—inexpressibles are expressly forbidden. We prefer ladies to approach courtship considering financial endowments only.

For exceptions, please write in with your explanation and measurements.

Ladies—we understand that short stays are more comfortable in the summer months, but for the sake of the gentlemen who must look upon you, please wear long stays. It creates a much more palatable silhouette! As always, for ladies, no exceptions shall be entertained.

We look forward to seeing you all there, as we support this year's debutantes in making appropriate, approved matches.
Sincerely,

The Neighborhood Association of Gentlemen Sweetbriarians (NAGS)

RIVETING RIBBONS

By Elle Equiano

With the commencement of the Rose's Season, ladies must wonder: What ribbon is best for one's first ball as a debutante? Mrs. Diana Vane's "blooms" have been presented, but they have not yet graced the dance floor.

Naturally, a young woman must select a demure color, such as pink or cream. This indicates that she is innocent, available, and unimaginative.

In terms of ribbon fabric, this writer suggests a tough textile. After all, since two have been murdered behind the Rose's closed doors, ladies must protect themselves against a killer at large in any way they see fit. A ribbon can be fashioned into a defensive lasso, if necessary.

Elle—

Unimaginative colors are such a chic suggestion! I approve of this fashion advice. My only note: The murder case is really a private matter, which Sir Huxley will handle discreetly. There is no need to cause any panic, especially during the precious Season!

Please revise accordingly and resubmit.

—*Your editor*

Dearest patrons,

We extend our deepest thanks for fifteen glorious years in business. Sadly, we shall soon close our doors, as we have not been granted permit to continue our artistic endeavors.

Since Queen Elizabeth's reign, our company has been honored to sculpt gargoyles for the community of Sweetbriar. Our creations flank the doorways of many townhomes, providing protection and decoration. However, the gentlemen of NAGS believe that these grotesques are too grotesque, and therefore mar the appearance of the neighborhood. They believe this neighborhood needs only "real" guardians (which is them, apparently).

Those who have purchased our products, we thank you. Those who have not, we pray you will find another way to protect yourself from the creatures which hunt by the light of the full moon.

Please be sure to visit the new supper club which shall replace our shop. It is open to all gentlemen of appropriate rank and fortune, so we sadly shall not see you there.

Yours always—

The Gargoyle Brothers (Jeff, Geoff, and Jeffrey)

CHAPTER TWELVE

A Makeover

Beatrice should have known that a London soirée would be completely unlike a simple country evening—but she still felt both impressed and overwhelmed when she and Miss Bolton were ushered into the upstairs ballroom at the Rose for the first dance of the Season.

There was no longer a corpse in the middle of an otherwise empty floor. Cecil Nightingale had been cleared away, his blood removed, and in place of the dead body there was something much more frightening: couples, everywhere.

The most fashionable woman in Swampshire, Arabella Ashbrook, had been obsessed with forcing everyone to learn complex dances. Beatrice had always thought these a particular hobby of Arabella's to show everyone she was superior on her feet, but she saw now that city folk preferred intricate choreography to a simple skip, hop, and turn. The women flung themselves around the room, defying gravity as they danced. Even the men spun in a circle, a complicated move for them that would have been unheard of in her hometown.

Instead of a small string section, there was an entire orchestra filling the room with dramatic, pulse-pounding music. Clearly, even the punch was stronger than a country beverage. Beatrice had only just arrived, but the guests' eyes already looked glassy, their voices loud and boisterous.

Groups of men gambled at small tables on the perimeter of the ballroom, throwing dice and laying down cards with joyful cries and angry shouts. Beatrice could not help noting how much money changed hands with each bet. If it were permissible for her to join them, she would have been tempted—those kinds of winnings could change her family's life—but she did not see any other ladies indulging, not to mention that she had no money for a buy-in.

"Do you have any idea how one secures dances with gentlemen?" Beatrice asked Miss Bolton as they stood against a wall, both nursing glasses of incredibly strong "signature Sweetbriar punch." Mrs. Vane had not actually been joking, Beatrice thought as she sipped it; the Londoners liked their spirits potent.

Perhaps the liquid courage would fortify her as she navigated this tricky social situation. After all, in her hometown, Beatrice knew everyone, but here in London she had not yet been introduced to most of the gentlemen meandering around the ballroom. Since ladies could not introduce themselves, it created quite the quandary, especially if one wanted to get close to a man for interrogation purposes.

"I was hoping *you* had learned," Miss Bolton said, taking a big gulp from her glass. "I'm a terrible chaperone! Things are so different from how they were in my day. . . ."

As she began to recount a ball from her youth that actually sounded *rowdier* than the current party, Beatrice felt a rush of relief when she located two familiar faces in the crowd.

Lavinia Lee and Elle Equiano had both just finished dances with identical-looking red-haired gentlemen. They curtsied in unison, and then Miss Equiano pulled a giggling Miss Lee away from the dance floor. Their heads were bent together as they exchanged some secret, and Beatrice felt a pang of longing.

When she first came to London, she thought she might have such a rapport with Inspector Drake—yet again tonight, he was nowhere to be found. She feared what his absence meant for their partnership—especially considering the words they had exchanged the day before.

How was it possible, she wondered, to feel alone in such a huge city? There were so many people surrounding her, yet she felt more isolated. Perhaps it was *because* the others were paired up like Miss Lee and Miss Equiano, laughing and dancing and drinking. Nothing made a person feel lonelier than watching others who were not.

But it was not to be tolerated for long: Mercifully, Miss Lee and Miss Equiano were making their way toward Beatrice and Miss Bolton.

"Miss Steele," Elle Equiano said, dipping her head in greeting. "And Miss Helen Bolton, so good to see you. We met the other evening, after I explained to her that you were testing out different perfumes in the powder room and might be gone a while," she told Beatrice, giving her an almost imperceptible wink. "Your chaperone is so knowledgeable about fashion. She gave me some very intriguing ideas for my next column."

"Two words," Miss Bolton said, nodding seriously at Miss Equiano. "More tassels."

"If you don't mind, darling, we were hoping we might borrow your charge?" Elle asked.

"Of course not!" Miss Bolton said, looking delighted. "Debutantes must stick together!"

"Yes," Lavinia Lee said, "we could not agree more!"

Before Beatrice could protest, or ask where they were taking her, Elle Equiano and Lavinia Lee had steered her straight into the ladies' powder room.

The place was a pink confection filled with bouquets of wild sweetbriar in glass vases. Clusters of ladies squeezed in front of beveled mirrors, reapplying powder and rouge and whispering about suitors. The air was thick with the smell of perfume and cosmetics.

Elle steered Beatrice toward a mirror, in front of which was an empty pink armchair.

"Sit," she instructed. "Before you disappear on any clandestine errands this evening, we must take care of a few things."

"It is for your own good," Lavinia said, nodding.

"*What* is?" Beatrice asked, growing nervous.

"You are wearing a gown which does not suit you, your hair is all wrong, and no one has done their rouge that way since seventeen ninety-nine," Elle listed off. "Beatrice Steele, my darling, we are going to give you a makeover."

Lavinia squealed and clapped her hands. It wasn't what Beatrice had expected, but she supposed she *did* need that sort of help. So far she had been out of her element at the Rose, and thus would take any assistance she could get. And a makeover, she told herself, was really just a type of disguise that she might use to her advantage.

"All right then," she said, squaring her shoulders. "What should I do?"

"Your hairstyle could use refreshing," Lavinia informed her. She began to rearrange Beatrice's dark curls. Beatrice could not see much of a difference but allowed Lavinia free rein. "And you must take off the rouge. Simply pinch the cheeks; it is nature's blush!"

"You can borrow this." Elle took a decorative chain from her neck and placed it around Beatrice's.

"Oh, I couldn't," Beatrice began. "I have a bad record of losing jewelry. . . ."

"I have sixteen more like it, darling," Elle assured her. "And it comes in useful, in case you need to examine any clues. Romantically, I mean," she added, showing Beatrice the small quizzing glass at the end of the decorative chain.

"I hope you won't need a magnifier to see the gentleman's good qualities," Lavinia said, aghast.

Beatrice shot Elle a grateful look. The young lady might have written a column about ribbons, Beatrice thought, but she was an investigative reporter at heart. It was clear that not much got past Miss Equiano.

"Now, are there any gentlemen who have caught your attention?" Elle inquired. "We can try to make introductions, if it's someone we know."

"And if it's Sir Huxley you're after, I promise not to stand in the way of true love," Lavinia said, though the very thought seemed to devastate her.

"I am not after Sir Huxley," Beatrice assured her.

"It's just . . . the way he looks at you . . ." Lavinia trailed off. "How *did* you two meet? I have been following his cases for years, and following him—I mean, in a friendly way. It's not like I broke into his office and sprayed perfume on anything last month. But he has always been so out of reach . . ."

"It was by accident," Beatrice said, recalling the chance meeting outside the Carnation's hedges.

"I wish such an accident would befall me." Lavinia sighed.

"He is handsome, I will give you that," Elle said, adjusting Beatrice's sleeves so they were puffed instead of wilted. "But once you marry, things become as dull as a stream with no trout. I took up fishing last Season," she added when Beatrice gave her a perplexed look. "The gentlemen talked about it so much, I had to see what all the fuss was about."

"You don't know that marriage would be dull," Lavinia insisted. "You have never been married!"

"And thank goodness for that, darling!" Elle said, tossing her hair. "I am having plenty of fun on my own. But we aren't talking about me; we are discussing Miss Steele. Now: Your first step is to stop pining over that tall man with an eye patch who abandoned you at your presentation."

"I am not pining," Beatrice said immediately. She could see two pink patches on her cheeks through the mirror. Evidently she did not need to pinch them to achieve a natural blush.

"Then I think you should prove it," Elle told her, a mischievous look in her dark eyes. "Dance with Sir Huxley. You have been introduced, after all. And everyone can see that he has taken an interest in you."

"He has not," Beatrice insisted, but Elle grabbed her dance card and scribbled something on it.

"Look, he already requested this dance!" she said, pointing to Huxley's name, now inked on one of the lines.

Lavinia took the card and examined it. "Goodness, that looks just like his writing!" she exclaimed. "Not that I have intercepted any of his mail so as to study his hand," she added, clearing her throat.

"I am a penmanship expert," Elle said with a shrug. "That includes forgery."

"Fishing, penmanship, social graces, ribbons . . . Is there anything you can't do?" Beatrice asked, only half joking.

"Bake scones," Elle said seriously. "No matter what I do, they always come out dry."

"Miss Equiano," Beatrice said with a rush of affection, "I am so glad we found each other. And you as well, Miss Lee," she added.

"Tell me everything Sir Huxley says." Lavinia sighed. "You

are *so* lucky." She adjusted Beatrice's curls one last time and then stood. "There . . . you are ready."

Beatrice blinked at the mirror, actually shocked by her reflection. In mere moments, Elle and Lavinia had improved her hair, added jewelry, and fixed her makeup, and the end result was that Beatrice looked like a Londoner for the first time. She still did not know what about her appearance had made her look so provincial, so Swampshirian, yet whatever it was, it was gone now. She was staring at a cosmopolitan young lady who actually belonged among the city dwellers.

"How can I ever repay your kindness?" she wondered aloud.

"This is what friends do for one another!" Lavinia told her.

"Trust me, I could *not* do this for you," Beatrice said, gesturing to her now-intricate hair and makeup. "But I will find some way to be a valuable ally." She felt warm inside at Lavinia's words. She was *not* alone here in London. *She had friends.*

"Enough dallying, my darling. We perfected the bait . . . now you must cast the line," Elle told her.

She and Lavinia pulled Beatrice back into the ballroom just as the orchestra began to play a slow, sensual tune. Before Beatrice knew what was happening, she was in front of Sir Huxley, and her dance card was in his hand.

"Well, well, well," he said with a smile. "It seems I already requested the honor. How could I have forgotten? Too much Sweetbriar punch, perhaps . . . but nonetheless . . . shall we?" He swept her onto the dance floor before Beatrice could protest.

He knew the moves well, his steps effortless and graceful as he swept her into a coordinated routine. She was surprised to find that, in his arms, she was able to dance somewhat elegantly as well. Apart from stepping on his feet two or three times.

It would be good, she told herself, to engage in conversation with the formerly mustachioed detective. After all, he *was* on the case—perhaps she might uncover something of use. This was the reason she had so easily accepted the suggestion that they dance, of course.

The strange fluttering she felt as he held her was something quite separate.

"You look radiant tonight, Miss Steele," Sir Huxley said once they had settled into the steps. "What need have we for the summer sun when you shine so brightly?"

"We really don't have a need for it at the moment, since it is night," she replied.

"You are so sharp, so quick-witted, Miss Steele. Most women can only swoon in my presence," Sir Huxley said. He lifted her hand and twirled her, making her feel much dizzier than she normally felt from a simple spin.

"Perhaps it is that you are not doing a very good job of listening. I have met several witty women here in London," Beatrice assured him. "Lavinia Lee, for one, is so kind, and wonderful to converse with—"

"It is *your* remarks I wish to hear. I believe I could listen to them all day. Or night," Sir Huxley replied.

"So it is my mind you are after? Now, *that* statement would make any woman swoon," Beatrice said, unable to suppress a smile. "If it were true."

"It is," Huxley insisted. "Though I suppose you will not reveal anything about what you might have seen from your hiding place in a certain closet, as it pertains to my current case?"

Beatrice's breath caught in her throat. She looked around to ensure no one was listening, before saying in a low voice, "I saw nothing."

"As I suspected," Sir Huxley said, nodding. "Which is why I *said* nothing."

"And here I was, thinking you stayed quiet so I would be in your debt," Beatrice shot back.

"How could I resist?" Sir Huxley's eyes sparkled. "You owe me a favor, Miss Steele." He suddenly pulled Beatrice closer to him. "I must have more than just a dance," he said, breathless.

Such a sentiment would have been scandalous in Swampshire, Beatrice thought, feeling slightly shocked. Were gentlemen in London normally so bold?

"Whatever do you mean?" she demanded.

"Will you come with me to the opera?"

Beatrice blinked, taken aback.

"The third installment of *Figaro* debuts tomorrow night, and Mr. and Mrs. Vane have reserved both boxes. They offered me one," Huxley said in a rush. "I would be honored if you accompanied me. We would have a real chance to talk, not just a few words exchanged over the course of one short waltz."

"You would go to *Figaro,* when the lead actor is your lead suspect in a murder investigation?" Beatrice blurted out.

"Percival Nash cannot commit murder while onstage, unless he sings atrociously enough, and we all know he has perfect pitch," Huxley assured her. "Besides, it is prudent that I keep a close watch on him. I may as well enjoy your company in the meantime."

"And this is the favor you want from me?"

"Of course not. It would be my gift to you," Huxley insisted.

Stunned, Beatrice looked up into his handsome face, with his chiseled features and those dimples. But before she could give a reply to his invitation, someone else took hold of her hands.

Inspector Drake had cut in.

"One normally waits until the conclusion of a dance to find a new partner," Sir Huxley said evenly. Whereas Drake's eye was flashing with fury, Huxley maintained a collected, calm demeanor.

Beatrice felt only panic.

What was Drake doing?

"I know what's going on here," Drake snapped at Huxley.

"Nothing is going on, apart from me inviting Miss Steele to the opera," Sir Huxley said, still calm.

"Aha," Drake said, tightening his grip on Beatrice's hand. "My theory was correct: You mean to do everything in your power to ensure that my investigative business fails. Starting by poaching my partner!"

"*Our* investigative business," Beatrice said, correcting him.

"This would be a purely social excursion," Sir Huxley said. Somehow he did not look awkward, standing on the dance floor with no partner, even while other couples danced around them. "You are welcome to join us," he added to Drake.

"What?" Drake sputtered with surprise.

"Yes, you must come as well," Sir Huxley said, nodding. "We have been at odds for too long, Vivek. This magnificent woman has brought us back together again; let us bury the hatchet in the box at *Figaro*. What do you say?"

He looked from Drake to Beatrice. Drake was obviously too conflicted to reply. Would he endure his enemy if it meant a coveted box seat at his beloved opera?

"We will be there," Beatrice said finally.

"I am delighted to hear it," Sir Huxley said, his face breaking into a smile. "I shall pick you up at eight."

With that, he whisked away, leaving Beatrice and Drake alone on the dance floor. Beatrice turned to depart to the side of the room, but Drake swept her up in his arms and they began to dance.

"You know how to waltz," she said, shocked to find that he not only knew—he was good at it.

"Do not sound so surprised. When you signed us up for the Season, I learned," he replied.

"You practiced dancing for me?" she asked, still shocked.

"Clearly I would do all manner of things for you," Drake said softly. "I mean, for our investigation."

"I thought you weren't coming," she said. She should have been relieved by his presence, but at the moment, all she felt was confusion.

"Of course I came," Drake replied, but despite the sureness in his voice, Beatrice knew his attendance had been anything but confirmed. She struggled to come up with a reply as Drake spun her in time with the music. She tripped, and he steadied her. She suddenly found herself very close to him, the subtle scent of cinnamon and oranges lingering in the air.

"Is that why you accepted a dance with Huxley?" Drake asked, his voice tight. "Because you doubted that I would attend this evening? Or because of some connection with him?"

"Inspector—" she began, but Drake interrupted her.

"You must know," he said, his jaw set, "Huxley is using you. He always does this."

"Does what? Invites women to the opera?" Beatrice could not help but laugh at Drake's seriousness. "That is hardly a cause célèbre—pardon my French," she added.

"No, I mean that he tries to court every interesting woman he encounters," Drake said, still stern. "But these flirtations never come to anything. No doubt he will drop you the moment a new debutante catches his eye."

"I am not pinning any hopes on Sir Huxley, Inspector," Beatrice assured him. She was not sure whether to be flattered or insulted by Drake's concern, but either way, it was misplaced. If Huxley was using her as a diversion, it did not matter—she was using him too, for access. Everyone could win.

"So you say." Drake's eye dropped down to her lips and then came back up to meet her gaze. "But I know how persuasive he can be. It is a distraction from the case you are meant to be solving with *me*."

"Yes, we are meant to be solving this case together," Beatrice said, a sudden irritation rising. Did he really think so little of her that he did not believe she could handle herself? Why was he doubting her, when he was the one who was being so unreliable? "Yet," she went on, "you have made it increasingly difficult to depend on you. You work without me, I never know where you are, you don't take the elements of our investigation that *you* don't like seriously. At every turn, you are not there."

"But I was—"

"At least Huxley thinks I am an interesting woman," Beatrice interrupted. "Evidently you believe I have nothing to offer this case, as you keep actively working without me."

"No, Miss Steele . . . that's not . . ." Drake faltered, his voice suddenly softening.

"Inspector Steele," she said, correcting him. "In spite of your behavior, I *am* still your partner. Though perhaps it isn't the investigation that you don't take seriously . . . but me." She tried to stay firm, but her voice wavered when she added: "You, of all people, should know how frustrating that feels."

Drake winced. "I assure you, I take . . . everything seriously."

"Good. Then thanks to the tickets *I* secured for us, I will see you at the opera. I doubt they will hold the curtain, even for their biggest fan, so I suggest that you arrive on time."

With that, Beatrice dropped Drake's hands and deserted the dance floor. She had had quite enough of dancing.

THE LONDON BABBLER

New *Figaro* Disappoints

Percival Nash reprises his role as Figaro in the newest installment of the opera saga at the Sweet Majestic. Tragically, even the charismatic Nash cannot save this comedy.

The latest sequel sees Figaro as a valet, "outsmarting" his employer. This unbelievable setup, coupled with the cartoonish portrayal of Figaro's gentlemanly employer, starts the opera off on a sour note.

Composer Mr. Dahan (who, readers will note, is not a member of the gentility, which explains how he was unable to capture the intelligence and poise of the upper classes) has tried to enliven the piece by adding in several arias. These are sung by Miss Felicity Lore, a charming soprano who cannot rescue a sinking ship, even with her soaring vibrato.

The audience laughed throughout the show. *At* it, not *with* it; an important distinction. After all, the idea that a barber would rise to the station of a valet, and then (spoiler forewarning) rise above even this, is laughable. Does "comedy" now mean "fantasy"?

Ultimately, Mr. Dahan should refrain from penning any further sequels. Sweetbriar audiences are tired of repetitive humor, didactic themes, and Figaro himself.

This reporter suggests that next time the Sweet Majestic try a tragedy. Then, at least, the audience's angst would be intended.

THUS FAR . . .

Introducing Figaro

We meet our hero Figaro, a modest but mischievous manservant . . .

Too Fast, II Figaro

Our hero is hired as a barber, but when he botches a judge's haircut, he must join a carriage-racing group and win back enough money to purchase the judge a suitable wig. . . .

Figaro III: Here We Figaro Again

Figaro leaves his position as a barber to become a valet. Yet when a young woman shows up on his doorstep, he must determine whether or not he is her father. . . .

CHAPTER THIRTEEN

A Threat

Though the Sweet Majestic was within walking distance of Miss Bolton's townhome, Sir Huxley insisted upon picking everyone up in his carriage. Drake refused to step foot in any carriage—especially one owned by his greatest enemy—so he sent word that he would meet them at the theater. Therefore Beatrice and Miss Bolton waited outside alone, watching the sun sink into the horizon as the heat of the day broke.

Miss Bolton wore one of her signature tasseled gowns and a hat that was comprised of a four-story dollhouse. For the first time, Beatrice wore a new gown that had been created just for her.

The order from the dressmaker's had finally arrived, just in time for the opera. Beatrice was shocked—and pleasantly surprised—to find that Miss Bolton had chosen tasteful dresses and accessories for her.

"I know you're less adventurous than I am when it comes to

fashion," she told Beatrice. "Still, I did have *one* shawl made with tassels . . . They just look so fetching on you."

The opera gown that Beatrice wore was made of a smooth, deep-green satin that perfectly fit her plump frame. It even had built-in pockets, so she did not have to carry her reticule. This was the one feature she had specifically requested, though it greatly confused the dressmaker. Beatrice could now store any clues or weapons needed directly on her person, without stuffing them into her bodice. Best of all, the gown was long enough that Beatrice could secretly wear comfortable, hard-soled walking boots, concealed beneath her skirt.

She was just starting to feel the chill of night ripple through the fine silk of her new gown when a dark blue carriage approached, emblazoned with "LH."

"Sir Lawrence Huxley really knows how to make an entrance," Miss Bolton observed as the carriage came to a stop at their stoop.

"One would think an inspector might prize subtlety," Beatrice murmured, though she was impressed in spite of herself. She had never seen such a large, grand carriage. Even the horses were beautiful, their blond manes arranged in a way that, she noted, looked just like Huxley's hair.

A footman opened the door and ushered Miss Bolton and Beatrice into the carriage. The interior was just as lush as the exterior, and Beatrice slid in to sit next to Sir Huxley. Tonight, the detective had donned a midnight-blue suit and top hat that perfectly matched his eyes, which sparkled at the sight of her.

She was surprised to find that he was not the only person in the carriage.

Mr. and Mrs. Vane sat across from them, both in stunning purple ensembles. Jewels gleamed in Mrs. Vane's ears and around her neck, and she twisted a ring around her finger.

It was the deep-red garnet that Beatrice had noticed in particular, due to its bloodlike hue. Its stone glimmered by the light of the carriage's torch.

How perfect, she thought, that she had found herself in a carriage directly across from her top suspect and his mysterious wife. Mr. Vane had much to answer for—but how might she draw him out?

"Miss Steele, Miss Bolton," Mrs. Vane said dreamily, nodding her head as the footman closed the door and the horses were brought to a trot. "We were delighted to hear that you were accompanying Sir Huxley in our other box this evening."

No doubt it was Diana's idea to attend the opera, Beatrice thought. Another show of support for her friend Percival Nash. Surely Horace had agreed to appease her, but it was all for show. Sir Huxley would keep an eye on his suspect—and Horace Vane would keep his finger pointed in accusation.

"It all worked out perfectly," Mr. Vane said, flashing his boyish grin at Huxley. "Though I never expected your latest conquest to be the woman who drenched herself in mud from our carriage. What will the society papers say?"

"I believe your carriage drenched *me,*" Beatrice shot back.

"Miss Steele is no *conquest,*" Huxley said, chuckling at Mr. Vane. He turned back to Beatrice and assured her: "It is my honor to escort you." He held her gaze as he lifted her hand to his lips, pressing a kiss to her glove.

Her traitorous heart actually *fluttered* at the motion. He really was good, she thought. But Drake need not to have worried—the only man she was truly interested in was her murder suspect. She respectfully withdrew her hand and refocused on Horace Vane.

"You probably do not know this, Miss Steele," he told her, "but your suitor is a very famous detective here in London. If you pay close attention to his conversation, you might learn a thing or two about solving cases. Not that this would be useful for a lady," he added with a laugh.

"I assure you, I am aware of Sir Huxley's fame," Beatrice said, sitting up a bit straighter. It was one of the first times Mr. Vane had addressed her directly, and she was determined not to buckle under his gaze. "I have read his column in *The London Babbler*."

"You flatter me," Sir Huxley said, clearly pleased.

"I read all of the columns in the *Babbler*," Beatrice continued. "For example—did anyone see the review of tonight's opera? The critic did not think highly of *Figaro*, to be sure."

"Ridiculous!" Miss Bolton said, shaking her head and sending a miniature love seat flying.

"We don't pay attention to such things," Mrs. Vane said wistfully. "We prefer to decide for ourselves."

"Not everyone does. I imagine that such a review will negatively affect ticket sales, which evidently are already dwindling, thanks to the erasure of the theater's pit," Beatrice replied.

"I see we have a bluestocking on our hands!" Mr. Vane laughed. "Miss Steele, you are very concerned with theatrical comings and goings."

"It is the goings which concern me. There seem to be so many of them, of late," Beatrice told him, watching his face for any hint of a reaction.

"Most concerning," Mr. Vane agreed, "but I assure you, my wife and I are doing everything in our power to help."

At these words, Diana smiled at her husband. Beatrice observed the two of them closely.

"How did you two meet?" she asked, adding, "As you can imagine, a hopeful debutante like myself is eager to hear the origins of London's most celebrated couple."

"We met at the Rose," Mr. Vane explained. "Before it was

what it has become today. It was merely another assembly room in London. Hardly notable. But after we found such success there in our union, we vowed to give the same gift to others."

He flashed Beatrice his boyish grin. The one, she had noted, that did not reach his eyes.

Who *was* this man? His very expression seemed to shift in the light, one moment innocent and charming, the next domineering and cold. When they had first met, he had refused to address her, and now he spoke as if they were old friends.

"I never thought I would end up with a man like Horace Vane," Diana chimed in. She began to rifle through her reticule, her expression unfocused.

"I would not accept a denial," Mr. Vane said grandly. "See here?" He took something from his pocket and held it out for all to examine. It was a frame that encircled two panes of glass. Between them, a rose had been pressed, thus preserved inside. "I gave this sweetbriar to Diana when I first asked for her hand," he explained. "She denied me, but I refused to give up. Eventually, I won the prize. And this I kept as my trophy."

Mrs. Vane had stopped rifling through her reticule and was now staring wistfully out the window.

"Wild roses symbolize a love which will never fade," she murmured. "I was always intrigued by such symbolism. I suppose I *was* a bluestocking. . . ."

"So you see, there is hope for you yet, Miss Steele." Horace Vane chuckled. "Even the wildest bluestocking can be tamed."

Tamed . . . or hunted down? Was the whole story romantic, or was Diana like the wild rose, trapped in glass?

Beatrice leaned forward. She had so many more questions burning within her—but alas, the carriage screeched to a halt.

"Miss Steele," Sir Huxley said, "may I be the first to welcome you to the opera."

As if on cue, Huxley's footman opened the carriage door, revealing a sea of ladies and gentlemen dressed in finery. Behind them, the Sweet Majestic loomed in all its grandeur.

Mr. Vane immediately escorted Mrs. Vane out of the carriage, his purple tailcoat smacking Beatrice in the face as they exited.

"See you inside," Diana called back dreamily before they were enveloped by a crowd of well-dressed ladies and gentlemen.

Sir Huxley stepped out next, turning back to extend a hand to Beatrice.

"If I may," he said gallantly.

But just as she reached for it, another hand appeared from outside the carriage.

"If *I* may," said Drake.

Beatrice found herself holding both Sir Huxley's and Drake's hands, the men flanking her on either side as she stepped from the carriage onto the candlelit front steps of the Sweet Majestic.

She turned to Drake, and her stomach flipped. He looked himself, yet different. His dark hair, normally tousled, had been combed back neatly, and he was clean-shaven, his usual stubble gone. He wore a dark green brocade suit and eye patch—both of which, she could not help but notice, perfectly matched her gown.

"Good evening, Drake," Sir Huxley said pleasantly. "Miss Steele and I shall advance from here, so you can escort Miss Bolton. It is ever so kind of you."

"But I—" Drake began, but Sir Huxley cut in.

"You would not want to leave a lady on her own, would you? I know you care little for society, Mr. Drake, but this is the opera. One must show some *respect*."

"There is no one who respects the opera more than Drake," Beatrice told Huxley, but Drake shook his head.

"It is fine," he assured her. "I have accepted past criticisms and I am henceforth dedicated to proper behavior and social commitments," he said, looking seriously at Beatrice, who was certain he had been replaced with an imposter—until Drake added, so only she could hear, "for the good of our investigation."

With that, he dropped Beatrice's arm and turned to escort Miss Bolton from the carriage. She exited slowly, taking care that her dollhouse hat's attic did not scrape the ceiling of the carriage.

Beatrice let Sir Huxley lead her away, into the swathe of ladies and gentlemen ascending the stone steps of the Sweet Majestic. Everyone was dressed in their finest, a colorful sea of jewels and gloves and suits.

Arm in arm, Sir Huxley and Beatrice stepped into a grand entrance hall. It was framed by curved archways and crowded with audience members, anticipation for the show palpable in their excited chatter. Beatrice could not help but share in the anticipation. She had never been to a performance before, apart from Miss Bolton's one-woman plays back in Swampshire. Something about the grand hall, her new gown, and Sir Huxley beside her made her finally feel as if she were living in the London of her long-ago dreams.

"I have solved several cases behind these doors," Sir Huxley told her conspiratorially. "Beyond the artifice of comedy lies terror."

She had been determined to resist his charms, but how could she, when he spoke such romantic words? "I do recall when you foiled a murderous plot against a prima donna," she blurted, before she could stop herself.

Huxley looked at her with a surprised, pleased expression. "I admit, I am truly flattered that you follow my cases in the papers," he said. Was that a blush upon his cheeks?

"I only read them once in a while." Beatrice felt flushed herself. She was meant to be an inspector in her own right, and Drake's partner. Not a gushing fan. Not anymore.

"That particular investigation was so challenging," Sir Huxley went on. "In fact, I thought I was stumped, until I received an anonymous tip suggesting that I examine the understudy's understudy."

"Because the understudy had a solid alibi—not to mention that the understudy killing the prima donna would be too obvious!" Beatrice exclaimed. "One had to consider that there would be a twist."

"Precisely!" Huxley agreed.

"What a genius suggestion this . . . anonymous person gave," Beatrice said, trying to affect breeziness.

She could remember writing that letter, back in the days when she was forced to serve as an armchair detective—solving cases from afar. It had seemed easier, back then, but perhaps part of that had been due to Sir Huxley's widespread influence and access, which came through in his articles. Tonight, she hoped, her proximity to Huxley would allow her a fraction of this privilege.

Because she was not going to get caught up in any fantasies. As always, Beatrice had a plan. After all, Huxley might have been acting like a doting beau, but she concurred with Drake's theory: Huxley meant to flirt with her, in order to irritate Drake and distract her from the case. However, what Drake hadn't considered was how Beatrice might use the situation to *their* advantage and get the opportunity to question the exact person they needed to speak to.

"Sir Huxley," she began coyly.

"Are you feeling ill, Miss Steele?" he asked, alarmed. "Your voice—something is not right."

She cleared her throat and returned to her normal tone. "I am fine. I merely wanted to inquire if we might be able to go backstage before the show. As you know, I have never been to the theater, and I am *so* enchanted by all of it. I would *love* to explore, and perhaps even meet a real performer! Like Felicity

Lore, the soprano? To do this all with the man who has solved so many cases behind these big, beautiful walls would be more than I could ever dream!"

Perhaps she was laying it on too thick—but Beatrice suspected that there was no such thing as "laying it on too thick" when it came to a man's ego.

"Miss Steele," Sir Huxley said gallantly, proving her suspicions correct as he took her hands in his. "I asked you here to impress you, and I plan to oblige. Come this way." He began to guide her through the crowded lobby.

"Sir Huxley!" Miss Bolton called, still trailing behind them with Inspector Drake. "The box is in the other direction—"

But Sir Huxley pressed on and did not stop until he and Beatrice had reached the edge of the lobby. Drake rushed to catch up, slowed down by Miss Bolton on his arm.

"Where are you going?" he called after them. "Late seating is disrespectful to the performers. We must get to our box before curtain!"

Ignoring Drake, Sir Huxley put his hand on the wall. He felt along the wallpaper, revealing a seam. With a thrill, Beatrice realized that there was a secret door concealed there.

"With *me,*" Huxley said, holding intense eye contact with Beatrice, "you can go anywhere you desire."

Thus, he pushed open the door and revealed—

Chaos.

Beatrice and Sir Huxley stepped into a backstage chamber to see actors and actresses in various states of dress—and undress. Some leaned in front of mirrors, retouching makeup; others drank from little bottles marked HONEY or THROAT TONIC. A man wearing only breeches helped a woman tie her ballet slippers, and a violinist walked around, calling, "For the last time—has *anyone* seen my rosin?" The air was thick with perspiration and excitement, and no one seemed to notice the group of audience members in their midst. They were preoccupied with their craft.

But what struck Beatrice the most was their demeanor. The performers were not standing pin-straight or editing every movement for the sake of an audience. Whereas ladies in high society were forced to perform whatever version of womanhood their gentlemen audience demanded, these actors were unbound.

No wonder the NAGS were so fearful of their influence.

Drake and Miss Bolton finally caught up to Beatrice and Sir Huxley, just as Percival Nash appeared in a cloud of powder and shimmer.

"Inspector Drake, Miss Steele!" He strode forward, arms flung out in welcome.

Tonight the actor wore a rich green suit, his thick auburn hair pulled back into a ponytail with a matching green ribbon. Beatrice could not help staring at his hair. *Was* it a wig? she wondered. One simply could not tell.

"How good to see you two—" Percival began, but broke off when he noticed Sir Huxley. His expression darkened. "What are *you* doing here?" he demanded.

"Are you acquainted with Mr. Nash?" Sir Huxley asked Beatrice, looking confused. After all, she had just told him that she had never been to the theater.

"I send him fan mail," she said immediately. She shot Percival Nash a look, and understanding passed over his expressive eyes.

"Yes, I never forget a fan," he said immediately—an adept improviser. "Miss Steele and Inspector Drake are the most doting admirers."

"I have seen every installment of *Figaro,*" Drake said, nodding. "Though of course, with the erasure of the pit, it shall be considerably more difficult to secure admittance—"

"But—you have never been to the opera," Sir Huxley said to Beatrice, still perplexed. "Why send fan mail if you haven't seen a show?"

"As a lady, I am"—Beatrice began, thinking quickly—"prone to flights of fancy and imagination! And the descriptions of shows in the *Babbler* were very vivid. Similar to the explanations of your cases, the opera reviews really . . . come to life."

"That makes complete sense," Sir Huxley told her, nodding. "Good reporting can really place one at the scene of the crime. Or, in this case, the opera."

"The *Babbler* finds *this* performance a crime," Percival Nash sniffed. "Didn't you see the latest review? The NAGS have issued the Sweet Majestic a 'temporary permit,' pending a rewrite."

"A travesty, and completely false," Drake assured him.

"No doubt *you* are pleased," Percival shot at Sir Huxley.

"I am no critic," Huxley insisted. "And I am not a part of the NAGS. I have nothing to do with any artistic decisions—"

"Your baseless suspicion of me has everything to do with it," Percival replied, still cold.

"If you gave an alibi for the night of either murder, I could easily clear your name," Sir Huxley told Percival.

"Obviously I was at the Rose the night of Mr. Nightingale's death, by Mrs. Vane's invitation," Percival snapped. "I was preparing for the performance, not committing murder. At least the Vanes support me," he added. "Their attendance tonight is assurance of their loyalty to the theater and its performers."

Sir Huxley pursed his lips, but he did not contradict this, though Beatrice knew he could have. Evidently Horace's secret accusations were safe with Huxley.

"We are all loyal to you, to be sure!" Miss Bolton chimed in, breaking an uncomfortable silence. She shimmied her way into their circle, her dollhouse hat swaying. "If you are ever looking for a new play, Mr. Nash, I hope you will consider my latest composition, *Altus* . . . It is an homage to both Latin and the most overlooked of singers, the altos. . . ." She launched into a description of the plot, while Percival listened politely.

"Felicity must be around here somewhere," Sir Huxley told Beatrice. He looked unshaken by Percival's ire, and Beatrice had to admire his composure. The gentleman detective seemed confident that he would find the truth in time. If only she could find the same certainty in her own sleuthing abilities . . .

"Ah," Huxley said, pointing over Beatrice's head. "There she is now!"

Beatrice spun around to find herself face-to-face with a woman. She had cascades of curls and wore heavy stage makeup, but even through the costume, Beatrice recognized her at once.

She would have known those cunning eyes anywhere.

"Caroline Wynn!"

THE ARTISTS' QUARTERLY

Nash and Lore Stun in New Sequel

The most beautiful ingénue who has ever graced the stage will appear in Sweetbriar!

Miss Felicity Lore will appear in the latest installment of the *Figaro* saga as the titular character's long-lost sister. Her stunning arias will enchant audiences, a delightful coupling with the ongoing plot of Figaro's social climbing. Her beauty is unmatched and her stage presence captivating. A standing ovation is not enough; Miss Lore deserves every rose in Sweetbriar.

Composer Mr. Dahan has created a balanced opera full of laughs, touching moments, and of course, scene-stealing solos for actor Percival Nash, who reprises his role as Figaro.

One hopes it is not the last we shall see of this beloved barber turned valet rising in the ranks. Considering the temporary permit issued to the Sweet Majestic, it very well may be. Fans should catch Figaro and his beautiful, incredible sister while they still can.

CHAPTER FOURTEEN

A Performance

"You are mistaken, madam." Felicity—or, rather, Caroline—batted her lashes.

But Beatrice wasn't falling for it. She'd have known Caroline Wynn anywhere. The young woman had last been seen posing as an innocent heiress in Swampshire. After Beatrice uncovered the truth—that she was a con artist, stealing money from men and then leaving them high and dry—Caroline vanished without a trace.

It seemed that she, like Beatrice, had decided to relocate to London.

"This woman is a thief!" Beatrice said, looking to Miss Bolton for backup. Caroline had taken jewels, money, and dignity from countless men. No doubt she was still up to her same tricks here in the city—and Beatrice wasn't going to let her get away with it this time.

"Beatrice, be respectful," Miss Bolton scolded. "We are meeting a professional actress! I am so sorry, Miss Lore."

"Not to worry," Caroline said. She spoke with an Irish lilt, which Beatrice was certain concealed her actual, disgustingly French accent. "Many are overcome when they meet a star of the stage."

"How do you not recognize her? She's Verity Swan! Caroline Wynn! Emmeline Clément!" Beatrice said frantically, shouting out some of Caroline's many aliases. But everyone simply looked at her blankly.

"Miss Felicity is several inches taller than Caroline Wynn," Inspector Drake informed her. "They couldn't possibly be the same woman."

"She's wearing heels!" Beatrice pointed out.

"Verity Swan had a beauty mark," Sir Huxley added.

"Haven't you heard of *makeup*?" she insisted.

"I'm confused," Huxley replied, looking from "Felicity" to Beatrice. "Do you two know each other?"

"I will explain, sir," Felicity assured him. "As an actress, it is my job to resemble any person you might encounter on the street. Or the most beautiful woman you ever met, once upon a time." Beatrice sputtered, but Caroline began to pull her away from Drake, Sir Huxley, and Miss Bolton. "Come, my dear, and I shall show you the costume room. You will witness the magic of the theater, and then it will all make sense to you."

Before Beatrice could protest, "Felicity" led her past a group of chorus members singing scales and through another door. It opened into a chamber filled with gowns, suits, and hats, all in different styles and colors. They hung on long racks, their fabrics glistening with golden trim and sparkling beading. "Felicity" closed the door behind them and then whirled around.

"*Bonsoir,* Beatrice," she said with a grin. Her French accent was now disgustingly prominent. She tore off her wig and wiped her hand across her cheek to reveal a beauty mark in the shape of a tiny heart.

Just as Beatrice had professed, Felicity Lore was none other than Caroline Wynn.

"*Bienvenue à Londres,*" Caroline said conversationally. The last time they had spoken, Caroline was escaping a crumbling mansion with her lover, naval captain Philip Peña. Beatrice had thought she would never see the woman again—but now here she was, in all her irritatingly beautiful glory.

"It was you who sold the squirrel statue to the pawnshop," Beatrice said immediately. "Is that where you came up with this ridiculous accent? You stole it from Mr. O'Dowde like you steal everything?" She wasn't going to waste any time. Caroline Wynn was an ephemeral woman; it was necessary to pry information from her as fast as possible, before she vanished like smoke.

"*Excusez-moi?*" Caroline looked genuinely confused.

"The bloodstained marble squirrel statue in the pawnshop," Beatrice said sharply. "The owner, Mr. O'Dowde, told me that you sold it to him. You were blackmailing Walter Shrewsbury and Cecil Nightingale," she said, now gaining momentum—and confidence.

"I am *très confus,* Beatrice," Caroline said.

To Beatrice's annoyance, she saw that the woman looked genuinely perplexed, her irritatingly beautiful face showing no trace of her usual duplicity.

"I did sell a squirrel statue to a pawnshop," Caroline went on, "but I have never heard of these men of whom you speak. The statue was a gift from an admirer."

"What admirer?" Beatrice asked quickly.

"I have so many, Beatrice," Caroline said, flipping her curls over one shoulder. "It could have been any of them. It was left by my dressing room with a note. Let me see. . . ." She pulled a wad of paper from her ample bosom and began to leaf through dozens of notes. "This is called fan mail," she explained to Beatrice. "Ah, *voici.*" She finally produced a small paper and passed it to Beatrice. Beatrice opened it eagerly.

I hope you treasure this as I treasure your performances.

"It's unsigned," Beatrice said, disappointed—until she looked closer.

Very faintly, at the edge of the paper, she could see a dark brown mark. It appeared in the shape of a fingerprint, as if someone had held the paper . . . with bloodstained fingers.

"Some admirers wish to remain anonymous. I'm sure you have noticed that artists are not exactly accepted into high society here in Sweetbriar," Caroline was saying. "People may not want to be so publicly outspoken in their appreciation of a transcendent performance."

"So you're saying someone anonymously gifted you a statue covered in blood, and you pawned it for cash . . . without even considering that it could have been a *murder weapon.* And this," Beatrice said, waving the note, "also has traces of blood, which I would wager is from the same corpse."

"*You* may wager, but *I* never gamble," Caroline said, batting her lashes. "And Mr. O'Dowde wasn't very concerned with where it came from. He merely appreciated that I was gracing his shop with my presence. His taste is impeccable, no?" She pressed a hand to her heart. "That collection of antique beveled mirrors . . . *très jolie,* at least when I stand in front of them. And his parties—of course you could never secure an invitation to one. He only associates with true *artistes.* But you are missing out on such grand fêtes—"

"If what you say is true," Beatrice interrupted, "and unfortunately, I believe your innocence in *only this case*—I think that your 'secret admirer' is actually a killer, who likely means to frame you for the crime."

"*La vache!*" Caroline swore. "I am aware that the NAGS dislike artists in Sweetbriar . . . but *I* am universally adored!"

Caroline had an (annoying) point; she *was* universally adored. Was one of the NAGS trying to frame Caroline in order to topple her from the pedestal onto which she had been raised, and thus poison public opinion of all performers?

Or, Beatrice thought, had someone framed her in order to clear his own name?

Someone like Percival Nash?

But no, that made little sense. Why would he target another artist when the community was so vulnerable? Even if Nash were guilty—which Beatrice did not believe—he would not turn suspicion onto one of his own.

Caroline was still talking. "Even Mr. Vane's paper praised me, despite the rest of its scathing review. I never expected this would affect *moi*!"

"Wait. *His* paper?" Beatrice asked sharply. "Do you mean that—"

"Mr. Vane owns *The London Babbler, oui,*" Caroline confirmed. "A little-known fact, but of course, I have my ways of finding out such things. His wife is a devoted patron of the opera, but clearly he must not be. Otherwise, he would not allow them to publish such terrible reviews. It affects ticket sales, after all."

Horace Vane owned The London Babbler. It explained so much, Beatrice thought. Sir Huxley's column, "Restoring Order," was printed in the *Babbler*. She had recognized that they were friendly—Mr. Vane had invited Huxley to go hunting, and they went to the opera together—but this went beyond casual companionship. Mr. Vane was, in a way, Huxley's employer. Whether or not Huxley believed Percival Nash to be guilty, he had great incentive to pursue Mr. Vane's preferred suspect.

"It might be time to take my leave of this city," Caroline murmured to herself. "I do love to bask in attention, but this light might be too hot, even for me."

Caroline grabbed Beatrice's hand, and Beatrice was surprised to find that the actress's palm was clammy.

She really *was* afraid.

"Perhaps you should leave too, *ma chère*. London is not like Swampshire. There are dangerous people here," Caroline said in a rush.

"Multiple people tried to murder me in Swampshire," Beatrice said dryly.

"Exactly. London is a much bigger city—think of how many more people probably want to murder you here!" Caroline exclaimed. "If you insist on solving murders—which seems a much messier way to enact justice than *my* line of work—you really should stick to solving the agreeable ones. Go back home. All this—London, the NAGS, art critics around every corner—it is a terribly nasty business." Her sickeningly beautiful face was twisted into a mask of concern. "At least promise me that you will be careful. I could not bear to lose my best friend."

"I promise," Beatrice sighed.

Caroline pulled her into an embrace, and Beatrice was flooded with the overpowering scent of her familiar floral perfume. But before Beatrice could press her any further, Caroline whisked away, and Beatrice was forced to follow her back to where Miss Bolton, Drake, and Sir Huxley waited.

"We have cleared everything up," Caroline said grandly, returning to her fake Irish brogue. "Miss Steele now finds herself as big a fan as any! She has requested a signed portrait of me after the show, which of course I shall oblige."

She winked at Beatrice, who scowled back.

"Good. The show is about to begin," Inspector Drake said, offering his arm to Beatrice as the sound of bells chimed somewhere in the distance. "We should take our seats." He ushered

Beatrice away, so Sir Huxley was forced to trail behind them with Miss Bolton, who had to walk slowly so as not to disturb the dollhouse contents of her hat.

"I discovered something which might be relevant to our case," Beatrice murmured. "Did you know that Mr. Horace Vane owns *The London Babbler*?"

"What?" Drake looked down at her with interest. "The *Babbler* publishes negative reviews of the Sweet Majestic. I would consider that further proof that Mr. Vane does not support local art, in spite of his claims."

"The face he presents to one person is different than what he wears for the next," Beatrice agreed.

"For a man who secretly hates the arts, he wears many masks," Drake replied.

"Was that a quip?" Beatrice asked, raising one eyebrow.

"I fear I am giddy," he said seriously. "You must forgive me—this is how I get just before an opera begins."

Drake expertly pulled Beatrice through the crowd of theater attendees and down another hallway, and then drew back a curtain to reveal their box.

"I have never sat in such a prime spot," he said, taking it in with reverence. "This box is wasted on Sir Huxley."

He sank into one of the plush velvet chairs of the box, and she positioned herself next to him. The swell of chatter from the audience echoed below. Drake's eye was alight with anticipation as he observed everything from high above in the stage-left box.

She realized, suddenly, that he was still holding her hand.

"Look there," he said, pointing with his free hand to the wings. "We will be able to see the actors just before they go onstage! And here," he added, indicating the flies. "We are so close to the backdrops. Perhaps we can tell something about the setting of the show. . . ." He craned his neck, trying to get a closer look.

As much as Beatrice wanted to share in his excitement, she felt an impatience entirely unrelated to the impending performance. They were growing close to the truth about the case at hand—she could sense it.

On the other side of the theater, at the box above stage right, Diana and Horace Vane entered the small compartment. Beatrice watched as Mr. Vane ushered his wife inside, the two taking seats on plush chairs identical to the ones upon which Drake and Beatrice sat. It would be hours before they would all be reunited, arias and arias before Beatrice could pursue the course of investigation to which Caroline's words led.

Like so many before her, Beatrice already could not wait for the opera to end.

The curtain to their own box opened, and Sir Huxley and Miss Bolton stepped inside. Beatrice immediately dropped Drake's grasp.

She felt a strange pang akin to guilt when she saw Drake ball his hand into a fist.

"The extravaganza," Miss Bolton said excitedly, "is about to begin!"

Indeed, boys in velvet uniforms began to race around the theater, snuffing out candles.

Miss Bolton and Sir Huxley took the seats behind Beatrice and Drake—Huxley looking irritated by the arrangement—and all four of them turned toward the stage just as the audience was cast into darkness. Two stagehands tugged on ropes to draw the curtains open.

"I only wish it weren't a sequel," Miss Bolton murmured as a hush fell over the crowd. "They're never as good."

But then Percival Nash stepped onto the stage, and the room broke into applause.

The actor had been commanding in their previous meetings, but Beatrice could see, now, exactly why he was so beloved. Onstage, Percival seemed larger than life. His chiseled features and roguish ponytail (which looked shinier than it had moments before. *Was* it fake? She simply *could not tell*) were perfectly accentuated by the stage lights, but it was his confident demeanor—his energy—that drew in the audience.

Percival paused at center stage, noticing a candle in the audience that the boys had yet to extinguish. He held up a finger to the audience, inhaled, and then let out a gust of air. Even from a distance, it was strong enough to put out the candle.

"The power of breath support!" he said, and the room broke into fresh applause.

Percival inhaled again, as if he were about to begin singing, but there was movement at the edge of the stage. He turned, and Beatrice traced his gaze.

A squirrel clambered up one of the curtains, its claws scratching into the velvet. Percival's eyes narrowed.

He did a fanciful spin, aiming a kick at the bottom of the curtain. The fabric rippled, and the squirrel came loose and tumbled downward. A stagehand dressed in black appeared. He caught it, perfectly, in a little basket and then disappeared offstage.

The audience broke out into applause again, and Percival bowed.

"*Now* we can begin!"

"Percival, I love you!" someone shouted, and Percival shook his head, grinning.

"I am not Percival," he said in a booming voice. "My name is . . ." He broke into song: "Figaroooo!"

A crowd of actresses danced onto the stage, joining the fast-paced opening number. They sang so quickly that Beatrice could not make out the words, much less the plot; she was already completely lost. (It did not help that the opera was in Italian.)

Beatrice leaned back to whisper to Miss Bolton.

"Do you have any idea what's going on?" she asked helplessly.

"There is a synopsis in the program," Miss Bolton whispered back. She handed the pamphlet to Beatrice, who took it and strained to see by the reflection of the stage lights. Unfortunately, it was also in Italian, so she soon cast it aside.

"I cannot believe that we are seeing *the* Percival Nash," Miss Bolton went on as the audience burst into applause, the opening number complete. "The most important performer of our generation!"

"I want to see more clearly. Let me use your lorgnette," Beatrice whispered to Drake. "You must have one."

He held a finger to his lips to shush her. She crossed her arms, and he relented, producing a pair of opera glasses from his pocket. She snatched them from his grasp, lifted them to her eyes, and focused on the stage.

Percival was stepping aside, exiting just as Caroline Wynn—or Felicity, as she insisted upon calling herself—stepped onto the stage in a sparkling gown. The audience broke into fresh cheers, and she waved a hand as if to say, *Stop! You're too kind.* She drew in a breath and then began to sing a devastating aria. (Devastating not because of its subject matter, which Beatrice did not understand, but because it was so annoyingly on pitch.)

Losing interest in the plot—which she had never grasped to begin with—Beatrice looked through the lorgnette at the crowd instead. This was where the real show was, she thought. She glanced over rows of rapt faces, many dabbing at teary eyes while Caroline sang.

"She is *so* talented. And she doesn't even know it," Sir Huxley murmured behind Beatrice.

Beatrice thought that Caroline definitely knew the degree of her talent but resisted a reply. Instead, she turned the lorgnette to the box directly across from them, where Mr. and Mrs. Vane sat.

While Mr. Vane looked adoringly at his wife, Mrs. Vane watched the stage, her face set in a dreamlike expression.

They were a strange match, Beatrice thought, but they shared one trait: Neither could be pinned down.

Mr. Vane leaned over and said something to Diana. She stiffened and then nodded. She stood up and, with a swish of the curtain, exited the box.

Now Mr. Vane was alone in the small compartment, his face aglow by the light of the stage. Beatrice regarded him.

He seemed tense. Had he and Mrs. Vane been arguing? Seconds before, he had gazed at her adoringly—so why had she left?

Something moved in the shadows behind Mr. Vane. Beatrice leaned forward, trying to make it out.

It happened before she could fully comprehend what was going on: A figure—she could not make out face or form—stepped out of the corner of the box and grabbed Mr. Vane, shoving him against the wall. He opened his mouth to yell, but the noise was drowned out by Caroline's ridiculously perfect belt.

"Drake!" Beatrice grabbed his arm and pulled him along as she rushed from her seat. She shoved aside the curtains of their own box, dragging Drake into the hallway beyond. Upon their exit, Beatrice broke out into a run.

"What's wrong? Is it the play?" Drake called from behind her. "It is *much* funnier if you understand Italian, I'm told—"

"Horace Vane is being attacked!" Beatrice cried.

At that, Drake asked no more questions; they ran side by side down the hallway, crossed the now-quiet lobby, and then raced down yet another hallway toward the stage-right box. Thank goodness she had worn her running boots, Beatrice thought—the distance between the two boxes was significant.

She feared they would not be fast enough.

They reached the box just as the aria ended and the auditorium erupted into applause. Drake pushed aside the curtain and Beatrice burst inside.

Onstage, Caroline Wynn curtsied and blew kisses, while in the box, there was a scene nearly as horrifying.

Mr. Horace Vane was splayed out in his plush seat, his face battered, a knife protruding from his chest.

Beatrice rushed to kneel next to him. She could see the slightest rise and fall of his chest, in spite of the knife plunged into his heart. *He was still alive.*

"We will help you," she vowed. "Just hold on, Mr. Vane."

He made a gurgling noise, and Beatrice leaned closer. He was trying to say something, the words strangled.

"The . . . actor," he choked.

And then he collapsed in the chair, and it was over. The show could not go on—for Horace Vane was dead.

Dear Beatrice,

I have not received any letters from you in some time—I trust the Season is going well? I had expected to hear of an engagement by now. . . .

Unfortunate news from Swampshire; your father has attempted another prank. This time he flooded the kitchens, so we have been forced to dine at Fauna Manor with Mary for the past two weeks. Your sister means well, but her idea of dinner is simply a plate of meat. A lady needs a vegetable and a bonbon now and then. We are not wild animals!

In any case, our financial need is dire. Please assure me that you have caught the eye of a duke or a prince; I am growing despondent.

Of course, you must not let your desperation show. Men like women who appear fun-loving. Perhaps you might attend a performance with Miss Bolton. The theater is a nice, innocent place to lighten the mood.

Your doting mother,

Susan Steele

CHAPTER FIFTEEN

An Interruption

"What did he say?" Drake demanded, sinking down next to Beatrice.

"'The actor,'" she whispered. At this Drake's expression grew, somehow, even more serious.

They turned in tandem to examine Mr. Vane's bloodied face. The attacker had beaten him in the same manner as Mr. Nightingale and Mr. Shrewsbury, and then stabbed him, Beatrice could see. It was a gory sight, and she deliberately looked away from Mr. Vane's mangled visage, focusing instead on the knife protruding from his chest. She withdrew the weapon, blood welling from the wound as she extracted it. The metallic scent filled her nostrils as she held it close to examine the blade.

Engraved upon it were the words THE SWEET MAJESTIC.

"Someone had to have custom-made this, to direct suspicion onto the actors," Beatrice surmised. "Once again, it is not retractable, like the prop knives you described."

Drake examined it. "Indeed. An obvious attempt at a frame job. A mark in Nash's favor."

They looked at each other, not voicing what they were both clearly thinking: The victim croaking out the phrase "the actor," just after being attacked, was a mark *against* Nash. And a fairly big one.

"Percival was offstage while this occurred," Beatrice told Drake. "He has never given any alibis for his whereabouts during any of the other murders. A killer could have taken advantage of his absence and planned the timing of the death accordingly. Or . . ."

"Or, Huxley is right, and Nash is the true murderer," he said, finishing her thought.

Beatrice looked toward the stage. Caroline still stood there alone, curtsying to ongoing, thunderous applause. Roses rained down upon her, and she lifted her arms, beaming at her admirers, oblivious to what had just occurred offstage.

She was a star—just like Percival. Had he grown addicted to fame? Beatrice wondered. Had his mind been addled by constant veneration, countless standing ovations, causing him to kill in order to protect his livelihood?

Could Horace Vane have been correct in his suspicions?

There was movement in the wings.

"Look," Beatrice hissed, pointing.

They could just make it out from their perch: Percival Nash had appeared, lingering offstage. He wore a serious expression as he watched Caroline bow. His hair looked pristine, though Beatrice noted that his signature ribbon was missing, and there was a sheen of perspiration on his brow. Was this from the exertion of performance—or had he just run from backstage to this box and then back again?

Once the cheers for Caroline waned, Percival plastered on a smile and strode onstage to fresh waves of applause. The music began again, and Caroline and Percival struck up a chipper duet.

The attacker had beaten the victims' faces, indicating a tremendous amount of anger. And, Beatrice thought as she watched him harmonize expressively, Percival Nash was a passionate man . . .

No, Beatrice thought. She mustn't fall prey to the real killer's clumsy attempts to cast suspicion upon Nash. He was innocent, and it was her job to prove it.

She began to rifle through Mr. Vane's jacket pocket. Her thoughts were turning too vivid, too dark, and she needed to focus on gathering evidence instead of grim theories.

"Here is his wallet," she murmured, withdrawing it from his pocket. "And his pocket watch . . . but no sweetbriar encased in glass."

"What?" Drake inquired.

"Just something of sentimental value to Mr. Vane," Beatrice explained. "He showed it to me on the carriage ride here. If the attacker took it, this is *definitely* personal."

"We know the killer stole a statue from the previous murder scene. Perhaps there is a connection," Drake suggested.

"The other theft seemed a ploy to frame Caroline Wynn."

"You mean Felicity Lore."

"Do you think someone intends to plant another 'clue'?" Beatrice asked, not bothering to correct him. Caroline's identity did not matter now; they had more serious matters at hand than stage names.

"We will keep an eye out. It seems probable," Drake said, nodding.

"Wait. There is something in here," Beatrice said, withdrawing another item from Mr. Vane's pocket: a familiar silver necklace in the shape of a heart. "My locket," she gasped, popping it open to confirm.

Sure enough, there were the painted faces of Louisa and baby Bee Bee, staring back at her in miniature.

"I don't understand," Beatrice said. "How . . . *why* . . . would Mr. Vane have this?"

She turned back to the body.

Mr. Vane's arm was splayed out at an odd angle, and a shiver ran down Beatrice's spine as she saw his wrist.

Sure enough, he possessed the same tattoo that had appeared on Cecil Nightingale's wrist—and on the threatening notes that Mr. Nightingale and Mr. Shrewsbury had both received. She withdrew Elle's quizzing glass from around her neck and examined it more closely.

Miss Equiano had been correct: When it came to clues, the necklace *was* useful. Under the magnifier, Beatrice could see that the skin around the tattoo was puffy and irritated.

Had he tried to remove it? Had he thought it was the reason he was being targeted and planned to save himself somehow?

"Beatrice," Drake said urgently, and she dropped the quizzing glass. He had picked something up from the floor of the box and held it up for her to see.

It was a green ribbon—just like the one Percival Nash always wore.

At that moment, someone flung open the box's curtains.

"Really, Drake," said Sir Huxley. "Miss Steele came here with *me,* and I will not have you trying to— Good heavens." He broke off as he took in the scene: Horace Vane, beaten and stabbed; Beatrice on the floor next to the corpse; and Drake, holding the possibly incriminating green ribbon.

Before Beatrice could process what was happening, Sir Huxley tore the ribbon from Drake's grasp and rushed to the edge of the box. He leaned out to the audience and waved it in the air.

"Percival Nash is a murderer!" he cried. His roar cut through the tinkling duet onstage. The orchestra broke off, violinists and cellists and a baton-wielding conductor all looking from one another to Sir Huxley in obvious confusion. A beat later, Percival and Caroline halted their song, both looking shocked and vexed by the interruption.

A hush swept over the audience as Sir Huxley spoke again, his voice ringing clearly throughout the theater.

"Horace Vane has been murdered, and I have evidence that Percival Nash killed him. You are all witnesses to his crime, and now, his arrest. Surrender yourself at once, sir!"

There were gasps and screams as audience members took in Sir Huxley's words.

"Sir Huxley, please—" Beatrice began, grabbing his arm. "We cannot jump to such conclusions—"

Even if the jump seemed like more of a hop, at this point . . .

But Sir Huxley did not turn to her. Instead he growled in frustration, and Beatrice traced his gaze.

Caroline Wynn stood onstage, now alone. Percival Nash had fled.

"The stage door," Sir Huxley said, whirling around. "I must apprehend him. *Move,*" he insisted.

Drake was blocking the exit to the box.

"I cannot let you arrest another innocent person with no solid evidence," he said firmly.

"And what is *this*?" Sir Huxley asked, shaking the ribbon in Drake's face. He tried to push past, but Drake blocked him once again.

"The ribbon is circumstantial," Beatrice insisted. "Evidence does not always indicate what you think it does."

"Exactly," Drake agreed. "We must have *better* evidence—"

"You have claimed that my weakness is my bias," Sir Huxley interrupted, addressing Drake. "But in this instance, you are the one with the bias."

"I love the opera, yes, but I also recognize that Percival Nash has no real motive to—" Drake began, but Sir Huxley interrupted.

"The NAGS have threatened Mr. Nash's career and community. I would call that a real motive. Everything that Percival Nash has ever worked for—fame, this theater, *Figaro*—could have been taken away by the three men he killed."

"The same could be said for any of these performers—" Drake began, but Sir Huxley interrupted yet again.

"Besides, the bias you possess has nothing to do with the opera. If you had not inserted yourself into this evening—"

"You asked me to come. I hardly inserted myself," Drake snapped.

"—then Miss Steele and I might have prevented such a thing from occurring. We would have been sitting *with* Mr. and Mrs. Vane, and the killer would never have dared attack with *me* there," Sir Huxley went on.

"We do not know that the killer would have been stopped," Beatrice cut in. "They could have attacked at any point. You can hardly blame Drake for—"

"He is distracted," Sir Huxley said, shaking his head. "And you have very strong opinions about how a case suffers when someone is *distracted,* don't you, Inspector?"

Drake's entire body stiffened, a muscle in his jaw visible. For a moment he was still, the words washing over him.

There seemed to be some understanding, something unspoken, between the two men, and Beatrice looked back and forth between them, trying to glean what it was.

"Step aside," Sir Huxley said, his voice softening. "Else a murderer will go free, and the blood of his victims shall be on *your* hands."

Beatrice expected Drake to push back, to force Huxley to stand down. But instead he pulled aside the curtain, making room for Huxley to pass through. Sir Huxley gave a nod of farewell and then disappeared from the box.

The theater below was in chaos, still. The audience had

erupted in terrified chatter peppered with shrieks, and they were scrambling from their seats, falling over one another as they tried to leave the Sweet Majestic.

Onstage, Caroline Wynn had finally exited. The empty set—a charming pasture scene—now looked foreboding, the fabric flowers and painted backdrop a haunting contrast to the murder that had just occurred. Stagehands rushed to blow out the candles lining the stage, and others cleared away the set pieces. One drew the curtain closed, casting the theater into shadow. Candle boys finally came around, relighting candles so the audience could find their way out.

"What are you doing? We must go!" Beatrice exclaimed to Drake, who had frozen. "We might be able to determine where Percival—"

"No. Sir Huxley is right," Drake said. His voice was low and tense, and Beatrice stared at him, shocked. Had he really just uttered those words? "I am . . . I have been . . . distracted." Drake went on, "I should recuse myself from the investigation, or else it will be ruined. I . . . I must go."

"But, Drake—" Beatrice began, completely confused.

But he did not wait to hear what she had to say. In the blink of an eye, Inspector Vivek Drake was gone.

For a moment Beatrice was alone in the box, apart from Horace Vane's body. She was unnerved.

Why had Drake been so affected by Huxley's words?

Beatrice had come all the way to London to partner with Drake, and he had just abandoned her . . . again. This time with a note of finality. Now she had to either deal with everything herself or simply allow Huxley to arrest the (potentially) wrong person.

A rustle of skirts sounded behind her, and Beatrice whirled around just as Diana Vane stepped into the box. She held up two glasses of champagne, her hands shaking.

"He . . . he sent me to fetch a drink," she whispered, her face pale as mime's makeup. "He said he didn't want to . . . miss anything."

"I am so sorry, Mrs. Vane," Beatrice said, taking Diana's arm. "This is not a sight you will wish to see—"

But Diana shook her off. She dropped the champagne, glasses shattering on the floor, and rushed to her husband's side.

"I don't understand. How could this have happened?" She trembled violently as she examined Mr. Vane.

"We will find the culprit," Beatrice assured her, though she had no idea if she could even make such a claim now. With Drake off the case, her own involvement was unclear.

And even if she found justice, it was not really enough. In a moment, Mrs. Vane's entire life had been forever altered.

The silver-haired woman suddenly recoiled.

"What is it?" Beatrice stepped forward. Mrs. Vane rushed to her feet.

"It's . . . it's just too much," she choked out. "Please. Will you take me away from here? Take me home."

"Of course. Anything you need."

Beatrice realized her opportunity. Drake had recused himself, but she had done nothing of the sort, and now she was alone with a woman at the very center of the case.

She held out an arm, and Mrs. Vane took it, allowing Beatrice to lead her out of the box.

Sir Huxley may have forgotten about the wife left behind, focused only on the man he wanted to pursue—but Beatrice would make no such oversight.

Dear Miss Bolton,

I read the manuscript you sent for your latest play, *Altus*. It was stunning. I must admit I guessed the first twist, but the next six? They came as a complete shock. I never thought theater could be so exciting! Please send the conclusion as soon as you have written it.

It is good that Beatrice rests often, so you have time to write—but is she quite well? I have never known her to rest so much! She's always busy sticking her nose in some business.

In other news, everything is peaceful at Fauna Manor. Your home and pets are well cared for. If you hear anything about a man with a pistol full of silver bullets who disappeared near your home, please disregard this. As I stated, all is well.

Your friend,

Mary Steele

CHAPTER SIXTEEN

A Decision

Outside the theater, it was as chaotic as the inside had been. The audience spilled out onto the front steps, voices raised in a terrified din after what had just occurred. The sky was dark now, illuminated every so often by foreboding flashes of lightning in the distance.

A storm was coming. Though really, Beatrice thought, it was already here.

She pulled Mrs. Vane through the crowd, dodging ladies and gentlemen and errant candle boys, until they had come to the line of carriages along the street in front of the Sweet Majestic. It was pandemonium as everyone tried to get into their carriage at once. Drivers attempted to keep control over their horses as guests wove through the line, looking to locate their carriages for hasty departures.

Thankfully, Sir Huxley's gleaming blue carriage stood out

among the sea of vehicles, and Beatrice pulled Mrs. Vane straight to it.

Sir Huxley's footman helped Mrs. Vane into the carriage.

"Please direct the driver to take us to the Vane estate," Beatrice told him, "and then to my town house in the Carnation Quarter. I am seeing Mrs. Vane home to ensure she arrives safely." And in the meantime, Beatrice thought, she would determine what the woman knew of the evening's events.

"Where is my lord?" the footman asked, looking around.

"He is pursuing a murderer," Beatrice said truthfully.

Evidently accustomed to this, the footman accepted the explanation and helped Beatrice into the carriage after Mrs. Vane. He closed the door, and they were finally enveloped in silence as the shrieks of the crowd were drowned out.

For a moment Beatrice did not speak, sitting quietly across from Mrs. Vane, who twisted her garnet ring around and around her finger. The poor woman had arrived for an evening at the theater with her husband and was now leaving alone. She deserved a moment to collect herself, Beatrice thought.

But to Beatrice's surprise, it was Mrs. Vane who broke the silence first. "How could he do this to me?" she whispered, her voice small and far away. "How could he put me through such a thing? I never thought this would happen tonight. . . ."

"We do not *know* that Percival Nash was the killer," Beatrice told her. Clearly Mrs. Vane felt betrayed by the actor she had supported, but they could not make assumptions. Beatrice drew in a breath. It would be difficult to extract, but she needed the truth. Before Sir Huxley arrested Percival Nash.

Before someone else was killed.

"Mrs. Vane," Beatrice began, "when you left to fetch drinks, did you see anyone in the hallway outside the box? Anything you saw could be imperative to the case at hand."

Diana pursed her lips. They were as pale as her face, her entire appearance ghostlike. "I was gone when everything occurred," she murmured. "I suppose he did that on purpose, so I would not have time to know what was happening. . . ."

"Likely, yes," Beatrice said with a nod. "Whoever killed your husband was obviously only targeting him. They waited until you left before striking, so you would not be involved—but also so there would be no witness to implicate them."

"I just don't understand how he did it," Diana said, her eyes becoming unfocused. Beatrice was losing her, she thought. "One moment Horace was beside me, and the next . . ." She did not seem to be speaking to Beatrice but to herself.

"If there is *any* detail you can remember about the attack—anything at all—it may help us find the killer," Beatrice pressed.

At this, Diana's eyes refocused. They sharpened upon Beatrice. "'Us'?" she repeated, raising an eyebrow.

Beatrice flushed. "I merely meant . . . we could help Sir Huxley, in his investigation. . . ."

"I know that you and Inspector Drake have been poking around," Mrs. Vane said, her voice weirdly dreamlike, though she was living a nightmare.

Now it was Beatrice's turn to sit silently in shock. Mrs. Vane *knew*?

"After I admitted you onto the list, I did some reconnaissance of my own," Mrs. Vane continued. "I have been running the Rose for many years, Miss Steele. I would not let a stranger in our doors. There is little which goes on there that I am not privy to."

"If you knew that Drake and I were investigators, why did you permit us to participate in the Season?" Beatrice asked, utterly confused by such a confession. "Sir Huxley had already been hired, after all."

"I reasoned that he could do with a bit of competition," Mrs. Vane said, her large eyes fixed upon Beatrice.

Yes, Beatrice thought, Mrs. Vane relished a challenge, lighting up any time one was before her. It seemed to excite her.

"And perhaps you have created such competition for both Sir Huxley *and* Inspector Drake, in more ways than one," Mrs. Vane continued.

"I don't know what you mean," Beatrice said, feeling flushed.

"I think you do," Mrs. Vane said, raising her eyebrows.

"You have misread the situation, madam," Beatrice said, now filled with embarrassment and indignation.

Why were they talking about *this,* after what had just occurred? They were meant to be discussing murder, not personal matters, especially those that Mrs. Vane clearly misunderstood.

"As I told you, Miss Steele, there is little which goes on at the Rose that I am not privy to," Mrs. Vane went on. "Sir Huxley requested to join the season late after meeting an intriguing woman, new to London. Though his presence ruined the balance of gentlemen to ladies, I allowed it . . . for your sake." Though Mrs. Vane held a handkerchief in her hand, her eyes were dry. She seemed perfectly collected. The color was already returning to her cheeks.

It was eerie.

"It is best for men to know you have other options. This ensures their loyalty. Their dedication," Mrs. Vane went on.

"Is that why you were courting a poet before you accepted Mr. Vane's marriage proposal?" Beatrice asked the question before she could stop herself. She immediately clapped a hand over her mouth. "I beg your pardon," she said in a rush. "It was an inappropriate question, at such a time—"

"You do have a knack for speaking your mind. A dangerous quality, here in Sweetbriar," Mrs. Vane said. But the corners of her mouth had curled upward in a hint of a smile. "Yes, I had other options before Horace. I did not think anyone still remembered Oliver. Of course, I never forgot him. . . ." She looked almost—wistful, Beatrice thought.

"How did Mr. Vane win you away from Mr. Oliver . . . ?"

"Beauchamp. Oliver Beauchamp," Diana replied. She turned to the carriage window, pushing the curtain aside. "Why aren't we moving?"

"Carriage jam," Beatrice told her. "Everyone is trying to flee at once. We will simply have to wait."

Silence stretched between them. Beatrice deliberately resisted the urge to fill it with questions. She had found that, when faced with such awkwardness, people would often volunteer more than they wanted to in order to end the quiet.

And there was something Diana was hiding. She felt certain.

"Horace was the appropriate match," Diana said finally. "He was inevitable."

"Inevitable," Beatrice repeated.

"Do what is expected of you, Miss Steele," Diana told her, "and you shall end up just like me."

Beatrice wondered if this was meant to be encouraging advice—or a warning. "Where is Oliver now?" she prompted.

"Ran off to the colonies," Diana said wistfully. "Some people don't belong here in London, Miss Steele."

At that moment the carriage moved forward, and Diana withdrew a cigar from her bodice. She stuck it between her teeth, unlit, then leaned back and let her eyelids close.

Was Diana Vane simply defeated? One never knew how a person might respond to grief, but Beatrice did know that she could not press Mrs. Vane further. It would be disrespectful, considering everything that the woman had been through—but most important, Beatrice could tell that the patroness of the Rose would not give her any more information. Not tonight.

She looked out the window as they ambled down the cobblestones, in line with the other carriages fleeing the Sweet Majestic, deep in thought.

What if Diana's former flame, this Oliver Beauchamp, was

responsible for the murders? He was a poet, the newspaper had said, meaning that he was a creative in his own right. Was there any chance that he had returned from the colonies and decided to enact justice on behalf of local artists? Perhaps he even meant to reclaim Diana, his lost love. . . .

It seemed like the plot of a tragic opera, she thought as they picked up speed, emerging into the wealthy Rose Quarter, where the Vanes' estate was located. Perhaps the person best suited to making sense of it all was the man who had been entangled in everything from the start.

After all, as an actor, Percival Nash understood drama.

The carriage pulled to a stop in front of an imposing manor, and the footman opened the door. He held out a hand to escort Mrs. Vane out of the carriage. She took it but then turned back to Beatrice.

"It wasn't Percival," she said, her voice hushed. Determined. How had Diana known what she had been thinking?

"You mean, he is not responsible for the murders?" she clarified.

"I don't know how . . . or who . . . I just know that Percival is not the killer," Diana told her. "You cannot let Sir Huxley arrest an innocent man."

"It may be too late for that already," Beatrice told her.

"It can't be too late. You must make sure of it," Diana said fiercely. "If the artists are silenced, I shudder to think what might happen to the rest of us."

"I promise that I will do everything I can to clear Percival's name," Beatrice said.

"Good," Diana said, nodding. "Good . . ." With that, she drifted away into the night, disappearing into her palatial home.

Beatrice watched her go, ensuring that the woman got safely inside, and then turned to the footman.

"Could you please inform the driver that I do not wish to return to my town house yet?" she asked.

"Of course, miss," the footman said with a bow of his head. "What destination shall I give?"

What destination, indeed, Beatrice thought. Percival Nash had fled. But to where? She did not think he would stay at the Sweet Majestic, for this would be the first place anyone would look. Really, anywhere close seemed risky, considering that Sir Huxley—and, thus, all of Sweetbriar—would be looking for the actor. His fame would work against him, in this case.

Perhaps at the edge of town, he might find refuge at some place where no genteel person would think to go. Where the buildings were crumbling, the gin was cheap, and desperate people sold antiques for quick cash . . .

What had Caroline Wynn said about Mr. O'Dowde?

His parties—of course you could never secure an invitation to one. He only associates with true artistes. . . .

A trapdoor that could have been hiding some secret chamber, an antique shop owner who adored performers, and a whisper about exclusive parties . . . It was a hunch, yes, but while the Drake was away, the Beatrice would follow her hunches.

"There is a pawnshop at the outskirts of town," Beatrice told the footman. "Dudley O'Dowde's. Could you take me there?"

"We shall have to take the long way, as Bibble Bridge is down, miss," the footman informed her.

"Yes, I am aware. Not a problem. Thank you ever so much," she told him. He nodded and closed the carriage door once more.

It was a long shot, Beatrice knew—but one she might as well take. What did she have to lose?

As the carriage took off once more, neither Beatrice, the footman, nor the driver noticed another carriage, following them.

Another curious soul, hidden in the shadows.

BULLETIN SERVICES FROM THE NEIGHBORHOOD ASSOCIATION OF GENTLEMEN SWEETBRIARIANS

(BS from NAGS)

Out of respect for the family and friends of Mr. Horace Vane, the Sweet Majestic will be closed for the foreseeable future.

All performances of *Figaro III: Here We Figaro Again* are CANCELED. Anyone found singing or humming tunes from the show will be FINED. Off-tune renditions will receive DOUBLE FINES. Street performers offering any version of the show (including mimed summaries or suspicious juggling) will have their permits REVOKED.

Anyone with information regarding the whereabouts of Mr. Percival Nash, please contact Sir Lawrence Huxley forthwith.

Cheers.

CHAPTER SEVENTEEN

An Interruption

Avoiding Bibble Bridge made for a long journey out of town, but Beatrice didn't even notice, as the events of the evening swirled in her mind: Diana's past love. The NAGS and their vendetta against local art. Sir Huxley's insistence that Percival Nash was guilty—and Horace Vane, the accuser, now dead. How to arrange such pieces?

The puzzle's image took shape, Beatrice had to admit, when she considered Percival's involvement. Sir Huxley was right; his motive made sense. And he had fled the scene. Was this an admission of guilt or the culmination of his fear that he would be blamed for a crime he had not committed? She had now promised both Percival *and* Diana that she would prove the actor's innocence, yet the current lack of suspects—and answers—made the feat feel impossible.

As the carriage pulled to a halt outside the narrow alley down which Mr. O'Dowde's shop was located, Beatrice felt more uncertain than ever before.

In her first case with Inspector Drake, she had known most of the suspects involved for all her life. It had made it easier to question them and find her way to the truth. But here in London, the stories of those around her extended much further back in history, before her time. She had only just met them, only uncovered the topmost layer of their secrets and lies. Would she ever make sense of it all, or had her first case merely been solved with beginner's luck? Had she been in the right place at the right time, but lacked any real skill?

The footman opened the carriage door, and Beatrice stepped onto the dark street, self-doubt sitting heavy on her shoulders. But when she strode toward the pawnshop's entrance, she could hear the sound of voices from within. And one of them, clear and charming, she recognized.

Percival Nash.

"I shall be back shortly," Beatrice told the footman. She tried to pull open the door to the shop, but it was locked.

"Shall we take our leave?" the footman asked, watching as Beatrice struggled with the knob.

"I *said,* I shall be back shortly," Beatrice told him. She withdrew one of her earrings, slid it into the lock, and moved it up and down. Something inside clicked, and the doorknob turned.

"As you wish, miss," the footman said. He looked both impressed and disturbed.

Beatrice was accustomed to such looks from men. She nodded her farewell to the footman, and then slipped into the shop.

It was dark, dust sparkling in the moonlight, but the voices she had overheard were louder now. She could pick out Mr. O'Dowde's Irish brogue and Percival Nash's expressive tones. And there were other voices, too, she realized—as well as music.

How many people were in here?

She carefully avoided stacks of footstools and lamps, finding her way to the bump where she had tripped before—the hidden trapdoor. She dropped to her knees and felt along the wood floor until her fingers located an indentation.

She slid her nails underneath and lifted, expecting to see a staircase.

Instead, she stared down at a brightly colored cushion. Evidently it was to be a sheer drop from the floor of Mr. O'Dowde's shop into its depths.

Well. She had never resisted entering a concealed secret room, and she certainly wasn't about to start now. She gathered her skirts and lowered herself through the trapdoor, tumbling down with only a tiny *oof* when she landed on the cushion below.

She righted herself quickly, expecting the inhabitants of the chamber to have noticed her entrance. But Beatrice saw, to her surprise, that there were even more people than she had guessed—and the little room she had anticipated was actually an expansive suite.

It was cluttered with heirlooms, like the shop above, but everything seemed touched by a creative muse: The walls were covered in portraits, directly painted onto black wallpaper. Their eyes seemed to glow in the candlelight of antique sconces. There were empty wine bottles, champagne crates, silk pillows, and old tapestries strewn about.

And there were artists everywhere.

It was like being backstage at the Sweet Majestic, except the mood was not frantic but somber. Clusters of actors in their opera costumes crowded around, speaking in low, serious voices as they sipped from chipped crystal glasses. Painters with acrylic-smudged smocks mingled among them, brushes tucked behind their ears and bobbing as they nodded seriously. Musicians wove through the crowd, playing snippets of mournful music.

Something crunched under Beatrice's feet as she stepped off

the cushion, and she looked down to see that the floor was papered with notices. She stooped to pick one up.

PERMIT DENIED, it read. *YOU MUST HERETOFORE CEASE AND DESIST YOUR "ART," IF ONE CAN EVEN CALL IT THAT.*

She dropped it and looked up, her eyes searching the crowd. She was certain that she had heard Percival Nash's voice.

Where was he?

"The lady searches for a myst'ry man," a voice said. Beatrice jumped, and turned to see a woman holding a skull.

"Please," Beatrice sighed, "no more sonnets—"

"Yet will she find him here amidst this crowd?" The woman continued, now addressing the skull. "This lady is no artist, yet she stands—with those of us who gather at O'Dowde's."

"You are correct," said a familiar voice. "This lady is no artist. She is a detective."

Percival Nash had appeared in front of Beatrice, his glossy auburn hair the only part of him that did not seem wilted in defeat.

"I am glad you are here," he said, taking Beatrice's hands and pulling her into a corner. He collapsed onto a cushion, and Beatrice lowered herself next to him. "Things are dire, Inspector Steele," Percival told her tearfully. "I escaped here with a few close friends—"

"A few?" Beatrice asked incredulously, glancing at the huge crowd of drunk artists assembled before them.

Percival nodded. "Unfortunately I had to leave many colleagues and admirers behind, but there was nothing to be done. Sir Huxley is convinced of my guilt. If he finds me, I am done for. Please tell me you have determined the true culprit."

"I am . . . close," Beatrice lied. Relief flashed across Percival's face, and Beatrice went on. "Still, I must ask once more—where were you on the night of Mr. Shrewsbury's murder? We all know that you were present for the deaths of Mr. Nightingale and Mr. Vane—"

"Which is how you know I am being set up," Percival interrupted. "I was *invited* to perform at the Rose the night of Mr. Nightingale's death. And of course I was present when Mr. Vane was killed; it occurred at the Sweet Majestic. An actor's *home* is the theater," he cried, pressing a hand to his chest.

"But *what of the night of Mr. Shrewsbury's death*?" Beatrice said again.

"I did not do it," Percival insisted.

"You have motive, Mr. Nash," Beatrice told him. He gasped at this pronouncement, but she continued. "You had opportunity. And you had means. The murder weapon was a knife with your 'home' engraved upon it. I have tried to clear your name, but each piece of evidence only leads me closer to you. Unless, of course, you can give me your alibi."

She let the words hang in the air.

"I did not do it," Percival Nash repeated. His cheeks were growing ruddy, and beads of sweat appeared along his brow.

His hair, however, remained perfectly coiffed. It showed no trace of sweat, not dampened in the least by the humidity of the room or Percival's stress.

"Percival," Beatrice said slowly, "where were you the night of Mr. Shrewsbury's death?"

"I cannot say," he insisted.

"This is a matter of life in prison or life onstage," Beatrice told him. "So I will ask you one more time: *Where were you the night of Mr. Shrewsbury's death?*"

"*I was at the wigmaker's*," Percival Nash cried, then clapped a hand over his mouth.

"What?" Beatrice drew back, floored by this sudden confession.

Percival looked around to ensure that no one had heard and

then leaned forward. He slipped a finger under the front of his hair and lifted it up ever so slightly.

Below the auburn hairline, Beatrice could see the truth.

He was bald.

"Are you satisfied?" he hissed. "It is true. I wear hairpieces. My wigmaker, Anastasia, can vouch for my presence in her shop on the night of Mr. Shrewsbury's death. She has a back entrance at her shop just for me and has been sworn to secrecy. Naturally when I fell under suspicion, she vowed to tell everyone of my innocence—but I made her swear not to. How could I maintain my reputation, or my status as a star, with this . . . this *cue ball*?" He motioned to his head, distressed.

"Surely your hair has nothing to do with your stardom," Beatrice began.

"You silly girl," Percival interrupted. "Of course it does. An actor's hair is everything. Without it, he cannot appear center stage and must be relegated to the shadows. He might as well be a *writer*," he spat.

"So you have an alibi for the evening of Mr. Shrewsbury's death," Beatrice said, trying to get back on track, "and for the others—"

"When Mr. Nightingale died, I was concealed in the powder room, fixing a piece of my wig which had come unglued from my scalp. And when Mr. Vane died, I was offstage, changing my first hairpiece out for a fresh one. I perspire under the light of the stage," Percival sniffed. "If *that* is a crime, then lock me up. But if I gave my alibis, I would be the laughingstock of Sweetbriar, likely banned from the stage because of my lies."

"As an actor, it's sort of your *job* to lie, though, isn't it?" Beatrice attempted to console him, but Percival shook his head.

"People want me to maintain an illusion. That is the whole *point,* Miss Steele. But if I do not tell, I shall be arrested and hanged for these murders."

"I suppose you must decide if you wish to give up acting or be hanged," Beatrice said.

"An impossible decision!" Percival cried.

Beatrice took his hands. "Mr. Nash," she said, "I know it seems dire, but all is not lost yet. Sir Huxley has not found you, and I am still committed to this case. Now that I know the truth, and am convinced of your innocence—"

"You weren't before?" Percival sniffed.

"—I *will* find the true killer," Beatrice finished. She looked around the room at the crowd of unfamiliar faces.

This was London, she thought. Too many murderers—and too many suspects.

She noticed, then, that the mournful music and conversations around them had been replaced by cries of fear.

Percival grabbed her wrist and pulled her to stand. Beatrice turned toward the source of the shouts and felt her stomach drop.

In the center of the crowd was a tall, handsome blond man, wearing a top hat.

Sir Huxley.

He locked eyes with Beatrice and then looked beside her. Beatrice tried to block Percival Nash, but it was too late. Sir Huxley pushed his way across the room and grabbed Percival.

"He didn't do it!" Beatrice said immediately.

"Step aside," Huxley said in a commanding voice. "I am placing this man under arrest."

The crowd immediately erupted into protestations. Artists tried to block Huxley's path, but he kept a firm grip on Percival with one hand and used his other hand to nudge people out of his way with his asp-topped cane.

"Let him go!" a dancer yelled. "He is innocent!"

"Percival would never kill anyone! At least, not offstage!" a chorus girl insisted.

"How did this *gentleman* even get in here?" a painter demanded, jabbing a brush toward Sir Huxley.

"Interloper!"

"Philistine!"

"He thinks the height of literature is the 'no mimes' sign at the local tavern!"

"He thinks the height of sculpture is a chamber pot!"

"Excuse you. I make chamber pots. They can be *very* artistic—"

Sir Huxley ignored the noise, dragging Percival all the way toward the trapdoor. Beatrice trailed behind them, yelling her own protests, but she was drowned out by the performers' impressive access to their diaphragms.

When Huxley came to the trapdoor, he halted. *Good,* Beatrice thought with relief. There was no staircase, so he would not be able to exit. They could still save Percival.

But then two figures appeared above, lowering a rope. Sir Huxley was no fool. He had brought backup: two burly Bow Street Runners.

"This is wrong! You are wrong. I can prove it!" Beatrice cried, but Huxley ignored her as he tied Percival's hands. The Bow Street Runners hoisted the actor through the trapdoor just as Beatrice reached Huxley.

"How did you even find this place?" she asked, watching helplessly as Percival disappeared into the ceiling.

"You took my carriage here, Miss Steele," Huxley replied. "I merely followed it."

There were fresh gasps amidst the crowd, and Beatrice could feel angry eyes upon her. Sir Huxley paused, then leaned in so only she could hear him.

"Consider this the favor you owed me." He winked and she winced. She could smell his cologne, expensive and musky, as he took her hand and pressed it to his lips. "I can't quite believe I'm saying this to a lady, but it is a pleasure to do business with you, Miss Steele. Let's do it again soon."

She tore her hand away, but he merely tipped his hat and then climbed up the rope to follow after his lackeys and his prisoner.

"How could you lead that man here?" someone demanded, jabbing a finger in Beatrice's face.

"She is no artist!" someone else yelled. "She is a *lady*!"

"Not according to my mother," Beatrice said weakly.

"How dare you joke at a time like this!" spat a clown.

"Get out of here, traitor!"

The crowd began to shove Beatrice. A group of mimes pretended to bind her with rope, and she took the opportunity to dodge them and leap toward the trapdoor.

It was useless, she thought; she could never jump so high.

But to her surprise, someone reached down through the trapdoor and hoisted her to safety.

After a confusing scramble that smelled of cinnamon and oranges, Beatrice found herself standing in the antique shop next to—

"Inspector Drake," Beatrice whispered. "Thank heavens you're here!"

"What have you done?" he said, his dark eye flashing.

A chain of acrobats formed a human ladder below the trapdoor, growing close to reaching them. Drake flipped the door shut on them and dragged a heavy vase on top.

"They will be trapped," Beatrice said, but Drake scoffed.

"They shall figure it out. They are creative."

For a moment it was silent, the tension thick between them—and then Drake turned on his heel and left the shop.

Beatrice did not hesitate. She rushed after him, frustration rising.

"I didn't do anything," she told him. "I was trying to *help*—what were *you* doing here?" she added, realizing: "You came without me."

"And you did the same, Miss Steele," he snapped. "Though *my* presence did not imperil the very actor we were meant to protect. I told you that Huxley always collects his debts. And now you have repaid him—by leading him straight to Percival."

Thunder rumbled in the distance.

"You never should have come here," Drake said darkly, raking a hand through his thick hair, obviously furious.

"To Percival's . . . or to London?" Beatrice asked, trying not to let her voice quiver.

Drake did not answer, and her chest clenched.

"You asked me to come," she said. "I am half of DS Investigations—"

"And perhaps that was a mistake," Drake said, not looking at her. Beatrice felt her stomach drop.

"Do you not think I have what it takes?" she said.

But instead of wallowing in defeat, she chose to let anger well up inside her.

"You didn't even give me a chance to prove myself," she went on. "You put my name on the sign of DS Investigations, and then you cut me out of this case at every turn. You do not trust me. Admit it."

"I told you from the beginning that I do not approve of Huxley's methods," Drake shot back. "That I do not want to fall prey to biases and let personal feelings get in the way of an investigation."

"I am not doing that!" Beatrice shouted. She could no longer bear his constant dismissal. She had done nothing but try to be the best inspector and had thought of nothing but the case at hand, yet Drake never seemed satisfied.

"No, you aren't," Drake said hotly, "*I* am."

"Because of what Huxley said? He was wrong, Drake. Your love of opera does not matter; Percival Nash is innocent. What he confessed tonight confirms it," Beatrice said in a rush.

"This is not about Percival Nash," Drake growled. "It's not even about the blasted investigation."

"I don't understand," Beatrice began. The rain was falling in earnest now. It clung to her gown, making the silk stick to her skin in an embrace as cold as Drake's words.

He raked a hand through his dark hair. "Huxley wasn't talking about my love of *opera*," he said. "He meant that I am distracted by *you*."

He stepped toward her, jaw tense. Her heart began to pound furiously at his sudden proximity.

"I have told you that you do not need to worry about me. I can take care of myself—" Beatrice began, but Drake continued.

"I am not *worried* about you, Miss Steele. I am jealous. Of Huxley. Getting close to you. Taking you to the opera. Dancing with you. Doing all the things *I* wanted to do."

Beatrice was breathless. The air had changed between them. What was going on?

Drake continued. "I have been . . . consumed. I think not of the case at hand, but of you. When I am around you, I cannot focus on evidence; I am overcome with *feelings*. Therefore I found it prudent to push you away. To cut you out of the case, so I could ensure an unbiased approach. It was not because of your shortcomings but mine."

"You were cruel because . . . you cared for me?" Beatrice asked, hardly believing that it was Drake—serious, stoic, logical Drake—who stood in front of her, speaking such words.

"Yes! But I failed miserably, and now have made a mess of this investigation," Drake said, his dark eye fixed upon her. "The truth is . . . you drive me mad, Miss Steele!" With that, he grabbed her face and kissed her.

Time seemed to stop as Drake and Beatrice embraced, rain pouring down from the heavens, pelting them with droplets. Beatrice hardly registered the storm.

After what seemed like both an eternity and a mere second, Drake broke away.

"Go home, Miss Steele," he said tensely. "Sir Huxley left his other carriage just down the street; the driver can take you back. It is all over."

With that, he left her, his tall, dark figure disappearing into the pouring rain.

Beatrice watched him go, more confused than she had ever been.

What did he mean by "it is all over"? The case? Their partnership? Or his feelings for her? And which of these did Beatrice hope for?

She did not know.

All she knew was that her mouth still tingled where his lips had met hers.

THE LONDON BABBLER

Breaking News

The streets of London are safe once more, thanks to the dashing Sir Huxley. He has arrested actor Percival Nash for the murders of Walter Shrewsbury, Cecil Nightingale, and most recently, Horace Vane.

Mr. Nash is best known for his portrayal of the cartoonish social climber Figaro. He performed at the Sweet Majestic, which has been shuttered indefinitely.

Sources indicate that Mr. Nash meant to eradicate the members of the NAGS, due to their "censure" of local art. Thankfully, the NAGS's numbers remain strong, in spite of losing three prominent members in Shrewsbury, Nightingale, and Vane.

The remaining NAGS have issued a ban on all art, performance, whistling, humming, and self-expression which goes against their traditional values. (Puns are permitted, as these do not require creativity.) Those in violation of this ban risk fine and arrest. Additionally, the Season at the Rose has been suspended, out of respect for patroness Diana Vane, who shall now be in mourning after losing her beloved husband.

"We have suffered great losses, but order has been restored," said Gregory Dunne, spokesman of the Neighborhood Association of Gentlemen Sweetbriarians. "Let this be a lesson to all artists: You cannot defeat the NAGS."

RIVETING RIBBONS

By Elle Equiano

Accessories can show personal style, but they can also make powerful statements. This past week Sweetbriar was shaken when Percival Nash, local celebrity, was arrested under suspicion of the murders of Walter Shrewsbury, Cecil Nightingale, and Horace Vane. Local artists are showing their support for Percival, and belief in his innocence, by wearing green ribbons—Percival's signature color—in their hair and caps. Ladies who wish to join in with the movement should say "Percival Nash is innocent" at Madam Gest's Dress Emporium to claim their complimentary ribbon.

Elle—

As you know, *The London Babbler* was previously owned by Horace Vane. Out of respect to Mr. Vane, the *Babbler* openly supports Percival Nash's conviction. Please rewrite this article accordingly.

Might I suggest a take in which you mention how garish green is?

—Your editor

Dear Mrs. Steele,

Please ignore my previous letter. You may throw it straight into the fire, for all is well here in London. As it turns out, Beatrice was not stolen by the one-handed Specter of Sweetbriar, and we shall have no ghostly poems written about her, for she is safe!

After the horrific events at the opera, Beatrice and I were separated. I feared the worst, which is why I wrote you that letter of resignation as chaperone and requested that I be arrested for shirking my duties, but happy days! Beatrice has just returned unscathed. Evidently she got lost in the scuffle after Mr. Horace Vane was murdered, but she is home now, resting peacefully.

I settled her in her chamber with a foot warmer and came straight to my writing desk to pen you this note of reassurance.

Therefore all is well, Beatrice is safe, and I remain

Her committed chaperone,

Miss Helen Bolton

THE LONDON BABBLER

More Breaking News

Though the Season has been suspended, the Rose Club's end-of-summer masquerade shall still proceed—albeit earlier than planned, and in spite of the tragedies the community has suffered.

"The deaths of Walter Shrewsbury, Cecil Nightingale, and Horace Vane have shaken Sweetbriar to its core," Sir Huxley told reporters in a statement. "Our neighborhood used to be a safe, serene place—apart from the squirrels—but thieves and murderers and mimes tried to change this. As always, though, justice prevailed. I have apprehended the killer, the actor Percival Nash. This terrible man murdered three men, *and*—as has recently been discovered—lied about his hairstyle. He will stand trial for his murderous acts and follicular deception, and everyone can rest assured that our streets are safe once more."

Thanks to the dashing Sir Huxley, the masquerade—which has traditionally been open to all in the neighborhood—can continue. As always, the festivities are complimentary to members of the Rose Club, their escorts, and their chaperones. Those outside membership may purchase a ticket for a lofty fee.

Artists will not be welcome.

As a reminder to all attending the masquerade, please pin down hats, hairpieces, and any valuables which could be snatched by flying rodents. Though the squirrels are not invited, they will likely intrude upon the event.

CHAPTER EIGHTEEN

A Puzzle

For several days, Beatrice did not leave her chambers at the Carnation Quarter town house.

There was no need, seeing as the Season had been suspended, and Beatrice was glad for this, because the last thing she wanted to do was put on a ball gown and dance a quadrille.

She was despondent. She had finally uncovered Percival Nash's innocence, only to unintentionally aid in his arrest. The papers proclaimed his guilt, and even his alibi had proven useless; no one believed an actor and a hairdresser over beloved gentleman detective Sir Lawrence Huxley.

As for Inspector Drake, he had not contacted her since that moment outside Mr. O'Dowde's shop. His silence told her everything she needed to know: Their partnership was truly over.

She was furious that Drake had cut her out because of his inability to communicate. The whole mess might have been avoided by a simple conversation. His attempt at restraint *was* admirably English—though his kissing had been indecently French.

If she were being truly honest with herself, Beatrice had suspected how he felt. But like Drake, she had tried to push romantic notions aside. They had both sacrificed personal considerations for the sake of the case—and it had ruined everything.

In the end, the voice of doubt inside her head was right: She did not have what it took to make it as an inspector in London. After all, Drake was gone. The case was out of their hands. The city had chewed her up and spit her out.

So Beatrice made a decision. She took out her trunk and began to fill it with books, papers, and her beautiful yet useless new wardrobe.

She would go home. Back to Swampshire—where she belonged.

Her window was open to tempt in a breeze, but the streets outside were still—and unusually quiet. All of the musicians, actors, and mimes had been banned from performing (Sweetbriar mimes were the worst offenders when it came to street noise, due to their obsession with tap shoes).

Beatrice could not believe it, but she actually missed the sound of sonnets. (Though she did not miss the kick-ball-changes.) There was something about the freedom of expression that was annoying, yes—but it *had* filled her with a certain inspiration.

She had just finished folding her final bit of frippery when her door creaked open and Miss Bolton entered.

"I brought refreshments," she said. She shuffled in and set a tray with a teacup and several lemon slices on top of Beatrice's trunk.

Beatrice could not meet her chaperone's eye. She was awash with a fresh wave of guilt; Miss Bolton was being so kind after Beatrice had disappeared and left her sick with worry. "Miss

Bolton, I am leaving," she said finally, "but you must stay. London needs you. *You* fit in here, with your understanding of fashion, and your plays, and—" Her voice broke.

"Beatrice. Whatever is the matter?" Miss Bolton said, rushing over to her. She put her hands on Beatrice's shoulders, forcing Beatrice to look into her chaperone's kind, puglike face.

"I never felt that I fit in when I lived in Swampshire. I thought that if I ever made it to London, everything would make sense here. *I* would make sense. But it's worse," Beatrice said in a rush. "Rules here are unspoken, relationships hidden, artists forced underground . . . literally . . . and I thought I could find the truth, but I don't know anything. Caroline Wynn was right." She choked a bit on those words but then continued: "I should go back to Swampshire. It would be better for everyone if I were not here."

Miss Bolton pressed her lips together and then turned on her heel and left the room.

Did she agree? Beatrice thought. Was this her polite way of saying so? She was about to flop down onto the bed in utter hopelessness when Miss Bolton reappeared.

She held something that sparkled in her palm. It was a beautiful brooch, made of mother-of-pearl carved into the shape of a frog.

"I was waiting for the right time to give this to you." She stretched out her hand, offering the brooch to Beatrice.

"Oh, Miss Bolton, it is far too fine. I couldn't accept such a gift. I won't have any need for nice things soon, anyhow," Beatrice said at once, but Miss Bolton ignored her and popped free the pin at the brooch's clasp.

"I remember the first time I traveled to London as a young woman. I had similar feelings—if only I could get to the city, all my problems would be solved," Miss Bolton said as she fixed the frog to Beatrice's frock. "And then you find out that wherever you go . . . you bring yourself with you."

"So . . . all is lost?" Beatrice asked miserably. If this was meant to be an encouraging talk, it was having the opposite effect.

"No!" Miss Bolton shook her head vehemently. "What I mean is that *you* are the key. Not Swampshire, or London, or anywhere else, for that matter. Your ability to thrive is not about where you live, it's about who you are." She pressed a finger to the center of the brooch. "You can hop from pond to pond, but that inexplicable luminescence is always within."

"That is easy for you to say," Beatrice said quietly. "You know how to trust yourself more than anyone I know."

"It takes practice," Miss Bolton told her. "You will get there."

"What if I am in over my head?" Beatrice asked, pressing a hand to the brooch as if it could transmit Miss Bolton's confidence into her through sheer proximity alone.

"You have been before. Think of all the times you fell into squelch holes!"

"I don't deserve any of this!" Beatrice finally cried. "I have been lying to you this entire summer, Miss Bolton," she confessed, the words coming out in a rush. "I have been sneaking out to investigate a murder, but it all went horribly wrong. Drake fired me—or quit, I'm not sure—and Sir Huxley betrayed me when he arrested Percival. Your entire perception of me is based on my horrible deception. I am not a well-behaved debutante. I am a failed inspector."

She held her breath, expecting Miss Bolton to gasp and clutch her chest in horror. Perhaps the woman would write to Mrs. Steele immediately and finish packing Beatrice's bags herself. No doubt she would agree that Beatrice must return to Swampshire.

But instead, Miss Bolton just pursed her lips and then patted Beatrice's hand.

"I thought that might be the case," she said. "You have never come off as well-behaved, dear."

"So . . . you're not furious?"

"I will only be furious if you give up before catching the killer!" Miss Bolton said sternly.

"But three men are dead, I have no leads and no partner," Beatrice told her, still miserable—but feeling the slightest spark of inspiration reignite, starting from where the beautiful frog brooch was pinned near her heart.

"Then it shall be just like old times," Miss Bolton told her, a mischievous look in her eye. "One should never underestimate an independent woman. That much I know." She picked up a stack of newspapers, which she had brought in with the tea tray, and handed them to Beatrice. "Perhaps to move forward, you must go back to the beginning. Remember who you are at your core."

She picked up the teacups, then, and gave Beatrice one. They clinked glasses, and Beatrice took a sip. She coughed, the liquid burning her throat.

"Is this—"

"Whiskey," Miss Bolton confirmed. "I thought we would need something a tad stronger than tea." She gestured to the papers. "When you are done perusing the crime columns, take a look at the social column. There is wonderful news: The end-of-summer masquerade shall continue! So drink up, read up, and then unpack your gowns. You must decide what to wear." With that, Miss Bolton flitted out of the room, saying something about needing to "brainstorm a costume that will truly 'wow' everyone . . . The hat, of course, shall be paramount . . . ," and leaving Beatrice alone with the crime column.

Miss Bolton was right—it *was* just like old times. And perhaps that was what Beatrice needed. To get back to a time when she trusted herself.

She flipped through the first paper—today's edition of *The London Babbler*. There was no crime column, Beatrice noted; apparently the *Babbler*'s reporter considered the case closed after the arrest of Percival Nash. She perused the rest of the stack, flipping through the pages of each *Babbler* until she found a column of interest.

"Curious Crimes" by Evana Chore.

Who *was* Evana Chore? Beatrice wondered. Sir Huxley wrote his own column, "Restoring Order," but this mystery woman had a completely separate crime column. It was admirable, really, and Beatrice was surprised she had not heard more of Ms. Chore.

But then Beatrice recalled something Elle Equiano had said once.

I only write of ribbons because my editor thinks it unbecoming for a lady to write about crime.

Why would her editor say this if a lady were already writing the crime section of *The London Babbler*?

Unless, Beatrice thought, staring at the byline, Evana Chore was no lady.

She took a quill and ink pot from out of her trunk, spread the paper out on her desk, and wrote out the letters, her hand shaking slightly.

EVANA CHORE

Now it was Lavinia's words that echoed in her mind.

The first letters in that headline spell "Rose." There were ninety-four words in that column. Nine plus four equals thirteen. "M" is the thirteenth letter of the alphabet. . . .

And then, Sir Huxley's reply—

Mr. Vane's wordplay inspired me; I thought I might have a little fun with my latest article.

Beatrice scribbled on the page. First she tried adding up numbers, attempting to copy Lavinia's methods . . . but finally she realized that the answer was simple. In fact, it was already there, in dark ink:

~~EVANA CHORE~~

HORACE VANE

She leaned back, staring at the words with grim satisfaction. It was an anagram. Horace Vane had been writing for his own paper—as the crime columnist, no less. While Mr. Vane had claimed to Diana that he supported the arts, "Evana Chore" had scorned the artists and subtly supported Percival's guilt from the beginning. Like the other gentlemen of the NAGS, Mr. Horace Vane wanted to discredit performers and diminish their influence. He simply used more nefarious, surreptitious means to do so.

Not that her discovery mattered, Beatrice thought with a pang of annoyance; Horace Vane could not be the killer. He was dead. And his anagram proved nothing, other than that Mr. Vane secretly wrote for his paper and appreciated wordplay. The latter of which everyone already knew.

People in Swampshire had their secrets, but the duplicitousness in London went beyond small-town skeletons in the closet. Everyone and everything had a public-facing persona with an entirely different character lurking beneath. Even Mr. O'Dowde's shop had a secret basement. No doubt the Rose had something similar. Perhaps even the NAGS were a front, Beatrice thought.

She sat up straighter.

"Yes," she murmured aloud, "what if . . ." She grabbed a jar of hat pins and began to tack pieces of paper onto the wall: Evana Chore's column, a sketch Drake had made of Cecil's moth tattoo, the old newspaper article about Horace and Diana . . .

It was almost as if she were back in her turret in Swampshire, solving Sir Huxley's cases by candlelight.

"Mr. Vane was close with Cecil Nightingale and Walter Shrewsbury," Beatrice murmured. "Gregory Dunne was jealous of their bond," she said, pinning an article in which Gregory had given a statement on behalf of the NAGS. "He is in the NAGS, but not in the inner circle," she continued. "Secret tattoos, a secret past . . . secret notes!"

She turned from the wall and wrenched open her desk drawer. On top was the paper she wanted.

Confess, or die. You decide.

It was the stiff, crinkled note she had stolen from Cecil Nightingale's pocket before his death. A strange texture, Beatrice had noted, as if it had gotten wet and then dried. Yet they had experienced a very hot summer thus far in London, with little rain. She smelled the paper.

Lemon.

Beatrice grabbed a candle from her desk and held it to the letter. For a moment, nothing happened. And then, as if by magic, a faint brown ink appeared.

Mr. Steele used such methods to send silly notes to his daughters. Yet, Beatrice reasoned, invisible ink could be used by others for more nefarious means.

She dropped into her desk chair and stared at the words that emerged on the back of the threatening note.

Horace—

I received this nasty little note this morning. Do you think it a joke—or something worse?

—Cecil

Below the first text, someone had penned a reply in a different hand.

Cecil—

Yes—I received the same. I fear someone has learned about what we did, but I will fix this. Do not be concerned. We are in it together. Umbra sumus.

Yours in the Brotherhood of the Moth,

Horace

"Miss Bolton!" Beatrice yelled. She took the newspaper with her and rushed downstairs, mind swirling with snippets of past conversations.

"Did you need more whiskey? I find the second serving is smoother!" Miss Bolton appeared at the bottom of the stairs with a teacup in one hand and a bottle in the other.

"You are writing a play in Latin, yes?" Beatrice asked, urgent.

"Yes!" Miss Bolton said, her eyes lighting up. "*Altus* is a sweeping examination of the way altos are overlooked—I suppose it's a metaphor, in a way—"

"Would you be able to translate a Latin phrase for me?" Beatrice cut in. She swore to herself that she would learn Latin in order to read Miss Bolton's play at some point, but now there was no time.

She was so close. She could feel it.

Miss Bolton turned and disappeared into the parlor. She reappeared a moment later, the teacup and bottle replaced with a book titled *Latin for Imbeciles.*

"I've been using it as a reference, while editing my play," she told Beatrice as she ascended the stairs. "As you know, I speak eight languages, but Latin can be so tricky."

"You speak *eight* languages?" Beatrice said, and then: "Never mind. I need to know the meaning of this phrase: '*umbra sumus.*'"

Miss Bolton flipped through the book. After a moment, she announced, "The best translation, I think, is 'We are shadow.' Or, to put it more poetically, 'We exist in shadow.'"

"Aha!" Beatrice cried. She waved the note in the air. "A close bond, strange tattoos, an exclusive social circle . . . a dark past, threatening notes, and this Latin phrase about shadows . . . Horace Vane, Cecil Nightingale, and Walter Shrewsbury were in a secret society!"

Miss Bolton gasped. "*No!*"

"Yes!" Beatrice said triumphantly. "And in their past, they did . . . something . . . which made the killer target them."

"And Percival Nash is innocent, of course!" Miss Bolton added.

"I never should have doubted myself—or him," Beatrice agreed. "But it is true that there is conflict between the artists and the NAGS." She paused. "There *is* someone who was left out of this group who sorely wished to be part of it. Someone who hated artists and would therefore have incentive to frame one for these murders."

His face crystallized in her mind: too-eager eyes and a visage overtaken by sideburns.

"Gregory Dunne," Beatrice whispered.

He would gain a prime power position by eliminating the three gentlemen who refused to admit him into their ranks. It was more than just a desire to be included, Beatrice could see now—Gregory wanted full control. And by framing Percival Nash, he would further the cause of the NAGS against local performers.

But he had not gotten away with it yet.

"We must get ready for the masquerade," Beatrice told Miss Bolton, a perfect mix of fear and excitement rising in her throat. "I have a plan to catch a man."

Miss Bolton gasped. "So you *have* found a husband?"

"No, even better," Beatrice assured her. "A killer." She turned on her heel and rushed back to her room.

Inspector Drake had abandoned the case, but that was no matter. He would only impede her now by claiming that her theories were too fanciful, too based on conjecture. She could practically hear him dismissing them as the folly of someone who read too many crime columns.

If she had time, she would pen him a note. Now she needed the two people who would not shy away from being fanciful, morbid creeps.

Dear Miss Steele,

Thank you for your letter, darling. I was not at the opera when recent events occurred, but trust that I am fine nonetheless—this is not my first Season. Remember that the London Menace was on the loose during the last Season—what a relief that *he* is gone, at least!

To answer your question: Yes, I would be happy to forge a note in Huxley's writing for the sake of trickery! As you know, I have already mastered his hand. What are friends for? I only hope that the contents you enclosed for the note do not indicate any attachment between you and the gentleman mentioned. In my opinion, you could do much better.

Please think of me for any future subterfuge, and I shall do the same for you. Consider the note sent, and I shall see you at the masquerade!

Your confidante,

Miss Elle Equiano xx

Dear Miss Steele,

A THOUSAND TIMES YES, I am available to dress you for the masquerade! Your costume idea is genius, and you are right; I am just the person to help you execute it.

I shall arrive in the morning at your town house with my crafting and costume supplies. We will need all day to prepare.

Your bosom friend,

Miss Lavinia Lee ♥

Dear Mr. Gregory Dunne,

Please meet me in the center of the maze at the masquerade, when the clock strikes nine. I want to discuss some concerns.

Sincerely,

Sir Lawrence Huxley

THE LONDON BABBLER

In Memoriam

Many will mourn my husband, Horace Vane. Ever since his passing, I have been trying to write a piece which encapsulates who he was at his core. Enigmatic at times, open at others—how could he ever be described in just one article? Too soon he was taken from us. All I can do is say that it was too soon. Too soon.

Dwelling on his life is the only way to cope with the grief. On many occasions Horace used his influence to improve our community. Caring for the wealthy was one of his passions. Kin was deeply important to him. Some thought Horace should have relented and allowed us our dipping pool at the Rose, but his views came from a place of love for nobility and tradition.

Who can ever really know another person? Even though I admit the validity of this sentiment, I think I did know Horace best. Essentially, at his core, he was a gentleman. So many try to define what that could be, but Horace exemplified it. Could I do anything to bring him back? All who know me trust that I would. Peer into my soul and know that I loved none but Horace Vane. Ending this obituary is impossible, for it requires me to admit that he is gone, and I cannot.

CHAPTER NINETEEN

A Disguise

The Sweetbriar pleasure gardens were in the center of the neighborhood, cordoned off by a tall hedge. Beyond the greenery walls lay a wild garden in the English style, thick with roses and peppered with stone fountains.

The air smelled of spices and fruit and baked confections, all offered by vendors on the outskirts of the gardens. But other than the chatter of guests securing drinks and refreshments, it was quiet.

Without any artists, the so-called party was more of a quiet shuffle through the garden. There was not even a single song with sweet notes to decorate the breeze. The NAGS had successfully created an event with no artists—and, Beatrice thought, it was as dull as to be expected.

"Punch?" a woman at a stand offered.

Miss Bolton took a long sip. "Lovely and strong," she exclaimed, "and thank goodness for that! My costume did not allow extra space for backup beverages."

Miss Bolton had transformed herself into an elegant squirrel for the evening, sporting a brown gown covered in fur that Beatrice suspected had been shed by Miss Bolton's dog. A majestic tail sprang from her back, and she wore a hat shaped like a giant acorn. Beatrice had helped sew tassels onto the ensemble, as Miss Bolton now considered them "necessary to any chic city garment."

"They must ensure we have plenty to drink, considering we cannot dance to silence unless inebriated," replied Elle Equiano. Fitting for a fisherwoman, she was dressed as a mermaid, with a gown of gold scales and sparkling lures as earrings.

Lavinia kept bumping into them, in a wide hoop skirt: She was the shepherdess from Sir Huxley's fourteenth case, the Murderous Herder. She had hand-embroidered a lavish pastoral scene across her gown and carried Miss Bolton's dog, Bee Bee, whom she had knitted into a sheep costume. It was a feat of crafting, but as they strode into the gardens sipping their punch, it was Beatrice's look that turned heads.

She wore heeled boots that gave her enough height to see the world in a new way, as well as—shockingly—trousers. She carried an asp-topped cane, wore a top hat, and had a full mustache affixed to her visage. The only off-theme accessory she wore was Miss Bolton's frog brooch, glistening on her lapel.

Whispers and giggles met her ears as she passed people.

"My goodness," someone said loudly. "She is Sir Huxley!"

"You really look just like him," Lavinia told her, tripping over her skirt and steadying herself with her shepherd's crook.

"Thanks to you," Beatrice said, affecting a gentlemanly bow. "I would trust no one else to know Sir Huxley's wardrobe and looks so intimately."

"It was nothing," Lavinia said, flushing scarlet. Bee Bee barked her approval.

What Lavinia did not know was that the costume was both playful *and* practical. Thanks to Elle Equiano's forged note, Gregory Dunne would be waiting at the center of the maze at nine o'clock, expecting to meet Sir Huxley.

And "Sir Huxley" would be there, ready to apprehend him for his crimes.

Until then, Beatrice had time to kill. Elle, Lavinia, and Miss Bolton were clearly enthralled by the masquerade, and she followed them from stand to stand, grateful for something to do.

She was buzzing with anticipation.

"This way," Miss Bolton said. "I must have some of those roasted nuts . . . such a snack will fit perfectly with my costume. . . ."

She and Lavinia joined the line at the booth, while Elle and Beatrice waited for them by a rosebush.

"You must explain this business with Mr. Dunne," Elle said the moment they were out of earshot of Miss Bolton. "I know you were skeptical about Huxley as a match, but Gregory is *much* worse. Think of the sideburns!"

"Do not worry," Beatrice assured her. "Gregory Dunne is not my top sweetheart. Only my top suspect." She held Elle's gaze.

"Hmm. I would like to hear more about *that,*" Elle said, nodding. "Perhaps you can tell me everything after the masquerade. Tea at my town house, at sunrise? I am certain Lavinia will want to join as well."

Beatrice's heart swelled. "Yes," she said immediately. "I will be there!"

If she could pull off what she hoped, she would apprehend a killer and then celebrate with her newfound friends, Beatrice thought. A dream come true—

If she could pull it off.

Miss Bolton secured her nuts, and they shuffled to the side of the crowd to stand along the hedgerow, watching clusters of costumed ladies and gentlemen pass by.

"I wish you could have seen it last year," Elle sighed. "There were acrobats on stilts . . . a portraitist who created the most comedic sketches . . . and of course, the Busy Nothings."

"The Busy Nothings?" Miss Bolton squawked. "I have not seen them since their tour in 1769, when I danced to their music all night, and they signed my bosom! That, er," she said, glancing sidelong at the young ladies, "that is what we used to call a reticule."

"Wait," Elle said, holding up a hand. "Do you hear that?"

The still night air had been pierced with the unmistakable sound of a quartet tuning their instruments. At once, Elle grabbed Beatrice and Lavinia and dragged them toward the noise. Miss Bolton followed, roasted nuts flying as she hurried to keep up.

Soon, they came to a larger opening in the garden maze, where a dance floor had been constructed. A cluster of musicians sat at the edge, tuning, and a crowd of excited guests began to gather.

"How did they get in?" Beatrice asked, looking around the crowd. "I thought no artists were allowed. . . ." Her eyes fell upon a hole in the hedge.

There was a door there that allowed surreptitious entrance into the maze. A pale hand held it open, a key dangling from one finger, a blood-red garnet ring flashing on another.

Diana.

She had clearly unlocked the hidden door, and more artists squeezed in through the opening: Jugglers, mimes, painters, and dancers dressed in colorful gowns poured into the party. The entire mood shifted nearly at once. Soon, the air was alight with excited chatter, poetry, and—

"Music!" Miss Bolton sang as the quartet struck up a tune. "Thank goodness, we can *dance*!"

But Beatrice was too distracted to dance. She moved toward the hole in the hedge. Diana Vane was meant to be in mourning, hidden away from society for the proper amount of time after the death of her husband. Yet here she was, making way for the artists of Sweetbriar to crash the masquerade. Before Beatrice could reach the woman, however, a figure blocked her path.

"Now, *here* is the best costume of the night. You look dashing."

It was Sir Huxley, dressed as a knight in shining armor. Of course. But Beatrice had to admit, the chain mail was flattering to his figure.

"All credit is due to Miss Lee," she informed him. "Now, if you'll excuse me—"

But Sir Huxley did not step aside, instead offering his hand to her. "Mrs. Huxley—I mean, Miss Steele—you must honor me with a dance."

Before she could protest, Beatrice found herself swept onto the dance floor in the arms of the man she had once admired.

"Really, such an impressive costume," Sir Huxley said again, pulling her into a spin. "I feel it is a testament to the perfection of this evening. Percival Nash is behind bars, and the deaths are also behind us." He shook his head. "Such a nasty business."

"A trivial description for what occurred, don't you think?" Beatrice said tartly.

"You are right, of course. It is tragic. That is where we are alike, Miss Steele. You and I understand the importance of emotion when solving cases. One cannot put aside one's biases, one's *feelings*. This is what Drake does not understand. Feelings are the core of a detective."

"Then why did you chide him for his?" Beatrice demanded.

"Because I knew it would drive him away from you." Huxley pulled Beatrice closer, enveloping her in his cloying cologne. "I cannot keep my own feelings obscured any longer," he murmured. "You are exactly the type of woman I have been searching for. Intelligent, interested in my line of work, attractive . . . You keep me on my toes, which I never thought I needed. After all, I am already so tall. Yet you raise me even higher."

Her stomach fluttered with a glimmer of the nervousness she had experienced with Inspector Drake on the rain-soaked street. Her lips seemed to tingle as they had before.

But in that case, she had wanted nothing more than for Drake to reveal his true thoughts. Now, she found, she wanted Sir Huxley to keep his to himself.

"I am a detective," she said firmly. "That is what I have always wanted. It is why I came to London."

"But you would not need to work," Huxley insisted. "Not if you were mine."

Unlike Drake's subtle scent of cinnamon and oranges, Huxley's expensive musk was overpowering. Stifling.

"Already your presence has made me an even better investigator," he went on. "Thanks to you, I swiftly arrested a wanted criminal."

"Because you followed me," Beatrice fumed. "And you arrested the wrong—"

"Think about it, Miss Steele," Huxley continued. "You would not have to solve my rejected cases. You would be the first to hear about my investigations, to contribute your opinion . . . if you were my sweetheart."

"So I would be waiting for you to regale me with tales of your adventures, and having none of my own," Beatrice summed up.

Somehow, she had found herself in the exact place her mother had always hoped she would be: between two men. But it was not quite how she'd imagined. Huxley wanted her as a paramour and not a partner, and Drake wanted her as a partner and not a paramour. At least Drake respected her as an inspector, though his attempt to deny his personal feelings had essentially destroyed their partnership.

They were both idiots, she decided, and she did not need either one of them now.

"I already belong to someone," she said finally.

"Vivek Drake?" Sir Huxley scoffed. "That sullen, serious, opera-obsessed—"

"I meant myself," she said, correcting him, and touched the frog brooch on her bodice. "My ability to thrive is about who I am. And I am a detective."

"Are you . . . *rejecting* me?" Huxley said, flabbergasted. "You do not care for me?"

"I thought I did, once," Beatrice said, thinking of the many cross-stitches she had completed that read, *Sir Huxley and Beatrice, sitting in a tree, i-n-v-e-s-t-i-g-a-t-i-n-g* . . . She had harbored feelings for him, yes, but she had also been interested in solving crimes.

And that was exactly what she was going to do.

The only idiot she needed to deal with now to do so was the person who had killed Horace, Cecil, and Walter. An idiot named Gregory Dunne.

Without another word, she left Huxley alone on the dance floor.

She rushed away, dodging out of sight of Elle and Lavinia. Miss Bolton had brought Bee Bee and was sharing a plate of finger sandwiches with her dog while they swayed in time to the band's music. None of them noticed as Beatrice wove through the hedges toward the maze's center.

Deeper into the maze, it was quiet. Beatrice passed a couple in the shadows, who whispered scandalously to each other, and dodged a group of contortionists who had gotten themselves into a pretzel she did not wish to see untangled.

She checked her pocket watch. It was nearly nine.

Beatrice picked up her pace as she made her way through the maze. The moonlight cast a silvery glow upon her path, and as she pressed toward the center, there were fewer and fewer stragglers.

The hedges widened. Stones crunched under her boots as she stepped forward. It was quiet, the air still warm. Somewhere, she could hear a clock strike.

"Detective."

A voice rang out behind her, and Beatrice turned to see a man step into the clearing.

He wore a long cloak and a mask that—she realized with a shiver—was fashioned to look like a moth. But behind the mask, she could still see his thick, unbecoming sideburns.

"Mr. Dunne," she said, affecting a low, arrogant voice.

Gregory halted. "Why does your voice sound like that?" he demanded.

"Er . . . too many cigars," Beatrice said.

"Ah. I have been there." Gregory shifted. He seemed nervous, Beatrice thought as she watched him lick his fingers and smooth his sideburns beneath the mask. "I received your note," he said finally. "You said you wanted to discuss something? Some . . . concerns?"

"You killed Horace Vane." Beatrice decided to go with a direct approach. Since she was dressed as a man, she felt that for the first time, she could get away with such forthrightness.

Even in the moonlight, she could see Gregory Dunne turn pale. "What? Of course I didn't!" he snapped. "How could you say such a thing? Didn't you arrest Percival Nash for the crime?"

"I was wrong," Beatrice said. *This* was a mistake she regretted immediately; Sir Huxley would never have admitted such a thing.

"When did you regrow that mustache?" Mr. Dunne said suspiciously, taking a step forward. Beatrice took a step back.

"Yesterday," she choked out.

"So quickly?"

"I am Sir Lawrence Huxley," Beatrice announced. "I can do anything."

Gregory Dunne halted and then sighed. "Yes. I appreciate how dedicated you have been to this case. You know that Horace and I were close. We were best friends, actually. So you can understand how offensive it is to suggest I had anything to do with his death."

She had not exactly expected a confession, but she felt thrown. Gregory seemed sincere.

"We are all in this together," Gregory went on. "You have done your job in arresting Percival, and now I will do mine. Just because Horace, Cecil, and Walter are gone, it does not mean that the NAGS will falter. It is up to me now," he said, squaring his shoulders. "And I have big plans. Just enjoy the distraction—I mean, the masquerade—and leave everything else to me."

With that, Gregory turned on his heel and strode away. Beatrice watched him go, his words ringing in her ears.

The distraction? Gregory Dunne was up to something, and she refused to let him get away with it.

She slipped into the shadows, following his form as he made his way through the maze.

Like a moth to a flame.

Dear Beatrice,

Thank you for your note. I agree that an unmarried woman writing to an unmarried man is wildly lewd, but I fear we are past such propriety.

At first, I thought you had drunk-quilled, as your ramblings were indeterminate. The annotated editions of *The London Babbler* you included also made no sense to me.

At first.

However, after several glasses of port (consumed in order to understand your own frame of mind, I assure you), I decided to apply your nonsensical methods to the most recent edition of the paper. Specifically, Mr. Horace Vane's obituary.

You are right. There is more to this case, and we must not give up. Please come to the office the moment you receive this. And, Beatrice—do *not* attend the summer masquerade. I fear only danger lies beyond the hedges of the pleasure garden.

~~Yours,~~

Most professionally,

Inspector Drake

CHAPTER TWENTY

A Sacrifice

Gregory slipped through the maze, footsteps sure, and Beatrice followed at a distance. As he wound around corner after corner, other men appeared and began to trail behind him.

What was going on? Beatrice thought. Where were they going?

The hedges opened up, and Beatrice realized that the maze spilled out at the front of the Rose Club.

The noise of the masquerade in the pleasure gardens drowned out the sounds of their footsteps.

A distraction.

Gregory took out a huge skeleton key and unlocked the gates. Another man was waiting just beyond the iron bars, holding some sort of fabric in his hands. Beatrice could see now that the fabric was a cape, and he held a mask fashioned to look like a moth, both identical to the costume Gregory wore.

As the other men following Gregory stepped through the gates, they each accepted a cloak and a mask.

A chill ran down Beatrice's spine as she watched them slip the masks over their faces, concealing their identities from view.

She fell into line, putting a hand over her face, shaking slightly.

If anyone recognized her, she was done for.

But her Huxley costume held true, a testament to Lavinia's talents. No one gave her a second look as she crossed beyond the gates and accepted a cape and mask of her own. She hastily tied the cape around her neck and slid the mask over her face, desperate for further disguise.

This was not what she had expected out of the evening—but she was not about to pass up the opportunity to infiltrate whatever was occurring.

She continued to follow the men, who stepped into the Rose.

Inside, the club was dark and silent. Beatrice fell into a single-file line of men walking down a long, narrow hallway. None of them spoke, and the swish of their cloaks sounded strangely like the flap of moth wings as they approached the end of the hallway.

Despite her heeled boots, Beatrice was too short to see where they were going. At first she thought the men were going into one of the club's rooms—the study, perhaps?—but then, when she finally got closer, she saw that they were approaching a large mirror on the wall.

Gregory pushed on the mirror, and it swung open to reveal a dark passageway, with stone steps leading down. He descended, and the line of moth men followed.

Finally, she was getting somewhere, she thought as she trailed them. Beatrice normally loved a lair . . . but this one filled her with a deep sense of foreboding.

The staircase stretched down several flights, leading deeper into the club until the air turned cool and the stairs opened up into a large chamber.

Unlike Mr. O'Dowde's artistic, hidden basement, this room

was not inviting or decorative. It was made of ancient stone, the walls jagged and windowless. The men formed a circle around the perimeter of the room, and Beatrice followed suit. They all turned to the center of the room, where the only furniture—if one could really call it furniture—was a stone slab.

On the slab was a glass jar. Beatrice leaned forward to make out the contents, and stifled a gasp.

There was a mummified hand inside. It still had some skin, but it was puckered and gray, peeling off in parts to reveal ivory bone. Men really had terrible taste in décor, Beatrice thought. A slab and a severed hand? That was sadistic *and* tacky.

As she stared at it, she noticed that around the hand's pinkie was a ring, encrusted with blood-red garnets. It was a ring she had seen before.

Why was Diana Vane's garnet ring on the finger of a severed hand?

The swishing sound of capes and footsteps stopped, and Beatrice looked away from the glass jar to see that the circle was complete. No more moth men descended the stairs, and the last to enter shut the door behind him, sealing them all in the underground chamber.

She felt a familiar spark in the pit of her stomach. It was the feeling she had experienced when solving her first crime, but until now, it had been dormant. It was excitement, the thrill of being just on the cusp of catching a criminal. It was the anticipation of justice about to be served.

That is, unless she was discovered.

She pressed her lips together, willing herself to stay calm, and focused her attention on Gregory.

"Thank you for coming," he said solemnly.

"Your note said this would be unlike a normal NAGS meeting," one of the masked men said. "I thought you meant because Walter, Cecil, and Horace are all gone. Not that we'd be forced to wear weird costumes and relocate to some disgusting basement. If we are to move our meetings down here, we should at least move the armchairs, as well. And where are our cigars and port?"

Some of the others murmured their assent. Beatrice, it seemed, was not the only one who disliked the room's décor.

"There will be time to redecorate later," Gregory said, raising his voice above the protests. "Now, we must focus on the problem at hand: Our leaders were murdered! Percival Nash thought he could stop us, but he was wrong. We will remain, stronger than ever. I have taken it upon myself," he went on, standing taller, "to ensure that Horace's legacy will live on."

"We will keep meeting, yes," another masked gentleman said, "but I do not understand what this is all about, Gregory. What *is* this place? Why are we dressed like insects?"

"We all know that Horace, Cecil, and Walter started the NAGS in order to protect Sweetbriar and uphold its traditional values," Gregory explained. "But they were even more dedicated than you all knew. This is where they met to discuss issues beyond what was raised at meetings. They were part of a brotherhood. A bond which went back to their schoolboy days."

"So what, you followed them here and eavesdropped on their conversations?" sneered another gentleman.

"As if that would get you invited into the group," another scoffed.

"And who is that?" someone asked, pointing at the hand. "I mean . . . who *was* that?"

"I . . . am not really sure," Gregory said, his confidence faltering. "I never overheard that bit. . . ."

Another man piped up. "Did they murder someone? I can't *kill* anyone!"

"Exactly!" another echoed. "We are gentlemen! If we want someone killed, or anyone's limbs chopped off, we will get our valet to do it for us."

"We don't need to kill anyone," another chimed in. "We have already won! Percival Nash has been arrested."

"But what is to stop another artist from taking up his mission to murder all the NAGS?" Gregory cried.

At this, a hush fell over the gentlemen.

"This is what I am trying to tell you," Gregory said, slowly regaining his self-assuredness as the men became attentive once more. "Banning the artists is not enough. We must have revenge! We must have order! Who do you think set the fires at the galleries to ensure any inappropriate portraits and landscapes were done away with? Who do you think sent mimes packing for Paris when their routines became too provocative? Who do you think disposed of manuscripts written by women? We all have been *talking* about what needs to be done . . . while Walter, Cecil, and Horace took *action*."

There were shocked whispers among the group. Gregory seemed satisfied; clearly the men had not known the extent of their leaders' efforts. But from the tone of their whispers, Beatrice deduced with dread, they approved.

"They had tattoos upon their wrists of the moth—a protector, cloaked in shadow. Now we are literally cloaked. As moths," Gregory went on. "We will take up the mantle the others left behind." He snapped his fingers, and the door opened once more. With horror, Beatrice saw two more men in cloaks and masks, leading Percival Nash to the stone slab in the center of the room.

The actor was pale, his eyes wide, his bare head wigless and exposed. He tried to fight back as the men pushed him onto the stone slab, but it was two against one. Percival was a performer, not a fighter—and he was outnumbered and easily restrained.

Surely these men did not mean to—

"Horace deserves justice," Gregory said loudly. "And we must send a message. We are in control. The consequences of dissent will be severe and final!"

Shockingly, Beatrice heard murmurs of agreement around the circle. They stepped closer in, and Beatrice felt panic ripple through her body.

There was one door that led out of the horrid chamber. What was Beatrice to do? This was the worst bind she had gotten herself into, and she had once gotten stuck in too-small stays.

"This sacrifice shall join us together in our common goal," Gregory said loudly. "It will be a secret we all share. And I will never be excluded again," he added under his breath, though his voice carried easily in the echoey room.

He took the torch off the wall and raised it high. Its flicker cast shadows across the men, their masks grotesque as gargoyles.

The rest of the men moved as one, and to Beatrice's horror, she could see that they all had taken knives from their pockets. They raised them in the air, toward Percival.

She had no gentleman's knife, no weapon, no way to save Percival. She had expected to eavesdrop, not witness some bizarre, ritualistic sacrifice. Why must everything in this city be so *extreme*?

The chamber was lit only by the light of that one small torch, Beatrice realized. A plan came to her in an instant, and she had no time to second-guess.

"Percival!" she shouted, tearing off her mask. "Use the power of breath support!"

Percival's eyes went wide, but he was a professional. He knew how to take a cue. He drew in a huge breath and blew toward Gregory's hand, extinguishing the light.

They were instantly plunged into darkness. There were shouts of confusion, the sounds of a scuffle, but Beatrice worked quickly. She knew she had only seconds.

She felt for the severed hand atop the stone slab, snatching it up. Then she lunged toward Percival and clasped her hand around his wrist, pulling him roughly toward where she knew the door was.

Someone reached for her cloak, and she felt it strain against her neck. She unclasped the fastener at the neck and slipped free, still dragging Percival, and shoved the door open.

But as the light of the stairwell beyond illuminated her, someone else grabbed at her hair. The blond Sir Huxley wig came off in his hands.

"Imposter!" he yelled. Beatrice kept moving forward, but another man grabbed her ankle, and she tripped.

"Go!" she yelled at Percival, shoving him to the stairs.

"Not without you!" He held out a hand, but Beatrice was being pulled back, back into the depths of the moths' lair. A moth man brandished his knife and slashed at her face, cutting her across one cheek. Another raised his own knife, aiming for her heart.

For the second instance in two days, time seemed to stand still. In the weapon's reflection of the light of the hall, Beatrice thought she could see the faces of everyone she loved: Her sister, Louisa, her red curls like flames. Her brother-in-law, Frank, with his crooked, flirtatious grin. Her niece, baby Bee Bee, with her wispy hair and round cheeks. Mr. and Mrs. Steele. A wolf, for some reason. Miss Bolton was there, of course, with dog Bee Bee—and—

Inspector Drake. Would Beatrice die without ever having the chance to tell him how she truly felt? If she even *knew* how she truly felt?

But Drake was not here. She was on her own. And one should never underestimate the power of an independent woman.

With this thought in her mind, Beatrice took Miss Bolton's brooch from her lapel and shoved it into the eye of her closest attacker. He screamed, and she withdrew the brooch—she could not lose such a precious gift, after all—then she ran.

She moves upon a cloud, my lady fair
For she was sent here from the skies above
The goddess who possesses silver hair
A huntress who has pierced my heart with love

Should I, a mortal man, ever deserve
To stand beside a moon so bright and true
Do I dare ask her? Do I have the nerve?
I fear I have to see this offer through:

My verses here, the worst I ever wrote.
I offer no great riches or great fame.
All I can do is hope you see this note,
Accept the ring I send, and take my name.

And when I look upon my hand, I'll know
The promise that we made those years ago.

Dear Oliver,

If you have already left for the colonies, perhaps this letter shall never reach you. Still, I must write, for I am both bewildered and heartbroken.

You wrote the most beautiful poems for me. I gave you my whole heart. We had a commitment to marry. Why, then, have you just sent word that you are leaving? Yes, there are opportunities for you abroad—but why not take me with you?

Horace Vane has made me an offer, as expected, but I wanted *you*. His pitiful puns are no match for your sonnets, as much as he tries.

I do not know what else to say. Evidently I cannot make you stay, so I will tell you this. I will marry Horace. He has money and influence, which is something. I will consider his dislike of the arts a challenge. I will transform him into a great supporter of all performers, painters, and even poets.

But know that, though I will rise to this challenge, I will never forget you. I will never remove the ring you gave me. I hope you keep yours, and that each time you look at it, you regret what you left behind in London.

Yours, still,

Diana

CHAPTER TWENTY-ONE

A Reveal

Percival and Beatrice moved up the stairs, through the Rose, and toward the iron gates as a cluster of men in masks pursued them. Beatrice could hear nothing but her pulse pounding in her ears as she flung herself at the gate—but it was locked.

"Stop!" Gregory yelled at them, but his instruction was not needed: They could run no farther without the key.

"I can't die!" Percival cried. "What will become of the Sweet Majestic? Of *Figaro*? My understudy is *pitchy*!"

"Leave it to me," Beatrice assured him. She used Miss Bolton's brooch once more, this time as a lock pick.

She struggled to see the tiny opening in the scant moonlight. She had to feel, rather than see, as she worked the brooch's sharp pin into the gate.

"It's the most secure gate in the city. You'll never—" Percival began, but broke off when the lock clicked.

They sprang free just as the men approached the gates, and

Beatrice slammed it shut behind them, the lock engaging once more.

"Get the key!" Gregory yelled, but the men merely rattled the bars in confusion.

"Who has it?" someone asked.

"I thought you did!"

Their voices faded as Beatrice and Percival rushed back through the hedge maze, pushing their way through crowds of masquerade attendees. Beatrice searched the crowd for a familiar face, but all she saw were blank stares behind masks.

She had to get Percival to safety, before he was recognized and apprehended. Before the NAGS sprang free.

She stared around wildly, feeling helpless, the crowd blending together in a whirl of colors and sparkles and fabrics and masks.

Until she spotted the beautiful sight of a tassel ground into the dirt. And then, several feet in front of it, another tassel.

Bless Miss Bolton and her fashion choices, Beatrice thought. And bless her own poor skill at sewing, for she had helped to affix the tassels to Miss Bolton's masquerade gown. So naturally, Miss Bolton was shedding them wherever she went.

Creating a clear path so Beatrice might find her chaperone.

Beatrice grabbed Percival's hand and pulled him down the tassel path. Before long, Beatrice was—for the first time—utterly relieved to see a squirrel blocking her way.

"Miss Bolton!" she cried, rushing toward her chaperone. She practically pushed Percival into the small woman's arms. "Get him somewhere safe," she instructed.

"You're abandoning me?" Percival cried.

"Take him to the town house," Beatrice continued. "Don't let anyone see."

"It would be my honor," Miss Bolton said at once. "But—are you not coming with us? Where have you been? What is going on?"

In reply, Beatrice held up the jar of severed hand. Miss Bolton recoiled.

"I must take care of something," she told Miss Bolton. "We have to part ways."

For a moment she thought Miss Bolton would protest. She thought the woman would insist that they stick together—that she accompany Beatrice wherever she might go. But to her relief, Miss Bolton nodded.

"Of course," she said. Miss Bolton removed her acorn hat and covered Percival's bald head with it, obscuring his identity from view. "I will take care of our star. You go—just do not let anything happen to you, Beatrice, or your mother will be *very* angry with me."

At that moment, someone hurtled toward them.

Gregory Dunne, his moth mask askew, was rushing at Beatrice, face twisted in anger. Just before he reached them, Miss Bolton held out her foot and tripped him. He crumpled to the ground in a heap of cape and mask and sideburns.

"A good chaperone knows when to put her foot down," Miss Bolton said proudly. "Now, Beatrice—*run*!"

Beatrice did not have to be told twice. She turned on her heel and rushed through the crowd, dodging jugglers, clowns, and mimes.

Gasping for breath, Beatrice finally made it to the other end of the pleasure garden, where a row of hired vehicles waited to take partygoers back to their homes at the end of the night. She and her chaperone had walked to the event, since Miss Bolton's hat was too high to fit into a carriage compartment—but perhaps Beatrice might co-opt someone else's vehicle?

Before she could attempt such a thing, the door of one of the carriages banged open.

"Get in," Inspector Drake instructed.

Without question, Beatrice flung herself into the carriage. The driver took off.

It was a small cabin, and Beatrice found herself seated across from Drake, who looked utterly panic-stricken.

"You got into a carriage? Willingly?" she asked incredulously.

Drake nodded but couldn't seem to say more.

"I am sure the driver is capable," she assured him, but he shook his head.

"It's not my fear of carriages—well, that is always present—but your face."

"It was a silly costume," Beatrice said, tearing off her mustache. Drake still looked concerned, and Beatrice was now aware of a stinging sensation. She lifted her hand to her cheek and withdrew it.

Blood.

"Oh, that. I was stabbed!" she said excitedly. "And look what I found!"

She held up the severed hand in triumph, and Drake drew back in disgust.

"What is *that*?"

"I am fairly certain it is the hand of Oliver Beauchamp," she told him. "You see this?" She pointed at the garnet ring on the skeletal finger. "Diana Vane has one just like it."

"Clearly you are far ahead of me. I shall require more explanation," Drake said, looking from the bloody garnets to Beatrice's bloodstained face.

"Horace Vane, Cecil Nightingale, and Walter Shrewsbury had a bond, going back to their school days. I believe they formed a sort of secret society," she told him.

"The NAGS," he said, but she shook her head.

"They were the founders of that group, yes, but I believe they had an inner circle within the larger group. Gregory discovered it, since he was always hanging about them. . . . The NAGS are just the surface. The fires destroying local art, the squirrel infestations, these are all the works of the inner circle," she explained. "The Brotherhood of the Moth."

"The moth," Drake repeated, his eye wide. "Their tattoo."

"A symbol of their secret," Beatrice said, nodding. "For years they operated in the shadows, surreptitiously enacting the darkest wishes of their members. But then the three of them received threatening letters, telling them to confess or die. But *what* did the blackmailer want them to confess? A simple fire or encouragement of unwanted squirrels is not bad enough for blackmail. Murder, on the other hand . . ." She shook the jar.

"Perhaps we might put away this prop," Drake said, taking the jar from her grasp and setting it aside with a shiver.

"Oliver Beauchamp was a poet," Beatrice went on. "He and Diana were meant to be married, until Oliver went 'off to the colonies,' or so it was said. . . . I believe that was a load of hogwash. Horace, Cecil, and Walter killed him."

She and Drake shared a grim, yet victorious, look. Any past annoyance, any tension between them, had gone.

They were *back.*

"They killed him . . . and kept his hand?" Drake said, prompting Beatrice to continue.

"No doubt they chopped off the limb he used to pen such perfect poetry," she told him. "Horace Vane said it himself . . . he saved trophies of his conquests."

"Miss Steele," Drake said, his brows knit together in concern, "sometimes I fear the places your mind goes."

"Thank you," Beatrice said, then went on: "Mr. Vane could have convinced Cecil and Walter to help him commit the murder. For him, it was personal, but he knew that Cecil and Walter hated artists like Oliver. No doubt he played upon this prejudice. I saw just now how far some of these gentlemen are willing to go to keep their power when they think it is at risk. But someone found out about Oliver and blackmailed the three of them. 'Confess, or die,'" she quoted from the nefarious note.

"Would they have faced any consequences, had the truth come out?" Inspector Drake pointed out. "It might be cynical to say, but I doubt the authorities would prosecute three upstanding gentlemen over the death of a poet most people have forgotten. Sometimes even murder is not enough."

"Yes," Beatrice agreed, "but love is. If the truth came out, Mr. Vane would have lost Diana. She is the reason he did all of this in the first place. She loved Oliver, and Mr. Vane killed him. That knowledge would certainly have put a damper on their relationship. It's almost romantic," she added thoughtfully. "Mr. Vane loved Diana so much that he was willing to kill in order to marry her."

"I shudder to think what kind of romance you are reading," Drake replied.

"None at all, Inspector," Beatrice said with a small smile. "You know I only care for the crime columns."

He returned her smile, but then his expression turned grim once more. "So they killed Oliver, and someone found out. Why would Cecil and Walter agree to keep quiet when their lives were on the line? *They* did not have loves to lose. They had nothing to lose, really, by speaking up."

"I think you are right. I think they *wanted* to speak up," Beatrice said, her heart pounding, palms sweating, as she put the pieces together. Her entire body was awash with the thrill of answers—at long last. "That is why I think that Horace Vane killed Walter Shrewsbury and Cecil Nightingale to stop them from confessing."

"He was on the scene for both murders," Drake said, considering this.

"He knew that Cecil Nightingale was dead, without confirming that fact," Beatrice reminded him. "We saw how he professed the death so quickly. He bashed in their faces first, because he felt guilty for killing his friends. He could not bear to look at them while doing the deed. . . ." She shivered at the thought, then went on. "Mr. Vane also could have planted the evidence against Percival Nash and Caroline Wynn. Thus he would get rid of his problem—two men who knew a secret which could ruin him—and frame artists he detested in the meantime. A perfect plot," she pronounced.

Until she remembered: "Dash it all. I keep forgetting—Horace Vane was murdered." At once, frustration replaced her short-lived triumph. "He might have stopped Cecil Nightingale and Walter Shrewsbury from speaking out . . . but the blackmailer killed him, too."

"Yes," Drake said with a nod. "I would dismiss everything you just said as wild conjecture, but I fear I have been indulging in some myself. And I believe I can add to what you have ascertained, and therefore make sense of the rest." He withdrew a copy of *The London Babbler* from his jacket pocket. "There is one surefire way to stop a killer from killing you."

"How?" Beatrice demanded.

"Die before they can do it," Drake said simply. He began to unfold the paper. "I have been considering the facts: Mr. Shrewsbury and Mr. Nightingale were murdered in private spaces. Yet Mr. Vane was killed in front of a crowd at the Rose. Almost as if there was meant to be an audience for this death in particular. Then there was the matter of the battered faces. While your theory that the killer did not want to look at his victim is plausible, it feels thin."

Beatrice began to object but then stopped herself. "That's fair," she allowed.

"He could have simply stabbed him from behind," Drake continued. "So I had to consider: What if the beating was not for the sake of the killer's emotion, but to conceal the face of the victim?"

"Conceal the face? For what purpose?" Beatrice did not follow. "We know the identities of all the victims. Walter was identified at the scene, we knew Cecil from his handkerchief . . . and Horace had his wallet. Though . . . he did not have his most prized personal effect," she recalled. "The sweetbriar, encased in glass. We assumed the body was him, without real evidence!" She gasped, finally realizing: "Horace Vane faked his death!"

Drake flipped to a page in the paper he had produced. It was an old edition of the *Artists' Quarterly,* Beatrice could see, and Drake turned to a page of classifieds and pointed at one. Beatrice began to read.

> ACTOR WANTED for exciting and unconventional role. Must be tall, dark, handsome, and willing to alter appearance for the sake of the integrity of the work. Please send inquiries to Miss Evana Chore at *The London Babbler*.

"When you sent me the note explaining that Evana Chore was actually Horace Vane, I recalled this unusual ad I had seen in the paper," he told her. "What if—"

"Mr. Vane hired a lookalike, and murdered him instead!" Beatrice cried. "Drake—'willing to alter appearance.' The body we saw in the box had a moth tattoo, but when I examined it with Miss Equiano's quizzing glass, I noted that the skin around it was puckered and raw. I thought that perhaps Mr. Vane had tried to remove his tattoo, to save himself—but what if the hired actor had been asked to get a *new* tattoo for the 'role'? That is why it looked raw; it was recently inked!"

Drake leaned forward and slipped his hand under the neckline of her shirt.

"Inspector!" Beatrice inhaled sharply—what was he *doing*? Why *now*?—but Drake's fingers caught the chain of her silver locket. He pulled it free from under her costume and ran his fingers over the heart shape.

"You found this in the pocket of the corpse who died at the opera," he said. "But there is no reason Horace Vane would have had it. It was stolen by—"

"Archibald Croome," Beatrice finished. She remembered the soliloquist who had blocked her path in the street with an irritating poem. She could see his visage upon the portrait he'd thrust into her hands. "A desperate actor. He would have taken any role . . . just the sort of person to answer an open call in the *Quarterly*."

"He did not know this role would be his last," Drake said sadly. His fingers slipped up the chain and brushed across her neck, but then he cleared his throat and drew back.

"So Mr. Vane killed Cecil and Walter, setting it up to look as though gentlemen were being targeted," Beatrice continued, "and then he put his plot into action. He sent Diana out of the box to fetch drinks."

"Archibald was likely hiding behind the box's curtains," Drake said. "According to the measurements of the box, which I studied in the theater's blueprints, a person could easily conceal themselves in the corner," he added.

"Then he came out the moment Diana left, thinking he was to be part of some performance, and instead Horace murdered him and put his personal effects into his pockets, though he couldn't bear to part with the sweetbriar. . . . *Drake!*" she cried, remembering with horror: "'The actor.' The last words he spoke—we thought it was Horace, telling us that Percival Nash had killed him, but it was Archibald Croome, trying to tell us the truth. That he was the hired actor, not Horace Vane."

"Precisely." Drake nodded. "Mr. Vane used the same method

of murder as in the previous two deaths so no one would question a thing. After all, it had already happened twice. But the third body was a doppelgänger—just like in the infamous prequel *The Figaro Trap*."

"So that is it," Beatrice said, feeling winded. "Horace Vane murdered his rival, then his two best friends, and then an innocent—though annoying—actor. Four people are dead, and he got away with the whole thing."

"Of course he won't get away with it," Drake said evenly. "This is *our* case. And we always get our man."

"We've only gotten our man once," Beatrice told him.

"And now we shall do it a second time. Two for two," Drake replied.

At this, the carriage came to a halt.

"Wait," Beatrice said, drawing back the carriage compartment's curtain. "Where are we?"

Outside the window, gulls screeched, and the moon shone down on a huge port filled with ships. Beatrice turned to Drake for an explanation.

He held up an annotated copy of the most recent *London Babbler*, pointing at Horace Vane's obituary. He had circled the first letter of each sentence, revealing a message that had been hidden among the words, spelling out:

MEET AT DOCKS. WE ESCAPE.

"Mrs. Vane wrote this obituary. Look at the message concealed within," he told Beatrice.

"She used her husband's own word-scrambling trick to send him a message!" She gasped and grabbed the paper. "So . . . Diana knew he wasn't dead?"

"Horace must have told her some version of events. As you said, everything he has done aligns with a wish to preserve his relationship with his wife. He would hardly let her believe that he had died," Drake replied.

"But he *would* let her believe in his innocence," Beatrice said grimly. "She doesn't know he is a killer!"

"This paper came out this morning," Drake informed Beatrice. "I checked the logs, and there is only one packet ship scheduled to depart tonight. What better time to escape than while everyone is distracted at the masquerade?"

"We must save Diana," Beatrice said immediately, "and apprehend Mr. Vane!"

Drake pushed open the carriage door. "Are you up for more peril?"

"Vivek Drake," Beatrice answered, heart pounding, "I thought you'd never ask."

My dear Diana,

I told you in the box at the Sweet Majestic, just before everything happened, that I would explain all in time. I told you to trust that I would be all right, and to fetch us drinks, and then sit tight until you heard instructions.

I am sorry that I was not with you to drink that champagne, but as promised, here are those instructions.

Someone wishes me harm. I cannot tell you why, for I do not wish you to be drawn up in the situation. My secrecy is for your safety. But we cannot stay in Sweetbriar any longer because of the threat. It is imperative that we leave London. We must escape—together.

I cannot include a return address with this note, for my own safety. You must burn this letter after reading it. But if you trust me—and if you will flee with me—book two tickets of passage on a ship bound for the colonies. Send me a message through the *Babbler* when you have done so, and I will know the plan is on.

I have never cared that I was your second choice. You were always my first.

Yours,

Horace

CHAPTER TWENTY-TWO

An Admission

The smell of brine and fish was thick in the air as Beatrice and Drake approached the water's edge. The Thames looked eerie in moonlight. The water sparkled silver and the ships' sails rustled in the night breeze, small waves sending the boats creaking from side to side. Most of the boats were quiet, their sails furled, captains asleep somewhere safe on shore.

Except one.

A packet boat rocked on the water, movement aboard drawing the eye. A few sailors walked around the deck, unfurling sails. A gangway stretched from the dock to the boat, and crew members carried boxes of mail and packages from shore to ship.

Though Beatrice had only dreamed of embarking on a voyage by sea, she knew that packets were the quickest way to travel from England to the colonies. They were used mostly to transport letters and a small crew, but a few passengers were also permitted on board. It appeared that this voyage *would* contain a passenger. He waited at the end of the gangway, two trunks at his feet.

Horace Vane—very much alive.

"I knew it," Drake growled.

Mr. Vane turned toward the sound of his voice, his chiseled features and salt-and-pepper hair illuminated by the moon. He let out a noise somewhere between frustration and laughter.

"Beatrice Steele and Vivek Drake," he said, "you two have a knack for turning up where you don't belong."

"We know the truth," Beatrice told him. "It's all over, Horace."

"Mr. Vane," he said, correcting her, his eyes crinkling as he smiled.

"You have not earned such respect," she told him.

"I don't have to earn it," Horace said, squaring his shoulders. "There is a hierarchy in the world, inherent things which gentlemen like me are due. I am your superior, Beatrice."

"That is Inspector Steele to you," Drake said. "And I do not think *you* could be considered anyone's superior."

"Why do you hate artists so much?" Beatrice demanded. "It was only one you were after, in the end. Oliver Beauchamp."

Horace's eyes narrowed. "Perhaps at first," he said in a low voice. "But I realized something important, *Beatrice.* Oliver was representative of the dangers all artists pose. I do not 'hate' artists. I fear them." He lifted his chin. "I am not naïve. I see the influence that a painting, a song, a performance, has on people's hearts and minds. It can effect change. Topple the correct ways and order of society. Give power to those who have never had it and therefore don't deserve it. Precisely the things I do not want." He held up his arm, drawing back his sleeve. "Before the NAGS, there was the Brotherhood of the Moth. A pact between myself, Cecil, and Walter. From the shadows, we would do what needed to be done to preserve proper principles. We created the

NAGS years after our schoolboy pact, so we could recruit others to the cause. But not everyone would go as far as us. The NAGS were our wings, but we were the thorax, ensuring what needed to happen would occur."

"Why the thorax?" Drake cut in. "I don't follow your metaphor—"

"It is just a little wordplay!" Horace snapped, his cheery tone faltering for the first time. "I never said I was a writer."

"*That* is obvious," Drake replied.

"You will face justice for what you have done. And I don't mean your faulty metaphors—I am speaking of murder," Beatrice told him, taking a step forward, but Horace just chuckled again, his affable countenance returning.

"I don't know why you are so angry with me, Beatrice. I have been nothing but nice to you. And I didn't have to be. I am a nice man."

"You killed four people," Beatrice said incredulously. "Two of whom were your closest confidantes!"

"Who betrayed me," Horace told her. He indicated his tattoo. "*I* took our bond seriously."

"This has gone on longer than the villain's speech in *Figaro and Don Giovanni*," Drake cut in. "A failed crossover," he explained to Beatrice, then turned back to Horace. "Your monologue is up; we are apprehending you now." He lunged forward, but Horace held up something that gleamed in the moonlight.

A blade, embossed with the words THE SWEET MAJESTIC.

"I had an extra one of these made," he said conversationally. "One should always have a backup. If you had done so with your dress back when my carriage first sprayed you with mud, *Beatrice,* all of this could have been avoided. Isn't life funny that way?"

"We know you made custom knives to try to frame Percival Nash," Beatrice said dryly. "It was hardly clever; Drake noted at once that they were fake."

"I also sent a squirrel statue to frame Felicity Lore," Horace replied, "just in case Percival ever came up with an alibi."

"You *do* always have a backup," Beatrice said. "Is that because you *are* a backup? Diana never wanted to marry you." She let the words hang in the air.

If she could unarm him somehow, they could still catch him, she thought furiously.

"Diana did not know what she wanted. And in the end, it wasn't her decision to make," Horace said pleasantly. He was frustratingly unprovoked. "An artist would never have been an appropriate match for such a high-class lady. She was always meant to be mine."

"A lady must have a say," Beatrice told him. "Or else it is not true love."

It happened too quickly for Beatrice to register: The moment the words left her lips, Horace raised his arm and hurled the knife through the air, straight for Beatrice. Drake shoved her aside, and the blade lodged itself in his arm. He crumpled to the dock.

Beatrice immediately rushed to Drake's side.

"Now, *that* is the appropriate use of your skills, Beatrice," Horace told her. "Assisting Mr. Drake."

"*Inspector* Drake," she snapped. His wound was deep, but it would not be fatal. Not if she could stop the bleeding—but she had to fast.

"Let it be a lesson to you: Never try to stand on equal footing with a gentleman," Horace continued. "Nothing good can come of it. Though," he added thoughtfully, "I suppose Mr. Drake is no gentleman, in the end."

Even with these final words, he still spoke amiably. Kindly. He *was* nice, Beatrice thought.

But nice did not mean much at all.

Horace turned on his heel and ascended the gangway. Two

valets appeared and dragged the trunks on board, and a ship hand pulled up the gangway behind them, collapsing the connection to shore.

The ship began to float from the port toward the horizon. The sky and water were the same pitch-black, blending together, and it was as if the ship were being swallowed by darkness.

"Drake," Beatrice said, focusing in on her partner, "are you all right?" She grasped the knife and pulled it from his wound, then tore a strip of fabric from her Huxley costume. She wrapped it around his arm, tying it tightly to stop the bleeding.

For a moment Drake was quiet as he composed himself. And then, he spoke in a low, angry growl.

"No one gets away with ruining an evening at the opera . . . or quadruple homicide."

"It's too late," Beatrice told him miserably. "The ship is leaving. He already got away with it."

Drake's mouth curved into a smile. "If you ever get to see an opera in full, you shall learn that the best ones have a twist in the third act. We have come to ours," he told her.

He winced in pain as he pushed himself to his feet. With his unharmed arm, he reached into his jacket and withdrew a small parcel. He tore it open with his teeth, took out the contents, and hurled them toward the boat.

As a handful of little balls hurtled through the air, Beatrice looked from them to the packet, and recognized the stamp on the container. Mr. McCrockett's Shop-o'-Tricks—her father's favorite brand of firecrackers.

The balls scattered in the wind, but they hit their intended mark. They smacked against the ship's sail, and the impact caused their casings to implode. Seven tiny explosions lit up, orange and red against the moonlit sails. There were shouts aboard as sailors rushed to the sails, but the damage was done. The sails caught fire, their rough fabric no match for pyrotechnics. Beatrice could see how her father had accidentally burned down a wing of their home back in Swampshire—he favored heavy-duty pranks.

The sailors began to scramble. Beatrice could just make out Horace on the deck, his face darkening. He glared at Beatrice, then turned and strode away, toward the ship's bow.

"Horace was right," Drake told her, turning back to Beatrice. "You should not stand on equal footing with me. You must stand higher." With fiery determination in his eye, he knelt down and interlaced his hands.

"But then you won't be able to follow me," she said, meeting his gaze. "I will have to go alone."

"Yes," Drake agreed. "I trust you will be able to finish the job."

Her chest grew warm with his words. She had longed to hear them since she came to London. Though she didn't need them now—she had learned to trust herself—she *wanted* them.

She placed her foot in Drake's hands, and her palms on his shoulders.

"Ready?" he said.

She nodded, swallowing back any nerves. "One . . . two . . ." she said. "Three."

Drake launched Beatrice into the air, and she hurtled toward the ship. She plummeted down just shy of the deck and landed against the ship's side with a smack. But she had anticipated this and flung out her arms. Her hands curled around the edge of the ship, and she managed to hoist herself over the rail. She scrambled onto the deck, her heart pounding.

"Oi! Stowaway!" one of the crew members yelled, but Beatrice shoved past him. The other deckhands were too busy putting out the fire in the sails to notice a lady half-dressed as a gentleman racing across the deck toward the back of the boat. Where she knew Horace and Diana would be waiting. He had two trunks, after all; his wife had to be somewhere on the boat.

As Beatrice ran, she could practically see Diana's face in her mind. Could practically hear her dreamy voice. She had no idea how her husband had betrayed her, that he was a killer.

Or did she?

If Diana had found out the truth . . . if she had learned of Oliver's murder . . .

There is little which goes on there that I am not privy to.

The woman had a dreamlike air about her. She seemed detached from the world, almost floating above it. Yet there was a sharpness behind that wistful exterior. Diana knew that Beatrice had been investigating. She insisted upon Percival's innocence. And she had defied the NAGS by letting the artists into the masquerade that very evening.

They had never determined, Beatrice thought with a chill, exactly who sent the threatening notes that Walter, Cecil, and Horace had received. Now she had a guess.

Beatrice rounded a sail and Diana's tall frame came into view. Her silver hair floated around her head in the sea breeze, wild tendrils framing her face. She stood next to Horace, both of them staring out at the water.

Beatrice thought she should grab Diana, get her away from her murderous husband.

But she had a hunch that Mrs. Vane was not the one in danger now.

"Mr. Vane!" Beatrice yelled, still running as fast as she could to reach the couple. "Step away at once—for your own safety!"

If Diana knew the truth, if she had been blackmailing her husband and his friends, she would have no plans to escape with Horace. She had always meant to hold him accountable.

They were a deadly pair.

"Oh, Beatrice, you are so dramatic," Horace said with a laugh, watching Beatrice race toward them, as if he did not have a care in the world. "A pity that art is dead in Sweetbriar—you might have made a fair playwright yourself. My dear," he said to Diana, "you may want to look away. This bloom is the root of our problems—and I am going to take care of the thorny issue, once and for all."

But Diana did not look away. She stared at Horace, fixing him with a piercing glare.

"I always thought that puns were the lowest form of wit," she told him.

With that, she pulled the hat pin from her hair and raked it across his chest. Horace's eyes went wide as the sharp tip pierced his flesh. He pressed his fingers to the blood that welled from the wound, in apparent disbelief, and then extended his arms toward his wife.

For a moment it seemed Diana was reaching back to embrace him—

But instead of taking his hands, she shoved him hard. He toppled off the boat, hitting the water with a stomach-churning *crack*. And then he sank into its depths, the Thames consuming his body.

Horace Vane had died and come back to life, and now he was gone forever.

Finally, Beatrice reached the edge of the ship. She was panting hard. Everything had moved so quickly. Now, time stood still.

As she approached Diana, something crunched under her boot. Beatrice looked down to see the glass-encased sweetbriar. It had fallen from Horace's pocket, and now the rose was free from the frame.

"You were the blackmailer, all along," Beatrice said, looking from the flower to Diana, who still faced the water.

"Yes," Diana said, not turning around.

"You found out about Oliver," Beatrice said, taking careful steps forward. Slow, now, after her sprint seconds before.

"When he first disappeared, I was heartbroken. I was certain he had left me," Diana replied, staring into the water. "And Horace swooped in. He said he loved me. I was so vulnerable. . . . I agreed to marry him. He had money and a good name. He made a case for himself. I thought we would have an agreeable life together. I never suspected the truth, back then."

Finally, she turned toward Beatrice. With her silver hair swirling in the breeze and her catlike features illuminated by moonlight, she looked like one of the Rose's statues. A vengeful goddess, Beatrice thought with a shiver. Horace had been evil, but Diana was something else entirely.

"Do you know how I found out that Oliver was dead?" Diana asked, her voice soft. "How I realized what my husband had done?"

Beatrice raked through everything she knew about the Rose. About Diana and her husband's indulgence.

To Diana's face, Horace had appeared the picture of support. He had assured her that he loved the arts. He had attended the opera with her. But in private, he had used the NAGS—and his inner circle—to sabotage the culture his wife adored.

There was only one time that Beatrice had seen Horace openly defy Diana. Only one time that Beatrice could recall when he had said "no" to her face.

Mrs. Vane suggested the dipping pool, Cecil Nightingale had said, *but Mr. Vane refused. The rose garden was part of the building's original construction. . . . One cannot simply change tradition.*

"The pool," Beatrice said finally.

"Precisely," Diana said, and her eyes met Beatrice's. "I wanted to install it, and Horace refused, which was very uncharacteristic of him. He was always so *nice* . . . yet he protested. Vehemently. He claimed we must keep up tradition by preserving the Rose as it was. I might have believed him. . . ."

"But the garden was not part of the original design," Beatrice finished.

Diana nodded. Beatrice remembered Drake's words: *One must always study the blueprints . . . the rose garden . . . was added about twenty years ago.*

"It was built around the same time that Oliver went missing.* I began to suspect what might be buried underneath the roses." Her voice broke, but she composed herself and continued, her story like a stream that could not be stopped now that she had begun. "Tensions were mounting between the NAGS and artists. Horace claimed he supported my viewpoints, but by then I doubted everything he said." She faced Beatrice, who stood next to her now. "I had to determine his guilt once and for all. He never did anything without his closest confidants—Walter and Cecil—so I sent notes to all three of them. Confess, or die. Whatever they had done, I thought, would come to the surface, whether it was murder of the arts or just pure murder. All I asked for was the truth," she said, her dark eyes glimmering. "I never thought it would lead to all of this."

She uncurled her fingers and let the blood-soaked hat pin drop to the ship's floor.

"'And when I look upon my hand, I'll know / The promise that we made those years ago,'" she murmured, twisting her garnet ring around her finger.

For the first time, Beatrice felt touched by poetry. The couplet was unremarkable, but to Diana, clearly, it meant the world.

The woman had married the man she was meant to, based on her rank and wealth—and look what had become of it. The NAGS claimed they were doing what was best for everyone by promoting their hierarchy, yet in the end they all had lost.

There was still chaos on the ship. Crew members raced to put out the fire, assessing the damage done by the fireworks. The

* Strangely, this was also when many began to witness the one-handed "Specter of Sweetbriar," reciting sad poems about a lost love.

flames had singed the canvas sails, and they were being forced to bring the packet back to port.

A piece of sail, still fiery, floated down on the breeze. Beatrice reached up and caught it.

"Finally—a light," Diana said. She took a cigar from her reticule and put it between her lips. Wordlessly, Beatrice held the flame to the end of it, setting Diana's cigar ablaze. "I tried," Diana murmured, between drags of her cigar. "I always believed in Percival. In all of them. They have the ability to change our society for the better."

"That's why you let the artists into the masquerade," Beatrice said quietly. "One last act of defiance."

"Haven't you learned anything from the *Figaro* franchise, Miss Steele?" Diana said, raising one eyebrow. "There's never a *last act*. Another sequel is always in the works. I will surrender myself," she assured her, "but it's not the end. Not yet."

As the ship changed direction, there was the sound of more popping—this time in the distance.

Beatrice and Diana turned toward the direction of Sweetbriar to see fireworks exploding above the pleasure gardens. In spite of everything, the masquerade had gone on, and the shimmering sparkles showered overhead, their glimmer reflected in the Thames. Though the night seemed all-consuming, the sun would rise again. Beatrice would have to get home to change. After all, Elle and Lavinia would be expecting her at tea, and she could hardly show up in her current ensemble.

Another firework exploded in a shower of gold. Diana offered Beatrice the cigar, but she shook her head.

"Good choice. Once you start down that path . . ." Diana trailed off, taking a long drag.

In a way, Beatrice thought, Diana had been the perfect gentlewoman—yet she had still been cornered. Manipulated. Lied to. If this was the best that ladies could hope for, why play a role in the show at all? And how much worse would it all be for someone without Diana's circumstances? At least the patroness had attempted to use the power she *did* have to advocate for such people. This bit, Beatrice could not help but admire. The murdering bit, not so much . . .

"You are smart, Miss Steele," Diana said as the ship brushed against shore. Crew members scrambled to drop anchor and tie the boat to iron poles, fireworks still crackling in the distance. "I can see you have a future as a detective. But if you think you have seen the worst of London, think again. My husband was merely the warm-up. There is true evil waiting in the wings. You must ask yourself: Are you prepared?"

As the crew members reconstructed the gangway, connecting the ship to shore once more, Beatrice considered Diana's words.

"No," she said. "But still, I will face it."

THE LONDON BABBLER

Curious Crimes

By Elle Equiano

Percival Nash is innocent, and Horace Vane is guilty—and dead.

Sweetbriar was shaken by a string of murders this summer, but thanks to DS Investigations (led by Inspectors Vivek Drake and Beatrice Steele), the culprits have been discovered.

Drake and Steele testified to authorities that Mr. Vane was the murderer of Oliver Beauchamp, Cecil Nightingale, Walter Shrewsbury, and a street soliloquist and aspiring actor called Archibald Croome, who—at the time of his death—was thought to be Horace himself. But Mr. Vane will not stand trial, for he was also murdered.

Mrs. Diana Vane, patroness of the Rose, was apprehended in connection with the death of her husband.

"Mr. Vane was being blackmailed, and faked his death to foil the plot," Inspector Drake told reporters outside the courtroom. "In a twist reminiscent of *Figaro's Follies,* Mrs. Vane discovered all and killed her husband. She vows to make a full confession explaining her motive . . . in the form of an original musical."

Speaking of *Figaro:* Mr. Gregory Dunne has also been arrested for the attempted murder of beloved actor Percival Nash, along with twenty accomplices.

All details of the situation have not been released,

but there are rumors that it involves a secret society, falsified negative reviews of local galleries and operas, fires, forced flying rodent infestations, and the exhumation of the Rose Club's garden.

Other than brief statements, both Steele and Drake have refused to provide accounts to any reporters other than this writer.

For a full account of all the scandalous details, you can read the exposé, available next week here in the *Babbler,* by yours truly.

It will also contain several tips about ribbons.

THE ARTISTS' QUARTERLY

New Artistic Collective to Launch

With the death of Mr. Horace Vane and the arrest of Mrs. Diana Vane, the Rose assembly hall's fate was hanging in the balance—until Mrs. Vane signed the deed over to Sweetbriar's local Figaro, Percival Nash.

"At best, that club was an exclusive cesspool with mediocre balls," Mr. Nash told reporters. "At worst, it was a place where men in hideous masks tried to commit ritual sacrifice in the basement. Therefore, I have decided that it shall henceforth be known as the Amaryllis. This flower, of course, symbolizes hard-won success, particularly when it comes to artistic endeavors. As the name indicates, the new club will be a haven for the arts, consisting of drawing studios, galleries, and the Archibald Croome Memorial Stage. The sacrifice and dances will no longer occur, unless as part of an interpretive dance, for it shall become a true commune for artists. A place we have needed for a long time."

Men and women of any rank are invited to attend classes and performances at the Amaryllis. Their opening production, *Altus,* was penned by local playwright Miss Helen Bolton, who will also be teaching a class on proper millinery choices.

EPILOGUE

The summer heat had finally broken, and the first whispers of autumn crept across London. The leaves were tinged orange and yellow, and there was a chill in the air as Beatrice and Drake walked arm in arm through Sweetbriar. He no longer had to wear a sling, as the cut on his arm from Horace's knife had healed, leaving only a faint line where the blade had pierced flesh. Beatrice, on the other hand, had a noticeable mark across her cheek where the NAGS had gotten her. With this scar, she felt, she was now a true inspector.

Miss Bolton led the way, sporting her latest obsession, inspired by tips from Elle Equiano's exposé—a cape of ribbons, which rippled in the breeze. A few leaves got caught in it, and Miss Bolton stopped in her tracks, attempting to free them before taking up her trot once more.

Several passersby tipped their caps as the three passed, and one even said, "Good afternoon, Inspectors!" Some, however, scowled. One even kicked a spray of dirt into their faces, though the wide brim of Miss Bolton's hat blocked it from its intended target.

Overnight, Beatrice and Drake had found fame and respect from crime and art aficionados, as well as scorn from those who believed that they had ruined the Season with talk of murder. (Never mind that they had not *committed* it.) Beatrice knew that the NAGS themselves had only been stopped for the time being. Though Horace, Cecil, and Walter were gone, and Gregory Dunne had been arrested, the group still had members and supporters in the city. The permit system might have been paused, but like the moths that came out at night, the NAGS were merely lurking in the shadows, waiting for their time to return.

But for now the admiration outweighed the scorn, at least in gold: Cases were pouring in, and for the first time, Beatrice had more than pocket money to send to her family. Percival had been right when he told them that rave reviews led to compensation. Reporters stalked them both, desperate for statements on the "Moth Murders," as they had been nicknamed. Yet both Beatrice and Drake had agreed: To ensure accurate reports, they would only speak to Elle, the new voice of the crime column. Elle had thus crafted a full exposé on the Brotherhood of the Moth, detailing their involvement in thwarting local art, complete with proof and witness statements. She had then retreated to Bath for a much-needed fishing holiday, imploring Beatrice to join her when business finally slowed.

Miss Bolton halted. "I shall never get used to it, without those gates," she remarked.

They were standing outside the newly refurbished Rose Club—or rather, the Amaryllis. The iron gates had been dismantled, and the front yard was now full of easels, acrobats, and half-finished costume pieces. Miss Bolton waded through the disarray, and Beatrice and Drake followed her through the front door.

Inside, it smelled of sawdust and paint. Percival had been hard at work overseeing the remodel, and Beatrice was impressed as she surveyed the change. Gone were the austere columns and the colorless marble; Percival had already hung paintings along the walls and retiled the floors in shimmering hues.

"Inspector Steele! Inspector Drake!" Percival appeared, his arms outstretched. He embraced each of them and then turned to Miss Bolton. "You are late. The actors have several questions regarding the stage directions in act five."

"Oh, yes. The hat number," Miss Bolton said. "It *is* challenging, yet pivotal. If you'll excuse me, I must oversee this. Opening night is in a week, and *we don't have a show*!" she told Beatrice and Inspector Drake, looking harried.

"I thought we were going to the office after this," Drake said, looking confused. "We really must reply to our mail, and lately we have had clients lining up to bring cases to our attention—"

"Oh dear, we never told him our decision," Miss Bolton said to Beatrice. She turned to Drake and announced, "I have resigned as Beatrice's chaperone."

"That doesn't mean . . ." Drake looked slightly panicked.

"We aren't going anywhere," Miss Bolton said immediately, following his thoughts. "I am simply allowing Beatrice the chance to be . . . alone. She is an independent woman now; she does not need me following her every move."

"Yes," Percival agreed. "She is a spinster. And she achieved that status in only one Season. Quite a feat, Miss Steele!"

"I don't mean *that,*" Miss Bolton said. "She is an *inspector*! And Drake is her partner! Chaperones are only meant for sweethearts. . . . Nothing is going to happen between these two."

"Yes," Drake said. He avoided Beatrice's gaze as he murmured, half to himself, "Nothing is going to happen. . . ."

"I certainly shan't complain," Percival said. He wore no hairpiece these days, his bald head gleaming in the sunlight streaming through the Rose's large windows—now the drapes were always flung wide so anyone could see in. "We need Miss Bolton to ensure that this first production goes off without a hitch. The box is reserved for you two, of course," he told Beatrice and Drake.

"And we won't bring Sir Huxley this time," Drake assured him.

"On the contrary. He has already assured me he wouldn't miss it for the world. He'll join you two in the box," Percival said cheerily, and Drake glowered. "He confessed that he never really believed I was the culprit," Percival went on. "It was all pressure from Mr. Vane to accuse me. Such a charming man, that Huxley . . ."

"Indeed," Miss Bolton agreed. She squeezed Beatrice's arm in farewell and then lowered her voice. "Just don't tell your mother about any of this."

"Never," Beatrice said with a smile.

With that, Miss Bolton tipped her hat (a scale model of the newly refurbished Amaryllis), turned on her heel, and disappeared with Percival into the chaos of artists.

"Shall we?" Beatrice asked Drake.

He offered his arm to her once more.

They took off down the street, now alone together.

Likely there would be gossip about this, among the pages of *The London Babbler*—but for the first time in her life, Beatrice did not care about her reputation.

She had participated in the Season and successfully snagged a fortune—but it was thanks to her own skills as an inspector. She would not have to rely on a marriage of convenience in order to support her family. Even her mother could not argue with cold hard cash. And she hadn't—Beatrice had not received any desperate letters in a fortnight, only notes of gratitude. For the first time she knew for certain that change was possible. She could feel it in the air, upon the breeze from passing flying squirrels.

Beatrice and Drake reached the stoop of DS Investigations. Drake opened the door, and Beatrice strode inside.

Their office had undergone a transformation in the months

following the Moth Murders case. Now the desks overflowed with letters from admirers and those hoping to have cases solved by the famous Steele and Drake. Every surface was covered with flowers and gifts.

To keep everything organized, they had also decided to hire a secretary.

"Oh good, you're here." Lavinia Lee rushed to her feet. "You had five clients come in with murder cases. I took notes . . . my penmanship is not as good as Elle's, I fear, but it is *mostly* legible. . . ." She shuffled a stack of papers on the desk, scrambling to bring them to Beatrice and Drake.

Beatrice noticed, with slight embarrassment, that Lavinia now wore a choker featuring miniature portraits of Beatrice and Drake. She was a devoted fan—but no one had a more encyclopedic knowledge of crime, Beatrice knew. Lavinia was the best woman for the job.

"I also had something I wished to discuss with you both," Lavinia said, setting down the papers. She crossed to the office closet and opened it to reveal a stash of wigs, jackets, and prosthetic parts. "I borrowed them from Percival," she explained. "I know I am meant to be a secretary, but some of these cases are going to require undercover work. Perhaps I might also be deemed your disguise creator?"

Beatrice and Drake exchanged a look. Beatrice nodded, but Drake crossed his arms.

"I shall agree on one condition: You both must promise to never dress anyone as Sir Huxley again. One of him is enough," he said sternly.

"This is wonderful," Lavinia said, clapping. "Of course, I agree; imitation is not nearly as satisfying as the real deal. Even though *I* admire both you and Sir Huxley, of course . . . I suppose there is room in my heart for the original *and* you two. Now, if you'll excuse me," she said, grabbing her bonnet and shawl from her desk, "I do have a few more pieces to pick up from Percival. I did not want to bring over the heavier ones, in case you said no. . . ."

She flitted out the door before Beatrice could inquire why costumes should be heavy and suggest that this might impede an investigation as opposed to helping it.

Now she and Drake were finally, truly, alone. They stood in the center of the office by the coffee table, both looking down, an awkwardness growing thick in the air.

Suddenly, Drake moved, reaching out—toward Beatrice?—but no, she realized with a flush. He was moving a piece on the chessboard.

He had finally taken her queen.

Drake cleared his throat and then strode over to his desk.

"We must be selective in what cases we take on next," he said as he sliced open a letter and pored over the contents. "After all, everyone is watching us." He held up the letter. "Ah. That man's spectacles *were* on the windowsill, by the way. He sends his thanks."

"Excellent." Beatrice swallowed hard as she plucked a note from a bouquet of angelicas and skimmed it. "'Congratulations on solving the case,'" she read aloud. "'Sending love to my biggest fans, from Felicity Lore.' And there is a portrait of her on the back of the note," she said, irritated, as she flipped the note over to reveal the painting.

"How kind of her," Drake exclaimed.

Beatrice rolled her eyes and picked up a box and opened it to find—"A miniature sword?" She pried it eagerly from the container. The small hilt was set with a black and white pattern that, she thought, resembled the streak of white in her own dark curls.

"I had Mr. O'Dowde send it over. You should not always have to rely on sharp jewelry to defend yourself," Drake told her. "Not with the cases we have coming."

"I love it," Beatrice told him, slipping the sword into her pocket, where it fit perfectly. "That was very thoughtful."

"Well, we broke half his shop. We owe him our patronage for years to come," Drake muttered.

Beatrice suppressed a smile at this as she continued to leaf through her mail. Drake, simultaneously, went through his own stack.

"Anything interesting?" she asked, absentmindedly opening yet another note, from a bouquet of pink camellias.

She flushed as she saw the message written there.

I am sorry I underestimated you. You are everything,
Beatrice Steele. Give me another chance?

Lawrence

Sir Huxley had sent her flowers. He had called her "everything." He was not bitter that she had solved the case, but admiring. After all, in the language of flowers, pink camellias meant one thing.

Longing.

She looked over at Drake. They had not discussed what had occurred at Percival's. There had not been time, what with catching Diana, and then the rush of business in the wake of their success.

But his words still lingered in the back of her mind. And their kiss still lingered on her lips.

"Drake," she began, "I need to say something."

It was now or never, she thought, steeling herself.

"Let me, first," Drake said. "I am sorry for everything that has occurred between us. You have my word. I will not cross the line again. I will maintain professionality and ensure our relationship is one of businesslike cordiality."

She kept her eyes fixed upon him, considering his words.

She had independent means now. Beatrice was no longer bound by some of the restrictions previously placed upon her. Perhaps—she hardly dared to think—her personal life could now be her own choice.

Drake rose to his feet. He slowly strode over to where Beatrice stood. "That is what you want, is it not?" he asked. He kept walking until he was just before her. "You came to London to solve crimes, not to court a beau."

"A lady," she replied, "*could* do both simultaneously." She took his hand and moved it to her waist, and he inhaled sharply.

She put a palm to Drake's scarred face, and he tightened his grip on her, pulling her closer to his chest. He leaned into her, and she into him—

Until the door to the office banged open, and they broke apart.

"My darling!" a familiar voice cried out. Beatrice turned to see her mother burst into the room—followed by her father, Louisa, Frank, and baby Bee Bee.*

"We know you have been so homesick," Louisa said, rushing over to embrace her sister. "So we brought Swampshire to you!"

"How wonderful," Beatrice said, met with a rush of both happiness and irritation. But she was grateful as she held Louisa tight, and then turned to embrace the rest of them. She really *had* missed them all.

"We received your money for the banister," Mrs. Steele gushed to Beatrice. "It is being fixed as we speak, thank heavens! We had nowhere else to stay during the repairs . . . but I told your father, 'Beatrice will be *happy* to host us.'"

Frank shook Drake's hand. "We read everything about your latest case in the paper," he told him. "Impressive, truly! I had to

* Mary was not there, as the family had forgotten to invite her.

write Louisa several sonnets to ensure she did not leave me for you. . . ."

"One may think poetry is the food of love, but I think crime solving may usurp its crown," Beatrice told him, shooting a glance at Drake. "Not to mix metaphors," she added.

"I should give you all a moment—" Drake said, flustered, but before he could escape he was blocked by Mr. Steele, who began to pump his other hand up and down.

"Now you see, Inspector, why a man must always carry firecrackers! I will need you to replace those, however . . . they *were* the last of my stock. . . ."

"Shall we take a stroll?" Louisa asked, passing baby Bee Bee to Frank, who bounced her on his hip. "After such a carriage ride, I must stretch my legs. And perhaps turn a few cartwheels—"

"I am certain your sister can show us all the best walking paths around Sweetbriar," Frank assured her. "She is a Londoner now."

"Let's go wherever is busiest at this hour," Mrs. Steele suggested. She adjusted her gown, a tasseled frock that Miss Bolton had helped Beatrice select and send to Swampshire. "The city must get to know the family of the wealthy, successful, wealthy Inspector Steele!"

Beatrice caught Drake's gaze, and the corners of his mouth turned up. She held his eye as she reached over to the chessboard and made her final move. "Checkmate," she mouthed.

A smile stretched across his scarred face.

They had more to discuss. There were cases to solve—and the matter between the two of them that also needed to be solved. But now they would take a turn about the garden with the Steeles and enjoy the cool evening air in Sweetbriar, out of the shadows, and into the sun.

As they left the office, no one noticed one letter sitting atop

Beatrice's desk. It was open, and had no postage, as if someone had simply walked into the office and left it there.

Dear Miss Steele,

> You have caught my attention with your skills at crime solving. I had paused my little game, as Sir Huxley proved inadequate at catching me. But now I find myself inspired to start again . . . with you as my opponent.
>
> I look forward to working with you.
>
> Sincerely,
>
> *The London Menace*

ACKNOWLEDGMENTS

It is a truth universally acknowledged that sequels—like murder—can be a terribly nasty business. They're a real challenge, but there is nothing like a team of incredible people to make that challenge possible. I am so incredibly grateful to everyone who made this book a reality!

First of all, thanks to YOU, dearest reader, and thank you to all of the librarians, booksellers, bloggers, and those on bookish social media who championed *A Most Agreeable Murder*. Your kind words and support have left me forever thankful. This job is a dream come true, and I am the happiest creature in the world to have such an opportunity.

To my editor, Emma Caruso, your patience, thoughtfulness, and astute notes constantly motivate me to improve. Jane Austen said that wisdom is better than wit, but I'm spoiled to have you as my editor, because you've got both. Talia Cieslinski, your positivity and enthusiasm is contagious; a true inspiration.

Thank you so much to the entire brilliant team at Random House: Vanessa DeJesus, Madison Dettlinger, Elizabeth Groening, Cassie Gonzales, Dennis Ambrose, Sandra Sjursen, and Rebecca Berlant. There is no charm equal to all of your brilliance!

Thank you to my copy editor, Aja Pollock, for your meticulous work, and to Anthony Troli for brainstorming another great title. Lisa Perrin, thank you for another gorgeous cover that exceeded all of my dreams.

Thank you so much to the authors who gave me indispensable advice and support: Kaitlyn Hill, Jacquie Walters, Erika Lewis, and Kate Stayman-London. How sooner one tires of anything but your incredible books!

To my early readers—Jeff King, Maddie Hughes, Schuyler Pappas, and Dan Crockett—thank you for your thoughtful notes, constant reassurance, and joke pitches.*

A huge thanks to my agents Rachel Kim and Richard Abate. I like you both very much—just as you are.

This book is dedicated to all of the kindred spirits who made L.A. another home. Erika, Nicole, Caitlin, Emlyn, Jeff, Artichoke Kevin, my Jane always, Maddie, and everyone in Sing! Sorry for singing opera at karaoke. I'll definitely be doing it again.

Lastly, thank you to my family for all of your love and support. Grandma Smith, who could definitely solve a crime or two herself; Dad, Andy, Meredith, Anderson, and Jesse, my life is festooned with happiness because you're all in it.

And to my mom, Pam, who taught me to read and write and made sure I turned out an obstinate, headstrong girl. All my love ♥

* One day we may break the Curse of the Moon. Until then, I am honored to have you all in my pack.

ABOUT THE AUTHOR

Julia Seales is the author of *A Most Agreeable Murder* and a screenwriter based in New York City. She earned an MFA in screenwriting from UCLA and a BA in English from Vanderbilt University. She is a lifelong Anglophile with a passion for both murder mysteries and Jane Austen. Julia is originally from Kentucky, where she learned about manners (and bourbon).

Instagram: @juliamaeseales

ABOUT THE TYPE

This book was set in Caslon, a typeface first designed in 1722 by William Caslon (1692–1766). Its widespread use by most English printers in the early eighteenth century soon supplanted the Dutch typefaces that had formerly prevailed. The roman is considered a "workhorse" typeface due to its pleasant, open appearance, while the italic is exceedingly decorative.